THE BIG BOOK
OF DOMINATION

THE BIG BOOK OF DOMINATION

EROTIC FANTASIES

Edited by
D. L. King

Foreword by
Laura Antoniou

CLEiS
PRESS

Published in the United States by Cleis Press, Inc., 2246 Sixth Street, Berkeley, California 94710.

Printed in the United States.
Cover design: Scott Idleman/Blink
Cover photograph: Roman Kasperski
Text design: Frank Wiedemann

First Edition.
10 9 8 7 6 5 4 3 2 1

Trade paper ISBN: 978-1-62778-068-1
E-book ISBN: 978-1-62778-080-3

"The Day I Came In Public," by D. L. King, previously appeared in *Yes, Sir: Stories of Female Submission* (Cleis Press, 2008). "All Work and No Play," by Anna Mitcham, first appeared in *Readerotica 3* (PriveCo Inc., January 2012). "Playing for Keeps," by Alison Tyler, previously appeared in *Bondage on a Budget* (Masquerade Books, 1997).

Contents

FOREWORD

Laura Antoniou

To dominate is a verb.

I have pronounced this line over a hundred times, maybe a thousand times.

And it's not just because of the thousands of morons out there who helpfully alert smart users of dating websites with clever, well-written ads like this:

Tall, handsome dominate with big dick seeks willing slave.

Or:

KNEEL b4 this DOMINATE bitch and beg for MERCY!

Or:

Seeking dominate goddess to force me to do these specific things until I'm done.

No, the confusion of "dominant" and "dominate" in text is merely a failure of literacy and attention span. Besides, it really does help weed out the people who can't read well or who don't care enough to proof their own invitation to the dating community.

What makes me stand up in front of thousands of kinky people all over the world, in small classes and at weekend conferences, and remind them that "to dominate is a verb" is that there are a lot of myths about dominance—and the people who practice it—and the worst one of all is that merely by saying you're dominant, submissives of all sorts will sway gently in your awesome presence and bend themselves to your will....

And then, after some kinky sex, they'll do your dishes, perform erotic dances, clean your bathroom, feed you breakfast in bed while dressed in alluring costumes, file your taxes, polish your boots in a leather bar and design your Etsy webpage for greater visibility. All without a single additional gesture from you, the beloved and submission-inspiring dominate.

Well, I have to call such a person something. And it sure isn't "dominant."

In actuality, to dominate requires activity. Ongoing focus, work, attention to detail, imagination. It also requires a high level of empathy, flexibility, a complete understanding of boundaries and limits and at the same time the ability to become distant, to maintain a certain rigidity, a willingness to take risks and the guts to accept responsibility when the risk doesn't pay off. It's not easy or simple, and it sure as hell isn't something practiced by acting passive while someone else does all the relationship heavy lifting.

Plus, you have to actually inspire those submissive reactions. Some lucky people get a gorgeous physical form with which to attract their potential prey. And that's all well and good, until they open their mouths or do anything. At that point, the shortest, most unassuming guy at the bar can out-dom the studliest stud there with just a well-turned phrase or the whispered command given at just the right moment. That skinny lady who peers at you over the edge of her glasses might have all the power and romance anyone might yearn to beg for in the topmost layers of her creative and engaging fantasies, while the buxom, corseted and spike-heeled cover model believes making the right fashion choices are the hardest decisions she needs to make all day.

Then there are the mysteries of what it means exactly to be a dominant person, a dominant partner, a dominant lover. Does it mean someone who must be in charge of all things, all the time? Does getting what you want make you sexy and demanding, or whiny and manipulative? Does it mean a partner who uses every item in a well-stocked dungeon, working his or her way into heat exhaustion with endless floggings, intricate bondage, fiendish devices and elaborate fantasy scenarios? Does the one who stretches back comfortably and purrs, "Please me," also fall under this umbrella term? And what if pleasing him includes beating or otherwise performing acts one might confuse with "dominance"? What if her power ebbs and flows?

The misunderstandings of how these complex power dynamics work leak from real life into fiction and back again with disturbing regularity. Readers of hot, steamy volumes like this one venture forth onto websites with predictably kinky names, seeking living avatars of their heroes and heroines in the stories. Real folk hold their own adventures up to the impossible world of romance novels and think the real reason they're not making things work is because they lack a twenty-room mansion, a staff of liveried servants, a dungeon of their own.

And we writers…ahh, well. We have our own Saint Andrew's cross to bear. Because we supply the impossibly good-looking characters and well-appointed play spaces and improbable coincidences. And while some excesses may be forgiven in the name of Making Shit Up because That's What Fiction Is, there are some crimes against both the tales and the readers that cannot be forgiven.

And one of those is how badly the poor dominants can be portrayed.

Because of the limits of space and word count, it's not always possible to show just how Mistress Malicious and Lord Larry *earned* the supplicating worship of Slave Salacious and Boy Baxter. But with no clue as to their worthiness, their dominance becomes a magical thing, given for seemingly no reason at all—aside from stunning good looks and an assortment of props and costumes. When they act, it appears to be by complete fiat, with no rhyme or reason; they are cruel and oddly thoughtless, selfish and...bland. Dominance becomes a state of being with no effort from the tops. They're not *performing* dominance; they are standing in for it. They're not sadistic; they're assholes.

Then there's the opposite situation. Drama often depends upon conflict. Conflict within a dominant and submissive world tends to be naughty behavior—or presumed naughty behavior—for which the dominant must then provide suitably dramatic punishment. So now, dominance becomes equated with punishment, or worse, unfair punishment, overdramatized for humorous or melodramatic effect. Even *bigger* assholes.

And then there are the magical tops. You know them. They have it all. Good looks, pinpoint accuracy, talent with the most esoteric kinky skills, and the ability to *read minds*. How do you know? Because they mysteriously understand exactly what will work, exactly how far to push, exactly what words to say to make their lucky victims tremble, hiss, whimper, melt, and drip with assorted bodily fluids. They never make a mistake, and they're never wrong and they probably ALL fly their own helicopters. You read them and simultaneously want to be/be with them, and think they're annoying as hell in their unreality.

I've done all those things in my writing. And you will find hints of them right here, as well.

But what you *won't* find are a tag-team of unimaginative, by-the-book, stand-and-model, inhumanly smart, precognitive, cutout characters standing strong for submissive feelings (and bodies) to be thrown against.

Oh, no. Here be *dominants*. Because not only do they inspire submission—and yes, some by beauty and style—but they also inspire jealousy. Or, they feel it! Deliciously, they feel it and let it wash over them because they have the power to *do* something about that pesky little feeling. And having the power is only step one. Figuring out how to use it and to what end is the real trick.

And also here you will find familiar tropes like birthdays and role-playing, a kidnapping and some public teasing. But while you think you might recognize a standard after-hours office scene, you might be surprised at who winds up where and how flirting can be very fun or very dangerous or both. Parties and music cross paths, but in unexpected ways. Not every party has guests who will appreciate whipping out the chef's naughty bits for some fun, and not all music is played in the background when you can *command* the musician.

And while some tops in this collection revel in their RKO evil menace persona (complete with costuming), there are also cozy moments of affection and love, crossing over an assortment of orientations and taste variations. A suitable mélange to tempt the palate for more complex flavors of seduction and coercion and the fine line between the two.

Some of these stories start in texts and via phones

and computers. The reality of those stories mingles with the surrealism of an almost noir flavor, hard-edged and defiant and sexy in a way that makes you hesitate before turning the page.

But you'll want to see what happens next. And enjoy the journey as these writers skirt the lazy tops and unimaginative overlords of lesser tales to show you just how deliciously complicated we can be. In our stories and our fantasies. And I'll bet a few of these tales will inspire some real-life adventures as well. I suggest binding someone to the bed while reading to him. Or lounging back and commanding her to read to you.

Either way, I suggest you embrace the verbs. To read. To excite. To entice. To enjoy.

INTRODUCTION

I was pretty thrilled when Cleis Press asked if I would be interested in editing *The Big Book of Domination.* Wow! Would I be interested? I'd been thinking about my next project and hadn't come up with anything really spectacular—and then: *The Big Book of Domination.* My mind started spinning and a little erotic slide show began playing in my head. I had to be snapped out of my reverie and asked again. *Yes, I would be interested in editing that book.* I think I might have started jumping around while saying "thank you" too many times. Yeah, I didn't play this one close to the vest.

I began thinking about what such a book should entail. Fem dom—of course there would be fem dom, because—D. L. King—hello! But I started thinking about all the possible permutations of domination, both from the dominant's perspective and from the submissive's perspective. I thought about male domination of women, female domination of men, domination between gay partners and between lesbian partners and, taking it farther, let's think about twinks, daddies, femmes, bears, butches, good girls, bad boys, first experiences, jaded doms, threesomes and more, forced domination, paid domination, learning the ropes, so to speak, and teaching skills to others. Really, when you begin to think about it, the possibilities are practically endless... Or at least they are when *I* do the math.

Domination. I roll the word around in my head and then the pictures come hard and fast. I visualize a club with which I'm familiar. I can see it: the room's dark. There are spotlit areas, but in my mind's eye, they're empty. I can fill them with my own subs and bottoms. I can cuff a boy to the wall here and fasten a girl to a spanking bench there. I can use rope bondage to tie up a willing slave and raise him off the ground with the help of a winch. There's a lovely, large throne over there, where I can be worshipped, and there's a table with about a hundred tie-down points. Neural synapses flash more and more pictures through my mind.

Next, I travel to a bedroom. I can see a man in leather pants and nothing else, wielding a whip. His girl is tied to the bedposts, on her knees, and she's begging.

But what is she begging for? Another taste of the whip? A slap? A caress? To be allowed to come? It's all up to him, of course.

Now I'm at a private play party. There are strangers and friends in various forms of undress but this isn't a swinger's party. No, this is definitely all about pain and bondage, dominance and submission, cuckoldry and humiliation, all at the whim of the dominants in the group.

I'm a fly on the ceiling of a longtime couple's bedroom. They might be married; they might not, but it's easy to see they love each other and have a history. The romance of her sighs and moans as he immobilizes her and forces pleasure upon pleasure on her—is it their anniversary? It's the little bursts of laughter peppering the action that make the scene all the more intimate, all the more real.

I enter a dungeon and see my bottom *du jour*, who has been so submissively awaiting my arrival. Before me is a table heaped with the tools of my trade. I run my hand over the toys that have been so lovingly laid out for me. My fingers twine in the falls of floggers and play with the tips of single-tail whips. I run my hands over paddles and clips, leather and metal cuffs, dildos and plugs made of silicone, metal and glass, various sizes of weights and clamps, rope, chain, locks, gloves and lube, leather bindings and more—it's all here, begging for my inspiration—waiting for the play to begin.

Are you like me? Are your nerve endings zinging? Have I whetted your interest? Try this on for size, from Anna Mitcham's "All Work and No Play":

> *I reach the top floor and enter the open-plan office, my heart pounding with apprehension and anticipation. I can't see my colleague anywhere so I wander in and sit down at my desk, suddenly paranoid that I have been taken for a ride or gotten the wrong end of the stick. I jump as a hand comes firmly down on my shoulder and a gruff voice whispers in my ear, "Time to put your money where your mouth is…"*
>
> *My colleague swivels my chair around to face him and I see that he has unbuttoned his fly and his cock is standing proudly, level with my face. "This is for distracting me during office hours," he murmurs as he winds his fingers into my long hair and inserts his penis into my mouth, pushing himself deeper and deeper.*

Just a little tease…

As I mentioned earlier, you'll find everything to do with domination here. There are fem dom stories and ménages, some female dominant, some male dominant and some both. There are lesbian stories and gay stories and some that defy the definition of preference. You'll find authors such as Alison Tyler, Rachel Kramer Bussel, Andrea Dale and Evan Mora. You'll also find many new names in erotic fiction, folks with whom I hope you'll want to become a lot more familiar. *The Big Book of*

Domination is a BDSM tour de force that definitely pushes my buttons. Hopefully, it'll push yours, too.

D. L. King
New York City

PLAYMATE

Katya Harris

I t's okay. Touch them."

"Are you sure? I don't want to hurt you."

Bent over the edge of my sofa, my smart pencil skirt pulled up and over my hips to display the bare globes of my upthrust ass, I looked over my shoulder and smiled. "Beth, how could it possibly hurt me more?"

It was true. The cane that had laid the stripes across my ass and upper thighs had been exquisitely painful. Even after two days, they were still a livid red against the creamy white of my skin.

Beth's pretty face was wracked by the most adorable uncertainty. Her curiosity won out though, as I knew it would. She'd asked, so tentatively, what being punished was like. I had shown her the marks because I knew she wouldn't be able to resist looking, touching.

Her hand lifted. Anticipation strung my nerves tight, millions of tiny filaments running through my body and singing with tension.

The first hesitant brush of Beth's fingertips on my ass made me gasp. The second, firmer and surer, made me sigh. I wondered if she could see the slick juices easing from my pussy.

"They look so painful, Demi." There was a quiver of excitement in her hushed voice.

My tongue darted out to dampen my dry lips. Flashes of remembered sensations flickered along the underside of my skin; the searing touch of the cane, Adrian's dominance bathing my skin in heat, and all the things that came after. "There's more pleasure in it than you might think."

Beth's fingers followed one mark from the top of my right buttock to my left thigh. My breath hitched, and released on a soft moan that made her pause.

"Pleasure?"

Straightening, I turned to face her. "Would you like me to show you?"

The flush on Beth's cheeks deepened. I didn't bother to pull my skirt down and her eyes kept dipping to my barely concealed pussy before jumping back up to my face. "How—?" She swallowed. "How would you show me?"

She was so sweet I wanted to lick her straight up.

Sitting on the sofa, I gestured for Beth to come closer. After only a slight hesitation, she did.

My hand shot out, grabbed hers and pulled. Beth cried out as she fell over my lap. Lying over my knees, she tensed but she didn't struggle or complain.

"Are you comfortable?" I asked primly.

"Yes." Her voice was a breathless whisper. "What are you going to do?"

Sliding her skirt over her bottom, I exposed the panty-clad curves. "I'm going to give you what you want." I paused. "That's why you came here, isn't it, Beth? To know."

She squirmed. "I—"

My hand came down on her buttock in a sharp little slap. It was unfair of me, but when it came to Beth I didn't want to play fair. I knew she didn't want me to either. I could see the darkened patch on the strip of ivory silk between her legs. A spot that grew as I landed a flurry of stinging blows on each quivering cheek. Carefully I counted in my head, rubbing each cheek a little between each smack. By the time I reached ten and stopped, I could feel the hot wetness of her arousal anointing my leg beneath her.

Beth hadn't uttered a word during her spanking, but she had moaned and gasped and squeaked. Now, she breathed hard, rasping pants that gusted hot against my calf.

"Did you like that, Beth?" I purred, rubbing my palm on the nicely heated flesh of her bottom. "Would you like more?"

Beth gulped and then whispered, "More."

The slap I delivered to her buttock made her squeal.

"More, what?" I demanded.

"More *please*."

The smile that stretched across my face was wicked.

"Well, first these need to come down." I peeled her panties down her thighs.

A shiver raced over Beth's skin.

Stroking over the nicely pinked cheeks of her pert bum, I purred, "There, isn't that better?" For me it definitely was. I could see the soft petals of her pussy, slick and flushed with arousal.

She moaned in agreement.

This time, I spanked her harder. Her bottom went from rose pink to a beautiful scarlet. Her hoarse little cries became more and more frantic, her cunt spilling its honey in a flood of sweetness I couldn't resist.

My hand dipped down, delving through the slippery folds of her sex. Beth stiffened, sucking in a startled breath. Her thighs parted in blatant invitation.

"I knew you were an eager little slut beneath those uptight clothes." Beth was always so prim and proper, her clothes so modest a nun could have worn them without shame. For her, a short skirt was one that came to her knees and her shirts were always a little loose and buttoned to her throat. She couldn't hide the killer body hidden beneath those sedate clothes though, just as she couldn't hide the desire that gleamed in her eyes whenever she looked at me or at Adrian.

With the pad of my forefinger, I touched her clit. It

was small and hard, throbbing with arousal. My touch sent a jolt through her, as if I'd just touched a Taser to her skin. Slowly, I circled that sensitive little knot of nerves.

"Demi!" She cried out my name, and I flushed with pleasure.

Round and round my finger went, each revolution stringing her a little tighter. From what she had told me, I knew Beth was about to have her very first orgasm. Twenty-four years old and she had never come before. Her old boyfriends had been worthless fucks, and the idea that I could give her what they hadn't sent a surge of satisfaction roaring through me.

"That's it, Beth darling," I cooed. She was so delightfully responsive. My finger slipped inside her, and even though she was soaking wet with arousal, she was tight. "You took your spanking so well, you deserve a reward."

My finger thrust into her. In and out. A little twist. A little flex. Beth cried out, her hands clutching at the carpet. I added another finger knowing that it would stretch her with a delicious burn. I hissed, "Yes," as I felt her cunt begin to spasm. Her internal muscles fluttered, and I could actually see the orgasm sweep over her body in a rush.

Beth's scream was a choked-off sound of utter surrender. I kept my fingers moving, letting her ride out every wave of pleasure until she finally lay limp across my knees with a sated moan.

"Well, isn't this a beautiful sight to come home to."

Beth yelped, so startled she fell off my lap and onto the floor. I wasn't surprised. I had heard the front door open and close, a noise Beth had been too preoccupied to notice.

Cheeks blazing red with embarrassment, Beth huddled on the floor by my feet. She didn't seem to realize that her skirt was still hiked up around her waist or that her panties were around her knees.

Sliding off the sofa, I sat next to her and enveloped her in my arms. She clung to me, her face snuggled into the curve of my neck. Watching Adrian prowl into the room, I asked her, "Did you like your orgasm?"

She gulped and nodded. "Yes." Her hands clung to me as she watched Adrian sit on the armchair catty-corner to the sofa behind us.

"And what about the lovely spanking that my Demi gave you?" Adrian's deep voice rolled over us, a lick of velvet. "Did you enjoy that too?"

Against my shoulder, Beth nodded. "Yes."

I nudged her and her cheeks got impossibly redder, her eyes so bright with arousal they nearly glowed.

"Yes, Sir."

Adrian's smile was beatific. "Very good." A sharper edge graced the curve of his mouth. Beth sucked in a breath. I could understand why. I had been Adrian's girlfriend and submissive for over three years now and sometimes his razor-sharp beauty still caught me off guard. Looking at us now with burning blue eyes, he looked a veritable devil, intent on wicked things. My thighs clenched, arousal surging through me at the thought of all the things he could do to me, to us.

Adrian beckoned to me. Exhilaration bubbled in my bloodstream as I untangled myself from Beth's clinging arms, stood up and went to stand between his spread legs. Catching my hand, the hand that I had used to pleasure Beth, he brought it to his mouth. His lips surrounded the two fingers that were still damp with Beth's juices. I shuddered at the feel of his hot, wet mouth, the velvety rasp of his tongue as he licked the taste of her from my skin.

Lust carved Adrian's face into savage planes. My heart leaped in my chest, recognizing that look.

Slipping my fingers out of his mouth, he turned over my hand and pressed a kiss to my palm. His eyes caught mine, and the familiar sensation of falling into their blue depths swept over me. So easily he could take me over. He wasn't Adrian anymore. He was Sir.

"Undress."

"Yes, Sir." My voice was breathless in anticipation as my fingers started to work at the buttons of my low-cut blouse. I wanted to tear my clothes off as quickly as possible, rush headlong to the next part, but Sir liked me to undress slowly. He liked to savor me. Beth's eyes were also on me and I knew that this was a lesson for her too. Arousal spiked, puckering my nipples to aching points as I unclipped my lacy bra and threw it aside. Shimmying out of my skirt and tiny thong, I was gloriously naked.

Sir's gaze moved over me, approval gleaming from his dark eyes. He moved his attention to Beth.

"And now you, Beth."

She hesitated. Arousal glittered in her eyes, but her teeth gnawed at her bottom lip, her fingers winding round and round one another.

Sir flicked a look at me and I glided toward her. I offered her my hand and, trembling, she took it. I drew her to her feet, gently leading her forward to stand in front of Sir.

"Let me help you," I murmured.

Standing behind Beth, I slipped buttons free, peeled back cloth. I revealed the swoon-worthy body I knew she possessed beneath her prudish clothes. I was long and lean, athletic. Beth was short and curvy. She had the body of a sex-pot and I could feel Adrian's growing arousal as keenly as I could feel my own.

"Stand up straight," I whispered to her. "Show Sir how beautiful you are."

Her entire body blushed. Taking a deep breath, she straightened her shoulders. Her plump breasts thrust out, capped by fat pink nipples that pouted for some attention. I licked my lips.

"Well done, Beth." Sir's voice was warm with praise. Sitting forward in his chair, he brushed the backs of his fingers over the curve of her hip. She shivered, a tiny gasp escaping her.

"Turn around. Let me see my Demi's good work."

My hands steadied her as she complied. A touch at

the base of her spine and she followed my silent direction, bending at the waist to show Sir her ass and pussy. I wanted to glow with pride. She submitted so beautifully already.

Sir made a deep noise of approval. "Lovely." His gaze slid to meet mine and I knew he didn't just mean Beth's body or her spanking. We had both wanted her for so long, ever since she had first started working with me. Her first day, I had pointed her out to Sir when he had picked me up. Since then I had worked steadily and carefully to entice her into our world. It hadn't been too hard. Beth had wanted us just as much.

Sir's hand stroked Beth's ass. He hummed in appreciation as he felt the heat of the marks I had put on her. She trembled as Sir's hand moved down to play with her pussy. Helpless little noises spilled from her lips, tremors racing each other up and down her body. I stroked her back soothingly.

"Shh," I crooned to her. Sir nodded at me, and I used my other hand to join his in playing with her pussy. I played with her clit as Sir slowly pumped two thick fingers in and out of her. She was even wetter than before and more eager, pushing back into our hands. When Sir took his hand away, she mewled desperately. I winced as his hand came down on her ass in a resounding slap. She yelled out, but I felt her clit pulse hard beneath my fingers.

"Behave," he growled.

"Yes, Sir," Beth whimpered.

Sir stood up behind Beth. She stiffened and I knew she was wondering if he was just going to unzip his pants and plunge his cock into her right then. I knew that she wanted him to.

"Undress me."

I moved, my willingness to obey him imprinted on my very bones. Only a couple of seconds passed and then Beth was helping me. With her following my lead, we undressed him together, sliding our hands over his skin as we bared him to our eyes and hands. When I dropped to my knees to take off his trousers, Beth was right there beside me. She gasped and then moaned softly as we uncovered Sir's cock, the long thick instrument that could give us so much pleasure.

If we were good.

"Demi, show Beth how to suck my cock."

I grasped the thick base of Sir's erection, angling it toward us. "Sir likes it wet. Like this." I licked along the shaft of his cock with long laps of my tongue. As always the taste and feel of him on my tongue was an aphrodisiac. Reluctantly, I drew back and with an encouraging smile, invited Beth: "Help me."

She was tentative, her dark pink tongue flickering out uncertainly.

"That's it," I encouraged her.

Beth's tongue lapped at Sir's dick, each lick more confident than the last. Her eyes glazed over as she gave herself to the enjoyment of the act, and she moaned. Dipping my head, I joined her. Our bodies crowded close together as we shared Sir's cock. We licked over the hard flesh of his erection, our tongues tangling together so we were kissing each other as much as we were pleasing Sir. Our saliva flowed down his cock, dribbled over his balls.

"Now, we take Sir deep."

I showed her how. Opening my mouth wide, I sucked Sir's dick into my throat. Swallowed around him. He was so big it was difficult. I came off his cock with a gasp.

Breathing hard, I looked at Beth. "Now you."

She licked her lips, fitted them around the head of Sir's dick. Her head slid down. She couldn't take him as far as I could, but that was just a matter of practice and Sir would give her plenty of that.

We took turns sucking on Sir's cock, until tension vibrated from his flesh.

"Mmm," he growled. "That's my girls."

We both moaned at his praise and moaned again sharply in disappointment as he pushed our heads away from him.

Fierce blue blazed down at us. "Demi, lie down on the dining table. Take Beth with you."

Pulling Beth up to her feet with me, I obeyed. Our living and dining room were open plan, so thankfully we didn't have to go too far. I wouldn't have been able to stand it.

Moving aside the chair at the head of the table, I lay down, my butt at the edge and my legs dangling and spread wide. I knew what Sir wanted, he had described the fantasy to me once.

I gasped and shivered at the touch of the cool wood on my flushed skin. Sir came to stand behind Beth. I watched his hands close lightly over her shoulders, stroke down her upper arms.

"And now you, Beth." Turning her around, he pushed her back, guiding her until she was lying on top of me, her back on my front, her legs hooked over mine. Her weight on top of me was sweet and knowing what was in Sir's mind, my heart kicked against my ribs in excitement, knocking against Beth's back.

"Demi."

Sir didn't have to vocalize what he wanted me to do. My hands moved over Beth's body as he came to stand between our legs. She writhed on top of me as I cupped her breasts, my fingers pinching and twisting at her nipples.

Sir looked down at us, laid out for his delectation. The smile on his face was wolfish. Beth and I watched as he took his dick in his hand. We both moaned as he ran the head of his cock through the slick folds of our stacked-up pussies, up and down, up and down, smearing our juices together, teasing our clits, our holes.

"Does that feel good, girls?"

"Yes, Sir," we chorused.

Sir's cock speared me, pushing deep. Held down by Beth's weight, I couldn't move as he stretched the tight sheath of my cunt. A familiar pleasure-pain. I bit my lip to keep from begging for more as he pumped into me slowly, once, twice before slipping out of me. On top of me Beth stiffened, a broken cry flying from her mouth as he did the same to her. "Oh god!" she moaned.

I pinched her nipples hard, eliciting another sharp cry. "Shh, Beth. Sir doesn't like noise."

"Not yet anyway." He laughed, a husky chuckle. "I'll forgive you this once since you don't know the rules."

I could feel him moving between our legs, and then he was inside me again.

Back and forth, Sir swapped between us. The decadence of the act was more than even I could bear. I orgasmed around him in a lush burst of undisciplined heat. My muscles squeezed him, tried to milk his own climax from him in greedy pulsations. I would pay for that later. Through my half-hooded eyes I could see the promise of punishment gleam in Sir's eyes as he enjoyed my helpless convulsions. I didn't care. It felt too good, and I knew his punishment would too.

Sir let me ride out my orgasm filled with his cock, and then he plunged back into Beth. His balls slapped against my clit as he fucked her with powerful thrusts. Each impact sent pleasure sparking though me, and I knew that I'd orgasm again soon.

My hands roamed over Beth's body, fondled her breasts, plucked at her clit. Her head was on my shoulder and I nudged her with my chin until she turned her face to mine. Catching her lips with mine, I teased her with flicks of my tongue until she opened to me. Lust was a sweet taste in her mouth and I ate at it hungrily, swallowing her moans and whimpers as Sir fucked her.

I could feel her starting to come. Violent tremors surged through her body. I strummed her clit with insistent fingers.

"Yes," Sir snarled. Sweat dripped from his brow as he fucked Beth with all his strength. His hands gripped her thighs bruising hard, holding her open to him. "That's it, Beth, come for us. Come for us now."

Beth screamed as she did just that. She bucked on top of me and the feel of her pleasure surrounding me, mixed with the sharp slap of Sir's balls on my clit, sent me over the edge with her.

Oh god, it felt so good I never wanted it to end.

"Get your mouths on my cock. Now."

The growled order brought us both back to our senses.

Inelegantly, our bodies not yet working properly, we spilled to the floor. On our knees, we sucked and licked Sir's cock, tasting him, tasting each other.

"Put your faces together."

Both breathless, we did so, and watched with anticipation and arousal thrumming through us as Sir grasped his dick. He pumped himself furiously and then, with a long, drawn-out groan, his cum was splashing on our faces, our tits. Thick white ropes of Sir's semen that just begged to be licked up. My tongue flicked out to catch a creamy glob from Beth's cheeks. She shivered, eyes dilating wildly, and then she was following suit. We licked each other clean as Sir watched with lustful eyes and then we licked him clean too.

Beth's face caught my eye. I couldn't stop myself from kissing her sweetly happy smile.

Sir's hands tangled in our hair, holding us to each other as our kiss deepened. The sound he made was hungry and satisfied at the same time.

"My good girls."

FROM INNOCENT TO SLAVE: THE STORY OF MY CORRUPTION

Olivia Summersweet

I stood at his kitchen sink, naked, collared and leashed, washing his dishes while he spanked my ass and thighs. *Disciplining you with many implements while we work on your obedience,* was how he'd described his plans for the evening in an email the day before.

"This, too," he said. He smiled and handed me a dirty pot I'd missed. He pushed the thin leather handle of the leash into my mouth, making me hold it sideways between my teeth. The situation suddenly struck me as absurd and I giggled.

"You think this is funny?" he said, and gave me a hard spank.

"No," I mumbled through the leather. My cunt was dripping wet. I moaned and dropped the sponge, closed my eyes and stuck my ass out behind me, trying to work it closer to his hands.

"That's 'No, *Master*,'" he said. "You just earned another spank. And don't stick it out. Hold still." He pinched my asscheek and fingered my pussy lips. "Back to work."

His name was Ethan; he was thirty to my forty-two. Only three months before, I'd met him at a birthday party for Yvette, a friend who was into kinky stuff. I was not kinky, although I'd had a few fantasies—a little spanking, maybe a little more, all gleaned from novels. There was an empty seat among the stuffed couches and chairs in the crowded pub where the party was being held and I'd sat down in it, next to him.

I didn't notice his good looks that night: his Roman nose, his appraising green eyes, his perfectly cut light-brown hair. His smile, which I later found held so many contradictions: tenderness and cruelty, gravity and wit.

I was feeling attractive and sexy. Other men at the party chatted me up, came on to me. He was just another young male; a kid, really. A quiet presence next to me, nobody to think twice about. We uttered no more than a handful of casual words to each other, introducing ourselves. Yet running into him on the sidewalk later on the way to my car, an impulse took me by surprise: I wrapped my arms around his neck and hugged him.

"It was nice to meet you," I said.

"Nice to meet you, too," he said.

When I got home, there was an email from him:

Hi, it's Ethan. Yvette gave me your email address.
Thanks for the hug after the party.
Hope you're being a good girl. ;)

Something about the phrase "good girl" made my
adrenaline spike. I wrote:

I'm trying to be. ;)

He wrote back:

Perhaps a spanking would help you to be a good
girl. ;)

Oh my god, I thought: *a spanking! This is just like in the*
books. I typed an answer and hesitated before hitting
SEND, wondering what I was getting myself into:

Perhaps it would. ;)

My head was spinning. I'd never been spanked by a
man. I barely knew this guy.

He suggested getting together, and I said it would
have to be in a public place. So a few days later, on
a Saturday afternoon, we met in a park. We sat side
by side on a wooden bench and carried on a mundane
conversation. He looked straight ahead. Didn't touch
me. Didn't make a move. He seemed barely interested in
me. Yet despite that, or perhaps because of it, my body

began inching up against him sideways, trying to make contact. Something in him drew me like a magnet.

"How're you feeling?" he said.

"How I'm feeling is, wouldn't it be funny if you pulled me over your knee right now and spanked me?" I said. I giggled, barely able to believe the words coming out of my mouth.

People in the park were walking, pushing baby strollers, jogging. He waited about thirty seconds and then, without a word, he pulled me over his lap. Holding me steady with a hand around my waist, he gave me three hard swats through my jeans.

I was stunned. His hand felt good, warm. My pussy reverberated with the sensation. Even the embarrassing position turned me on. And although shy, I was beginning to enjoy the thought of shocking the people in the park.

"Oh my god," I said. "Please, do that again."

He pulled me back up. "We should meet in private," he said. "When are you free?"

A week later he arrived at my doorstep for our first real "date." I was nervous as hell. I walked into the kitchen, offering him tea, and he followed me, alternately hugging, spanking and caressing me until I didn't know what was coming next. He was smiling. Faced with confusion, my brain disengaged. I gave it up, let go and, just as I'd done that first day outside the pub, I pushed my body up against him. I moaned, groping him, shocking myself: I'd never behaved that way before with a man.

He took my hand and led me back into the living room. He sat down on my couch. Gently, he pulled me over his lap. He stroked my ass a few times. Then he began to spank me in earnest.

"Count," he said in a soft voice.

"One," I whispered.

"Louder," he said. "And with each count, I want you to say, 'Slut likes it.'"

I was mortified, but some instinct compelled me and I forced myself.

"Two, slut likes it," I mumbled.

"I can't hear you," he said. He yanked my jeans and panties down and gave me a stinging slap on my naked ass.

"Ow! I think…"

"Did I tell you to think?" He spanked me twice. "Do sluts think?"

"No," I whispered. I knew, in that moment, that being ordered not to think was what I'd longed for my entire life. Something at my core gave way. My cunt flooded with juice.

He continued spanking while I counted. At ten, he pulled me up and stroked my ass.

"You're nice and wet," he said, touching my pussy. "On your knees."

I sank to my knees, my obedience to him no longer surprising me.

Here is what they don't tell you in the novels. The

realization came to me in that instant. Domination is not force. It is seduction. Submission is willing. All these years, I'd misunderstood. I wanted this man with every fiber of my being. I was willing do anything he wanted. Anything.

"Hands behind your back," he said, in a voice he'd use to casually order a pizza, taking my compliance for granted now. He pulled out his cock and presented it to my mouth. He did not have to order me to suck. I thought it was beautiful. I took him into my mouth willingly.

He left without fucking me and I spent the rest of the night aroused, just lying in my bed, thinking about him and touching myself.

The next morning, there was an email from him:

Such an obedient little slut last night. ;)

Reading it made me wet all over again.

We had a few more dates like that. I had lunch with Yvette and told her about our budding relationship.

She laughed. "That's not a 'relationship,'" she said. "Ethan likes to train girls as slaves in his spare time. It won't last."

"You're kidding," I said. "That's ridiculous."

"No, I'm not. And I've heard he's one of the more experienced ones. You're lucky."

"Ha, ha," I said. "Right."

Yvette just smiled.

Over coffee and dessert, she began trying to educate me about what she called "the scene." She said there were public "dungeons" where it was safe to let someone tie you up because of all the other people around. I'd told her that was the one activity I'd resisted with Ethan: when he pulled out a length of rope or a set of handcuffs, I panicked and drew the line. But she said my fears would dissolve in the safety of a dungeon. So I mentioned the idea to Ethan.

"Take me to a dungeon and you can handcuff me and chain me to a leash and make me crawl around on all fours, for all I care," I told him, hoping I came off as fearless and adventurous. I really didn't know whether I was joking or serious. I thought we'd never go anyway, so it didn't matter.

But he called my bluff, and we set up plans via email to meet at a dungeon club. He asked me if I had a butt plug. I said yes, embarrassed to admit I owned such a thing. I told him nobody had ever used one on me.

He wrote:

You'll bring it with you to the club.

The thought of him sticking that thing in my ass in public both excited and unnerved me. For the second time, I wondered what I was getting myself into.

A few days later, I arrived at the dungeon for our date. Yvette had advised me on proper attire for these kinds of places, and I wore a crotch-length, see-through black top that served as a very short dress. Below it, hot-pink, thigh-high fishnet stockings left about two inches of my thighs bare. I'd worn a large overcoat on the way to the club, but once inside, I took it off. The outfit made me feel exposed and vulnerable.

I found Ethan sitting on a couch toward the back of the club and I walked up to him, trying to pull my "dress" down lower over my crotch.

He smiled. He didn't say a word. He stood up and hugged me, then turned me around so that my back was facing him. He slapped my ass. He took a black leather collar out of a backpack on the floor and gently wrapped it around my neck, snapping it shut.

I moaned and reached for him behind me.

"Is this too tight?" he asked.

"No, it's okay," I said.

Out of the corner of my eye I could see other people milling around: a few couples, some individuals. I'd expected to feel ashamed at being seen like this. Instead, I felt pride. I looked at Ethan and for the first time, realized how handsome he was.

He pulled a chain leash out of his bag and attached it to my collar. I felt the environment around me begin to fade away; all I could see was Ethan. He pulled out a set of handcuffs and without any ado, not expecting any resistance this time, he gently attached one around each of my wrists, checking, as he had with the collar, to see if they were too tight.

He slapped my ass again, then got in front of me and

yanked the leash, pulling me along. I was shocked. At first, I stumbled. I felt humiliated. But as on that first day in the park, even the humiliation turned me on. And suddenly, I felt proud to be at this man's beck and call.

He led me to what looked like a sawhorse with a rectangular hump on it lined in black leather.

"Get up," he said in a barely audible voice. He often talked so softly that I had to ask him to repeat himself.

I climbed up onto the contraption; it allowed me to rest my arms and legs along the pieces of wood below the leather hump.

"Facedown."

I lay facedown on the leather, my ass protruding over the edge.

"Back up a little," he said. "Stick your ass out more."

I pushed farther back until I was stretched tight.

"You're going to be a good little slave," he said.

Maybe Yvette hadn't been kidding after all, I thought.

"From now on, and for the rest of the night, whatever I say to you, you are going to answer, 'Yes, Master,'" he said.

"Okay," I said.

"What?" he said. He lifted my "dress" and spanked me.

"Yes, Master," I whispered.

"Louder," he said. "I can't hear you."

"Yes, Master," I said, audibly this time.

"That's better," he said. He pulled my thong aside

and stroked my ass, slipping a finger into my cunt and along my pussy lips. I moaned.

"Do you have cummy panties?" he said.

"Yes, Master," I said.

"Good girl!" he said. I felt as if I'd won the Nobel Prize. He slapped my flank.

I heard him rooting around in his bag and turned around to look. He was pulling out metal clips. One by one, he used them to fasten the handcuffs on my wrists to the bench. He attached restraints to my ankles and clamped them to the bench, too. I moaned, realizing how helpless and exposed I was.

I felt something cold across my asscrack; he was dripping lube on it and spreading it with his finger, then pushing it in. The combination of pleasure and shame was beyond my wildest imagination.

"Does slut want her butt plug?" he said.

"Yes, Master," I whispered.

I felt the cold tip of the plug pressing against my hole.

"Push out," he said.

I pushed out.

"Good girl," he said, as the first notch slid in. He spanked me.

I moaned.

"Another one," he said. "Push it out."

I pushed again, letting the second little protuberance on the plug slip in.

"One more," he said. He slapped my ass as I pushed and the last one slid in.

I was skewered. Stuffed. Humiliated. Helpless. I'd never experienced such ecstasy in my life. I heard what sounded like tape being torn off a dispenser; I felt him attaching the plug to me with several strips of tape. After it was firmly attached, he spanked me over the plug, making me feel it inside me.

"Does slut like that?" he asked.

"Yes," I said, quickly amending it to "Yes, Master."

"Such a good little slut," he said, and stroked my back.

I wanted badly to touch and suck his cock, as had become my habit while he spanked me over his knee at my house. But my hands were attached to the table and I couldn't move them to reach him.

"I want your cock," I murmured.

"What?" he said.

"I want to touch your cock, Master," I said.

"Say, 'I want to suck your cock, Master,'" he said.

"I want to suck your cock, Master," I whispered.

"Louder," he said. "I can't hear you."

"I want to suck your cock, Master," I said. He made me say it twice more, demanding I say it louder, spanking me harder each time until finally I was screaming it out. I was mortified. I was sure everyone in the place could hear me.

He positioned himself in front of me, pulled his cock out of his flannel pants, and held it to my mouth, letting me suck. But only for a few seconds. He withdrew, went back to spanking me and ordered me to beg again. Finally, he unfastened my hands and feet from the bench.

"Get up," he murmured.

I pulled myself off the bench and stood up.

"On your hands and knees."

I crouched onto all fours on the floor and he pulled me along, crawling, on the leash. I saw that I was headed toward a small cage with iron bars only a couple of feet high. I stopped and looked up at him, trying to smile. For a moment, I panicked. Then I made myself crawl into the cage.

He slammed the cage door shut and came around the side. Oddly, I felt safe inside it. He pulled out his cock and presented it to me through the bars. I crawled over to it. I was nearly drooling as I took him into my mouth. It was my reward. He was hard as a rock and pulsating and I sucked him hungrily until he came, and I swallowed his cum.

He let me out of the cage and I stood up.

"Good slut," he said. He held me for a few moments, then took my hand and led me to a bed in a corner, where he cuddled and massaged me. I was in a fog.

He drove me home; I barely remember the ride.

The next day I got an email from him:

Such a good, dirty little slut last night. Tomorrow I plan to work on your obedient-slave training. Showing yourself to your Master. Washing dishes while taking your punishment and necessary spankings, naked with only a leash and collar.

Whoa, I thought. Each time I thought I'd lost all my fear, he managed to escalate. I answered:

I am scared but I trust you, Master.

He wrote back:

I enjoy pushing along your limits and boundaries to see where I can expand them. Are you sure you want to learn how deep this rabbit hole goes?

All my life, I'd been an untrusting, contrary person. For the first time in my life, I felt trust in every cell of my body. I felt the ecstasy of unconditional surrender. I felt only the desire to say yes to him. I answered:

Yes, Master. I'm sure.

He wanted me to wear white underwear at our next meeting. I answered:

Okay.

He wrote back:

No, it's 'Yes Master.' You'll be spanked hard if you forget to say 'Master' after every sentence you speak to me.

The next afternoon I rushed home from work and tried on all my white underwear. I settled on a silk off-white French bra, white lacy panties and the white fishnets I'd bought during another recent shopping expedition for "slutwear."

It was the first time we were meeting at his place. He lived in the rented-out bottom floor of a mansion. I pushed my way through the wrought-iron gate as he'd instructed, walked down the long driveway and knocked on his door. He'd told me to arrive at 7:15; I was a few minutes late.

He opened the door and stood aside as I entered.

"Take off your jeans and T-shirt," he said.

I stripped down to my underwear, which he removed for me, pinching my nipples as he took off my bra.

"On your knees," he said.

I knelt in front of him. I was already wet and moaning.

Casually, he attached a collar around my neck and handcuffs to my wrists. He attached cuffs to my ankles and fastened them to a long metal bar between my feet. He attached a leash to my collar. He stood in front of me and pulled on the leash.

"Crawl," he said.

I crawled a few inches, then a few more as he pulled again.

"Good bitch," he said.

It was hard to make progress with the bar between my feet. But that was probably the whole point. I was, as usual in his presence now, dripping wet.

He led me to the kitchen, where he pulled me up and made me wash his dishes as he spanked me.

Then he made me crawl again, leading me on my leash to an open suitcase on the floor. In it lay paddles, floggers, whips and odd implements like kitchen spatulas.

"Pick something you want me to use on you," he said.

I picked out a leather paddle and handed it to him. He took it from me and led me crawling back to the couch, where he sat down and pulled me over his lap.

"Why were you late?" he said. He gave me a few stinging spanks with his hand.

"Ow!" I said. "I don't know."

"You don't know, *what*?" he said. He spanked me with the paddle.

"I don't know, *Master*," I said.

"Maybe a good spanking will help you remember why you were late," he said. He never raised his voice. "A good little slave is always on time. You need to learn respect as well as obedience."

"I was trying on underwear," I said.

"Oh, so now you remember?" he said.

He was spanking me harder and harder, faster and faster. Something deep inside me began to melt and I felt tears. But not from the pain. All the sadness, all the grief I'd ever felt in my life was coming out and I sobbed like a baby.

When it was all over, he held me on his lap.

"It's okay," he said, holding me and stroking my hair.

I wanted to melt into him. I wanted him to hold me forever. My pussy was soaking wet even as I continued crying.

He unchained me and led me to the bed. He gave me a massage. He took me into the shower and washed me all over with a rough pad, using shower gel. He washed my hair and my face and when we were through, he spread lotion all over my body.

The next day, there was an email from him.

Subject: A New Master
I don't have time to train you anymore. But you are ready. I have found you a new Master. Be there tonight at 8:00 o'clock. Make me proud. Show him how well you've been trained.
—Master Ethan

I couldn't believe it. I cried, lost it, begged him not to give me away. But he was as indifferent to me as he was that first day in the park. As indifferent to me as he was that night in the pub, as indifferent, in fact, as I suddenly realized he'd been all along. Of course it could never last.

I love Master Ethan. He taught me trust and obedience. And so I trust and obey the new Master he has given me to. My new Master is just an extension of Master

Ethan: when I suck my new Master's cock, I think of Master Ethan's cock; when I massage my new Master's body, I think of Master Ethan's body. And when my new Master calls me "good bitch," I am happy, because that is what Master Ethan called me.

I am content.

CAUGHT LOOKING

Angela Sargenti

I'm out for drinks with some of the guys from the team, and the player I've been crushing on for months is here.

In the first five minutes, I know I'm taking him home. What a tush he's got on him! I don't care that he's a forceful, aggressive, Asian guy. In fact, that's one of the things I like best about him.

He catches me looking at him, and I think that's when he first notices me, because in all the times we've been at the same parties together, he's never said a word to me before.

Not that I talked to him before, either.

What, are you kidding me?

He's way out of my league.

Being socially awkward is a terrible burden.

He looks at me again, though, and I can see his interest is piqued. I once had a therapist tell me you can't determine a person's mood just by the look in his eyes, but I know that isn't true.

Anyone who believes that has never seen Kisho Urakami's eyes. Long, black lashes to die for and a look that says he's up to anything and everything.

He's tough, too, way tougher than I am. The last time I watched him catch, he got hit square in the nuts by the ball, but he was up and ready to go again in less than five minutes.

I hope that's how it is tonight, too.

Our glances meet again and finally he speaks.

"So, what do you do again?"

"I'm one of the team's statisticians."

He looks impressed and smiles.

"What do you think of my stats?"

"You're definitely coming out of your slump."

What man doesn't like a compliment? He warms to me right away.

"Your name again?"

"Maury."

"Well, Maury, whatcha drinking there?"

I feel the need to lie and name a manly drink, so I say the first thing that pops into my head, something I saw last night on television.

"A shot of tequila with a beer back?"

He grins again. My heart's pounding, he's so near, and I can't believe he's buying me a drink.

It's true.

The great Kisho Urakami, best catcher in the Majors, is buying me a drink.

"Awesome. Get the waitress over here and we'll all have one."

Thank god he hasn't noticed there's no shot glass on the table.

Yet.

Well, tequila always goes right to my head, and after I drink the shot and half a beer, I start to loosen up a little. Kisho and I talk about our jobs, like we have to in front of the other guys, but I think maybe he's starting to like me. He tells me all about his hobby of riding a fast crotch-rocket, and I'm thinking how much they terrify me, but I lie and say I adore motorcycles.

He orders up another round and changes seats.

"I'm sick of shouting over you," he tells the guy next to me, and when the guy gets up, Kisho takes his place.

He touches my knee under the table and gives it a little squeeze and my heart's pounding out of my chest, because I know it's game on. We finish our drinks so we don't look like we're in a big hurry, and then Kisho stands up and stretches.

"Well, I'd better be getting home," he tells the others. "Early game tomorrow. Want to share a cab, Maury?"

"Sure. Why not?"

I'm nervous in the back of the cab, but he sneaks a hand down to squeeze me again. He has to be careful what he does in public, so I don't say or do anything to draw attention.

Kisho takes me to his place in Sausalito, one of the famous houseboats. The place is to die for, I'm telling you. He pays off the cab and leads me inside. A wall of glass reveals a stunning view, and I can see the lights twinkling across the bay.

Of course, with his kind of money, his place is much bigger and nicer than mine.

I live in a third-floor walk-up in Chinatown, to my poor Jewish mother's despair.

"Oy, *a broch*, this son of ours," says my mother, beseeching God and anyone else who'll listen to help her understand. "What did I do that I should deserve this? On my worst enemy I wouldn't wish it."

And my father, who's in the other room reading the paper, says, "So he'll eat a little chop suey. It's not so terrible."

"A stab in the heart is what it is. Why don't you meet a nice Jewish girl and settle down?"

"Ma, I'm a Buddhist."

"Since when? Maury, you're killing your mother. When I'm in my coffin, you can become a Buddhist. Until then, you're Jewish."

And then she feeds me, whether I've just eaten or not, and she tells me all about my sister's husband, the dentist.

"He gets weekends off, that Jonas. Just think of it. With weekends off, you could come visit your mother once in a while."

"What, because Jonas is a dentist, I shouldn't work in baseball? Says who?"

But there's nothing I can say to convince her I don't identify as a Jew.

Never mind the fact that I'm gay.

But you can't really escape being Jewish, and we believe in destiny, so I'm thinking it could be fate, and Kisho might be the one. He might be my Mr. Right.

We get just inside the door and he kicks it shut, then he backs me up against the door and starts kissing me. And he doesn't just kiss me. He sweeps me off my feet. Never in my life have I been kissed like that. I'm so short that guys usually treat me like I'm fragile, but not Kisho.

He goes right in for the kill.

I know I'm standing there like a dummy and I should respond in some way, so I slide my arms around him and kiss him back, trying to match his passion.

Suddenly he pulls back.

"I've always wanted to talk to you," he tells me. "I've noticed you before, but you're always so quiet."

"I don't know how to talk to strangers."

"I'm not a stranger anymore, am I?"

"No."

"Then talk," he says, unbuttoning my polo shirt and pulling it over my head. "Tell me all about yourself."

I don't know what to say, so I just reply, "I went to Stanford."

He nods and undoes the button on my khakis.

"Uh-huh."

"And I was at the top of my class."

"Mmm. I bet," he says, unzipping me. He drops to his knees and jerks my pants and underpants down to my ankles. "Go on."

"And I used to be Jewish?"

He smiles and grabs hold of my *schwantz*.

"Good. Is this thing kosher?"

"All beef."

What a guy like him sees in a guy like me, I can't say, but he bends his head closer and tongues the tip of my cock.

I feel weak at the knees and sag against the door, grabbing hold of the knob to steady myself. The last time I had a blow job, it was given by a klutzy twenty-year-old when I was still in college, but Kisho's not klutzy at all and he gets the job done in record time.

His hair's thick and glossy. I run my fingers through it, but it's too short to grab, so I take his head in both my hands and spend into his mouth. He sucks me dry and I almost black out, it feels so good, but I moan and call his name out loud instead.

He laughs, and then he stands up and kisses me again. Things heat back up pretty fast, and before I know it, we're in his bedroom and he's stripping off his clothes.

"Come on," he tells me. "You do me now."

He throws down a towel and grabs a bottle of lube,

and then he drops it down beside him and gets down on all fours.

I kneel beside him on the bed and squirt a little lube into my hand, massaging it in. I stroke his dick, too; Kisho's pretty hung and I'm relieved to see he's circumcised. Some things from your upbringing aren't as easy to shake off as others.

"Say some Jewish stuff," he tells me, and I can't think of anything else, so I start chanting the Haftora from my Bar Mitzvah. I climb up on the bed behind him, and I can see he's really getting off on this.

The truth is, so am I.

I've never felt this relaxed and confident with a man before. I hold onto Kisho's hips as I pump in and out of him, and he feels so crazy-good I can't help myself. Before I know what I'm doing, I rear back and slap his ass hard.

"Oh yeah. Fuck yeah. Keep going, Daddy."

So I do. I smack his ass again, and then a few more times, saying all kinds of wild stuff.

"Just wait," I say to him. "Just wait until we're done here, because you're going straight over my knee for a good, sound spanking, do you hear me, young man?"

He mumbles out a response and I stop. I hold him still and give him a few more swats, getting into this game for real.

"I said, 'Do you hear me?'"

"Yes, Daddy. I hear you."

We fall silent as I drill into him. He meets my every

stroke, until suddenly he throws his head back and starts to groan.

"Not yet," I tell him, though I'm almost there myself. "Don't you dare."

But he's too far gone, and he falls down on one elbow and grabs his cock. He finishes on the towel, and I finish inside him.

I pull out and drop down next to him, grabbing him and dragging him up against me. I'm smaller than he is. Ideally, he should be behind me, but somehow, against all probability, I've fallen into the dominant role, so I take it and run with it.

"You're in big trouble now, Mister. Just you wait. I'm going to spank you like nobody's business."

"Oh my god," he says, snuggling up against me. "I always knew you'd turn out to be the strong, silent type."

And he's right.

Suddenly, I am.

"You'd better believe it," I tell him. "Now quiet down before you get yourself in more trouble."

And he says, "Yes, Daddy," and promptly falls asleep in my arms.

FAKING IT

Tilly Hunter

Y ou'd be surprised how many men—strong, powerful, intelligent men—long to kneel at the feet of a dominant woman."

Beth so wanted it to be true. It was her favorite line in the latest book she'd bought, the one she'd hidden at the bottom of the pile of spanking and bondage stories. But it was bollocks. Wishful thinking. The book—*Female Dominance and the Men Who Crave It*—was meant to be nonfiction, but that line was turning out to be pure fantasy.

Beth knew this because she'd chosen a suitably kinky dating site and placed an ad.

Wanted: submissive male. No wimps. No panty-wearers. Intelligence essential, college education prefer-able.

Maybe she'd found all the nut jobs because she hadn't said anything about herself or the relationship she was looking for. Casual fling or longer term? She didn't actually know that yet. What she'd found were the men daft enough to turn up at her house, knowing next to nothing about her, and follow her instructions to kneel at the door while she made them wait.

She'd made her decision on the latest one in a millisecond. But she found it mildly amusing to keep him waiting while she went online to assess other candidates. Not that he knew what she was doing from where she'd locked him in the cupboard under the stairs. Time to let him go and move on.

Beth bent down to slide back the bolt. The cupboard was a little triangle of space she used to store muddy boots and damp umbrellas.

"Out."

Tim crawled out, naked, his slight paunch hanging beneath him like a baggy T-shirt. He stared at the floor, staying obediently on hands and knees, silent.

"You may get dressed and leave."

"Yes, Mistress," he whispered, his voice higher than it should have been. Higher than she wanted it to be, anyway. The man in her fantasies had a deep voice that she would relish breaking into a desperate whimper. The man in her fantasies did not have a slight paunch. She knew she was being mean. She knew it wasn't how real life and real liaisons worked, casual or serious. But this was her fantasy, where she called the shots. For now.

Tim was struggling into his clothes, shoulders hunched and still staring at the floor. But as he pulled on the last garment, he raised his head, dared to look her in the eye and asked, "Mistress, may I ask how I displeased you? So I may learn from it."

Maybe he wasn't so pathetic after all. His look was almost endearing.

"You arrived wearing a cardigan. I cannot abide cardigans on men."

"Thank you, Mistress." He turned and walked down the hall, shutting the front door respectfully quietly behind him. Beth turned back to her screen and read.

Mistress, please allow me to introduce myself. I am a submissive man who would love to kneel at your feet, give you pleasure and accept any correction and punishment you may wish to inflict upon me. I am a senior manager in private business, have a degree in psychology, as well as an MBA, and I work out several times a week.

Tick, tick, tick, tick and tick. This was looking promising. His profile picture was acceptable enough—at least he'd avoided the "here, look at my erect cock" approach. Beth was partial to cock, but choosing a man from a row of purple, veiny members was not her idea of online dating. UseMe79 had neat, dark hair, a hint of stubble and an open, inviting sort of demeanor. His write-up confirmed that he seemed to be a normal human being who just happened to enjoy bondage, tease and denial, corporal punishment and pegging. Bingo.

> *Hi UseMe79, if you want to be used, be at 86 Fairoaks Avenue, Ryton, at 8:00 p.m. tomorrow. Knock, then kneel and wait.*

Simple instructions really, but three guys had already failed by being on their feet when she opened the door. One was rooting around in his pocket for his phone, saying he'd started to doubt he'd got the time right. Another said he was too embarrassed to do it at all; the whole thing was new to him (that wasn't what he'd claimed in his profile). The third said he'd come to show her that as a woman, her natural place was at his feet. Those three didn't make it inside. Then there was John, who had pink frillies on under his jeans, Simon, who had a plastic cock cage on under his and tried to give her the key as a gift, and cardigan Tim with the paunch. Hopefully, UseMe79 would be lucky number seven.

Beth went to bed and gave herself a lazy hand-job.

UseMe79 was bang on time the next evening. Beth shut down her laptop, took a moment to draw her long hair into a high ponytail that made her feel like Queen Bitch, and eventually sauntered to the door. He was kneeling as instructed. He wasn't wearing a cardigan. He looked pretty much like his photo, which she'd discovered was unusual; most of the guys looked anywhere from five to twenty years older.

"What's your real name?"

"Pete, Mistress." His eyes were downcast.

"I'm Beth. Go into the living room and strip."

She pointed and stood back to let him pass. Her front door was screened by shrubs, or she'd have thought twice about the kneeling thing. Mrs. Stubbs at number 83 was probably already counting up the men beating a path to her door.

Pete crawled inside, but then stood and walked into the lounge. Beth hadn't yet decided whether she preferred them to crawl or walk. John had walked; Simon and Tim had crawled. For some unfathomable reason it made her think of a children's farm she'd visited once with her nephew, where they'd staged a race with sheep. Beth pictured the two men instead, racing down a narrow grassy strip on hands and knees with teddy-bear jockeys strapped to their backs and bridles on. She liked the image of the bridle, but she was coming to the conclusion that walking was better, less pathetic. More satisfying when she got to order them to their knees again.

Pete undressed efficiently and left his clothes in a neat pile by the radiator. No paunch. No frillies. No cock cage. No pubes either, which was a surprise.

"Kneel and put your hands on your head." His cock semi jerked. He sank with a practiced grace and raised reasonably toned arms to link his fingers on top of his head. He lowered his gaze to Beth's Converse-clad feet; she couldn't bring herself to do bitch heels too.

He'd gotten farther than anyone else. But she didn't want to give in to wishful thinking. Time to make sure he wasn't too nuts. "Pete, you do know how foolish it is to turn up at a stranger's house without any idea of what they might do to you, strip at their command and kneel at their feet?"

"Yes, Mistress, but my roommate is expecting a text in a while and I gave her your address, just in case."

"Just in case, I see. Her? Do you fuck?"

"No, Mistress, she's gay."

"Is she? Perhaps I should have invited her over instead."

"She's not submissive, Mistress."

"Domme? Vanilla?"

"A domme, Mistress. Sometimes she practices her ropework on me."

"Do you enjoy it? Even though you know there's no fuck?"

"Yes, Mistress."

Apart from the fact that "Mistress" was starting to grate and make her think she should be wearing a PVC catsuit, she reckoned Pete was earning plenty of brownie points. He held a high kneeling position without his legs wobbling. His eyes remained respectfully downcast, and his answers were clear and articulate.

"Pete, would you please get onto all fours and press your forehead to the floor between your hands."

She hadn't got this far with any of the others, so she wasn't prepared for the thrill that shot through her cunt as this buff-looking guy genuflected on the wooden floor in front of her, sticking his ass high and showing the sharp edges of his shoulder blades.

"You say you like pegging. How much experience have you had?"

It was the first "um" and Beth held her breath as she waited for her fantasy world to come crashing down. That didn't happen. It became apparent that the "um" was not because he'd never done it, but because he struggled to remember individual occurrences, he'd experienced it so often.

"My last girlfriend did it to me a few times. Before that, Adele, a girl I was with for four years used to do it regularly. Maybe once a week or so. On average. A few other women…" He trailed off.

Beth was starting to feel out of her depth. The fact was, she'd never fucked a man with a strap-on. And if Pete was that experienced, she feared he would somehow work things out and call her out for the fraud she was.

Beth wasn't really a domme at all. It was her girl-friend, Talia, who was the domme. Talia was the one who got to use the strap-on and leave Beth guessing which hole it was going in. She was the one who made Beth kneel and watch while she made herself come with her vibe even though Beth would have loved to press her face between Talia's thighs and do the job with her tongue. Talia was the one who spanked Beth's ass to throbbing redness.

And then Talia had caught Beth holding the strap-on

to her own hips one day, running her hand over it and wondering what it must be like to thrust it into someone's body.

"You fancy strapping it on, do you?" she'd asked, sneaking up behind her.

"I was just wondering what it's like."

"Well you don't get to find out on me." Talia fucked; she didn't *get* fucked.

"I had a look at that new book of yours too," she'd said.

Beth had flushed.

"Yeah," Talia said. "Funny title. *Female Dominance and the Men Who Crave It*. What about the Women Who Crave It? Like you?"

"I know. It was just a bit of silliness."

"No it wasn't. You want to fuck a man don't you? With my cock."

"Well, I wondered..." Beth had kept hold of the plastic dick, but she'd moved it away from her body as if it might bite her.

"Yes or no?"

"Yes."

"I have an idea," she said. "I worry that you don't get enough cock anyway. Real cock."

Talia wasn't so keen on guys, but Beth liked both. It made her feel greedy.

"We need a subby boy for you to play with. I'll top you and you top him. Place an ad pretending you're a domme and find a good one." And so the quest for their

Pete had begun. Beth had been exclusively Talia's for a while. What she hadn't realized was that Talia worried about that. She was like that, a domme who cared for Beth's needs, even if she sometimes chose to deny them for her own amusement.

"When you've found him, call me over." She made it seem so simple. But Beth knew she'd have to tell Pete first. He was too decent a guy to keep in the dark any longer.

"Pete, I have to tell you, I'm not really a domme. My girlfriend is. She told me to find another sub to play with by pretending I was dominant."

"Um, okay, Mistress." The poor sweet thing still had his forehead pressed to the floor and his voice came out all muffled.

"So you don't have to call me Mistress or do as I say, Pete. You can get up."

He rose, but only back to his kneeling position, putting his hands back behind his head. His cock was hard. Beth wanted to get down there, shuffle her head between his legs and drag him onto her face so she could suck him. "Please, Mistress, I'd prefer to keep doing as you tell me. You've seemed pretty dominant so far."

"Okay, in that case, stop calling me Mistress. And tell me whether you're happy for me to call Talia over— my girlfriend."

"Yes, Mis… Er, Ma'am."

"Jeez, just call me Beth. It's freaking me out. Are you sure about this? Any questions?"

"May I call my friend to let her know everything's okay?"

"Sure, but is that wise? You still don't know what's going to happen."

"I'm sure everything's going to be fine, Beth. More than fine." He smiled.

"How can you know that?"

"I'm a submissive guy who gets off on letting strange women do bad things to me. Being able to suss someone out quickly is kinda important. And you're offering me the chance to have two strange women do bad things to him." He looked up at her through his eyelashes and grinned.

"Who you calling strange? Make your call."

Pete retrieved a phone from among his clothes and went into the hall. Beth called Talia. "I've found him."

"On my way."

The wait was a little awkward. Pete offered to lick Beth's clit but she declined, afraid Talia would disapprove. "Tell you what Pete, I'll just kneel next to you. She'll like that."

Talia had her own key. Beth glanced at Pete as she heard it enter the lock and gave him a nervous smile. Talia let herself in to find the pair of them kneeling with hands on heads.

"Well, that's a nice sight," she said. "But Beth, I'm going to need you to get up and put this on."

Beth climbed into the strap-on harness and buckled up, while Pete sneaked glances up at the purple dildo and started to breathe more raggedly.

"What's your name?"

"Pete, Mistress."

"Well, Pete, I'm going to call you slut. Bend over the back of the sofa, slut, so Beth can fuck you."

"Yes, Mistress."

Pete arranged himself over the couch, head hanging toward the seat cushions, ass high, thighs taut. Beth couldn't see his face but she could see his rib cage heaving. She stroked her hand up her plastic shaft.

"Beth, use plenty of this and get that cock inside him." Pete groaned. Beth felt a flush across her throat as she took the bottle of lube. She squirted it into her hands and rubbed it up and down the plastic before moving her hands to Pete's ass. She looked up at Talia, who nodded encouragement. Beth pressed her slippery fingertips to Pete's hole and rubbed the lube around the entrance, then inched a finger inside. He was making a low, guttural sound into the upholstery. Beth wondered if his sweat was soaking into the fabric yet.

She brought the tip of her cock to his hole and pushed. Whatever kind of relationship she'd had in the past—vanilla or kinky, with men or women—she'd always been the one getting fucked. Getting fucked in the pussy. Getting fucked in the ass. Getting fucked in the mouth. Now she was fucking a man, reducing him to a sweating, moaning mess.

"Oh fuck, that's good," Pete groaned as she slid the shaft inside him and pushed until the base of the harness pressed into his cheeks. Beth slid it back, watching the purple plastic emerge from his tight sphincter. She pulled all the way out and felt a wicked pulse in her pussy as she thought about sliding it in and right out for each thrust instead of fucking him properly. She wanted to tease him. She wanted to open him up afresh with each thrust, see the head of her cock pierce him. She pushed one hand onto his lower back to press him down, wishing he was tied in position. She rested the head of the cock against him again and watched his ass gape for it as he pushed his hips high, trying to push back onto her.

"Enjoying yourself?" Talia asked from beside her, grasping Beth's ponytail. "Enjoying fucking someone? Bending him over and thrusting your cock into his tight hole, forcing him to take you all in?"

"Yes." The hand on her hair made her pause with the shaft halfway into Pete. It overrode the feeling of power and made her want to collapse over the back of the couch herself.

"Well, carry on then. Don't let me stop you. I'm enjoying the view."

Beth pushed all the way in again, but she could no longer coordinate her hips properly. She thrust in short, sharp jerks.

"No, not like that," Talia said. "I liked it when you pulled it right out and I could see his ass close before you put it in again. Do it like that. Bring it right out every time."

Talia kept a firm grip on Beth's hair so Beth could only just see the shaft leave Pete's body. She thrust in again and saw Pete's hands scrabble for the edges of the cushions, gripping them tight. It was a feeling she'd never experienced before, a dizzying feeling of reducing someone to a fuckhole, and knowing they liked it. Craved it.

Smack. Talia's hand came down on her ass as she pushed in, making her hips jab forward. Pete exhaled sharply. Beth cried out. And pulled out. *Smack*, Talia's hand came down just as she had the tip inside him again, and she drove the cock home hard. Beth didn't know how she even managed to stay on her feet. It felt like the grip on her ponytail was the only thing holding her up as Talia continued to spank her butt. It made each thrust brutal and Pete groaned out a wordless stream of throaty noises somewhere halfway between ecstasy and pain.

Beth could feel her pussy growing slick and swollen and calling out for attention, but it was Pete who spoke.

"Permission to come, please Mistress?" His voice was high, desperate.

"No," Talia said. "Beth, stop."

Beth didn't want to stop. She whimpered and gave another thrust, but without the pounding of Talia's hand on her flesh it was a pathetic little movement.

Talia pushed down on her shoulders and Beth allowed herself to be bent forward until she was lying over Pete's back, pressing him down with her cock still inside him. Talia took her arms and placed them across her back, pushing them up to pin Beth into place. Beth felt her girlfriend's other hand smooth her stinging ass, then move between her legs. She parted them to let Talia find her clit more easily, coming onto tiptoes with her weight crushing Pete into the hard back of the couch. She flicked her tongue out to taste the sweat on his spine, wishing it was a mouthful of spunk.

Talia's fingers found her clit and rubbed. No tease. No buildup. Beth could tell Talia wanted her to come. Fast. So she did. So fast it took her by surprise. She pressed her open mouth to Pete's skin as the orgasm overtook her and stifled her own scream against his slippery flesh. Her hips juddered, making her climax ripple into his ass. Her legs used his for purchase, pressing out against them and feeling his muscles tense.

"I want both of you on your knees, back to back."

There was no time to recover before Talia gave the order and let go of Beth's arms. Beth pushed herself off Pete, feeling her skin peel away from his and her cock slip from him again. She knelt, hyperaware of the shaft jutting from her crotch. It suddenly felt huge and obscene, and she wanted to take it off. But she didn't dare. Pete moved slowly as he straightened up his crushed body and knelt behind her, shuffling back until she felt his buttocks press just above hers and his back against her shoulders. Beth wondered if his cock was sticking out too.

"Reach backward around each other. I'm going to tie you together, use my crop on you then decide which one of you gets to make me come with your tongue."

"But…" Beth wouldn't normally question Talia. It wasn't that she was afraid to. It was that she didn't want to. She wanted Talia to be in control.

Talia looked at her. "What?"

"I was enjoying fucking Pete, that's all. I thought I was having a go at topping."

"You were. Now you're not." Talia pulled her crop out of a bag and tapped it against one of Beth's nipples. She only did it lightly, but Beth shuddered nevertheless. "Don't worry, you'll get another turn sometime. If Pete wants to."

She turned to Pete and Beth heard the tap of her crop and felt a shiver run through him.

"Yes, Mistress," he said. "I'd love to."

PLAYING
FOR KEEPS

Alison Tyler

Scared of you, girl. Scared of you…")

I work for *Mayhem*. You've probably seen it on the stands. One of those glossy, avant-garde magazines that popped up about six years ago and made it, despite the critics who claimed there wasn't a market for another "mean sex" zine. There's always a market where sex is concerned. Trust me.

I'm a reporter. *The* reporter, if you ask my editor, Jimmy. I'm the one who doesn't fear any assignment. The one who will walk into a coven and start asking questions. The one who sits placidly by while some frightened eighteen-year-old gets her clit pierced. The one who tried blood sports before writing up a piece, just so I would know what it was all about.

I'm also the one who doesn't cry. No matter how

much pain is involved. If you cry, you lose a bit of yourself. A part of yourself I'm not willing to lose. (Wasn't willing. *Wasn't.*)

"Scared of you, girl." That's what Jimmy says to me whenever I hand him a new article, one fresh from the printer, ink still wet and smeary on the page. "Scared of you, Sarah. What's this one about?"

"Ah, you know, Jimmy. It's the piece on carving."

"Carving?"

I roll up the sleeve of my faded denim work shirt, showing him the fresh marks there, the scabbing wound on the inside of my left bicep. "Carving," I say, quoting from my own story. "Different from tattooing or scarification. A new form of blood sports. When you're through fucking, the top carves a design or a symbol into the bottom's flesh."

"Scared," he says, "scared of you, girl." A shake of his head, of his thick blond hair, and then a kind smile flashes on his handsome face. "How far will you go?"

"What do you mean?"

"For a piece. For a story. How far will you go?"

I leave his office without answering, without looking back. He knows what I would have said, so why voice it? I go as far as it takes. To hell and back, if necessary. 'Cause I've been to hell, hand in hand with Dillon. Though, honestly now, I'm not sure if we are ever coming back.

I met Dillon at the office Halloween party nearly two years ago. *Mayhem* always holds our parties at ritzy hotels, and this was at the B— on Sunset, in one of the finer suites.

("Sweet...yeah...yeah...oh, don't stop....")

No decorating committee had fixed up the place. The owners don't go in for frills. The guys who own and run the magazine, Louis, Jimmy, and David, are ex-frat brothers. Parties to them mean alcohol and sex. More alcohol. More sex. A few spidery cotton strands were draped over the chandelier and red bulbs replaced the white ones in the hallway. The coke in lines on the glass coffee tables was real. The slicked-up, silicone-enhanced girls who looked like call girls *were* call girls. There was expensive booze and plenty of it. There were many rooms and many beds.

I was with Kevin. At least, I *arrived* with Kevin. He's in advertising and ranks himself slightly higher than anyone else does, but he's pretty, so he can get away with it. We were a little beyond fashionably late, and the party had already peaked and was on a downward arc. Most of the rooms were taken. Most of the alcohol had been drunk and some had already been puked into various corners. Nasty. I wanted to turn around right then, but that's when I saw him.

("Faster...bitch, c'mon, open your mouth wider!")

There were a few people in the main room, a few couples dancing together near the bar. The music was on low, very low, so that you could hear noises from the hallway: Lou's dark voice ordering a woman, a whore, no doubt, "Faster, bitch...c'mon..." It simply added to the mood, bringing it up a notch or down a notch, depending on your point of view. A drugged-looking bartender was making out with one of the secretaries in the corner. My editor, Jimmy, had his hand down the art director's panties, digging for treasure, and David was working on her from behind. Normally, I would have joined in the orgy, but when I saw him, when I saw Dillon, the rest of the crowd melted away.

Dillon is Lou's brother, older by about two-and-a-half minutes. I'd heard of him, had even read his work—he writes for a competing magazine doing the same sort of articles that I do—but we'd never met. On first glance, I was surprised that I found him more attractive than Lou. I decided that it was the attitude, the way he carried himself, since he and Lou are identical twins. Still, they do have their own looks. Lou is coated with the sheen of an ad man, a polished surface with little going on beneath. Dillon has the same ebony hair, near-translucent skin, and bottle-green eyes. But he's more substantial, more together. Though on Halloween, he was definitely out of his element, dressed down in a pair of worn jeans and a casual sweater.

We made instant eye contact, and then he walked my way, drink in hand. Kevin didn't mind. He'd already spotted Jacqueline, the ditzier of our two reception-ists, sprawled across a black velvet couch, her red skirt up and G-string visible. As far as I could tell, she was dressed as a slut.

Without a word, Dillon took my hand and led me

through the room to the deserted balcony. "You're Sarah?" he asked when we were standing outside.

"Yeah." I was already holding his hand, so I simply gave it a shake, looking into his dark eyes, seeing my own reflection there.

"Lou's told me a lot about you...."

I let it hang. I'd had a brief fling with Louis my second week on the job. Not too professional, I suppose, but I had been drawn to a promise I saw in his eyes. A promise he failed to keep. Somehow, we'd managed to let the affair dissolve without a lot of office gossip. I wondered now what Dillon knew, whether he'd heard of my "assignments" bent over the boss's desk, panties down, skirt up, gritting my teeth to steel myself for the pain.

He motioned to his attire, "I just got in, and my luggage was lost. Otherwise, I'd have been in costume."

"Lou could have loaned you something of his," I said. "You could have gone as an asshole." That line won me a look, but not a verbal response. After a long beat, I apologized for being so vulgar, and only then did Dillon continue.

"We came here straight from the airport. I'm staying in a room down the hall."

I nodded, retrieving my hand and wrapping my arms around myself. I was dressed as a nymph, a water sprite from one of Klimt's paintings, though I didn't expect anyone to get it. I'd sewn the costume myself: gold swirling fabric, ethereal, sheer. My face was made up dramatically, my deep brown eyes rimmed in kohl. It was a beautiful outfit, but not too well chosen for the chill of October.

When Dillon saw that I was cold, he moved in closer, behind me, wrapping his arms around my own. I wondered, briefly, how we'd gotten so quickly to this point, but then I let it go. That's what office parties are like. At *Mayhem*, anyway.

"Lou is in the master suite doing double time with a set of twins he ordered just for us," Dillon said next. "But I was waiting for you. Why were you two so late?"

I shrugged. "We fucked first."

He started to let me loose, but I snuggled back against him, craving the heat. "Just a fuck," I told him. "To get in the mood. We're not anything. I mean, we've got no ties." I motioned back through the sliding glass door to Kevin and Jacqui, now locked in a sixty-nine on the lounge.

"Then let's go to my room."

I turned in his embrace and stared up at him. Dillon is nearly a foot taller than I am, but I had on spikes, had on a costume, and was filled with confidence. "What did Lou tell you?" I asked. "Why were you waiting to meet me?"

The neon from Sunset filled the hollows beneath his eyes. There was a purple cast to his glossy black hair and his skin looked beyond pale. Vampiric. Then he smiled at me, and at once I understood. Where some smiles can soften a severe countenance, his let me see his true nature: that of a sadist.

"I know you," was all he said, all he needed to say. "I'll give you what you want."

Louis had told him.

"I'll give you what you need," he went on, staring into my eyes. "I need to give it to you."

Lou hadn't been able to keep up the intensity, not to the level that I like. And that was our reason for parting. He kept me on staff, I believe, because I frighten him. Anyone who can take the level of pain that I can...well, you gotta beware.

"I'm not like Lou," he assured me, dragging me by my wrist down the hall. "When I play, I play for keeps."

Once we were in his room, in his space, Dillon had no qualms about stripping my gold dress from my trembling body, wrapping his leather shoelaces around my wrists (we had to improvise), gagging me with my own thin panties, and thrashing me with the heavy leather of his well-worn belt. He worked me, keeping me on the verge for a long, long time. And when he finally used his buckle, he made me come from the pain. That takes someone special. It takes someone in control.

Afterward, when I calmed down, when my breathing grew slow and steady, I looked at him. He'd settled himself in a maroon leather chair across from the bed, regarding me with a curious expression. The only light in the room came from streetlamps outside, but I could see Dillon clearly, his eyes, his skin, and I felt a cold shiver rush through me.

"You're going to be mine," he said.

"I...?"

"You'll fight it, I know. And it might take a while. But I'm patient. I have plenty of time."

"What?" I finally managed, not recognizing my own voice. "What might take time?"

He moved them. I felt the motion rather than saw it—it happened so quickly. At first, he was seated in the chair, legs crossed. Then he was at my side, on the bed, stroking the hair away from my eyes. "It will take time," he repeated. "But, Sarah, I will break you."

I nodded. I thought I understood.

Anyone can beat you. Anyone can give you pain. But it takes an artist to turn that pain into pleasure. To uncover the rough-dirty-seedy-gritty part of it and make it beautiful. And the mix of dark and light, sweat and sin, coming together in such a swank place, made it all the more desirable to me. Crisp white sheets that I bled freely on. Windows opening up onto the Hollywood Hills, letting in the night air, air that cooled the heat of my wounds. The sounds of the city a muted background to the sounds of *our* style of lovemaking.

My training began as soon as we'd moved in together, on the first night in our new house.

"Let go of the headboard, Sarah, and we'll have a much more humiliating lesson tomorrow," he assured me.

Staying still for a whipping, staying still on my own

accord, is nearly impossible for me. Being tied down is so much easier. So much less work. There is no choice involved. No mental trauma. But holding steady, wrists over my head, body clenched, back and thighs and cunt whipped severely. That takes will.

And I failed.

"I don't ask for much," he said sadly as he fastened my wrists with metal handcuffs. "I don't ask for much, do I?"

"No, Dillon."

I watched over my shoulder as he quickly removed the cane from the stand by our bedroom door. I saw the grandfather clock by the stand. It read five to midnight, and then the hands moved faster, at super-speed, and it was suddenly the witching hour. And then, instead of chiming in its normal deep tones, I heard the clock tick: PAIN. That word radiated through my head. I couldn't stop it. I couldn't shut it out: PAIN. PAIN. PAIN. PAIN. Twelve times.

"Close your eyes, child," he said, his voice gone dark. "It's gonna hurt. It's gonna hurt a lot. It will be better for you if you close your eyes." Then a whisper. "Do this much for me, Sarah?" Don't make me have to blindfold you, as well."

I shut my eyes. And waited.

And waited.

And waited.

And then...he began. A white-hot stripe found the roundest part of my ass. Instantly, it was followed by a second, like an echo, a fresh throbbing line right below the first. I howled. But I kept my eyes sealed shut.

There were twelve, total. Burning me. Scalding. And after—after, when he should have held me, when he could have loved me, he left, and I was alone. Wrists cuffed. Body throbbing. Bed shaking with my choked sobs, but my face dry. (I am the one who does not cry.)

It started that night, that first night in our beautiful house. It started, and I immediately understood. I am not by nature a competitive person. But he threw down the glove, and I picked it up.

How long will it take you to break me? How much of your sweet poison can I happily drink...and hold out my cup for more?

It started that night, and every night, at midnight, he brought me the pain I crave, the pain I need, but he did not take me to the edge. Did not bring me to tears. It's what I most wanted, and what I most feared, and sometimes, waking early in the morning, I would see him seated on the edge of the bed, watching me, his lips curved back in a harsh smile, his teeth so white. I would see him, clearly, even in a midnight-black room, and I would hear his voice whispering, "When I play, Sarah...when I play..."

"Tonight," he told me, as we were dressing this past Halloween, dressing for our one-year anniversary. "Tonight, you will become mine."

I turned to look at him from my vanity table, my hand poised midway to my lips, about to slide on the crimson gloss. "What, Dillon?"

"You heard me."

"Yes."

"You'll cry, my darling. And when you cry..." Then he smiled, canines bared, and I felt the chill start at the base of my spine and work its way through my body.

He'd let me heal for the entire month of October because he'd chosen a sheer dress for me to wear. We were attending the *Mayhem* office party, and I was going as his muse, his dream, his prize. The string-backed chemise was cinnamon-hued, of the softest, sheerest silk. Dillon was playing himself: my Owner.

This time, the party was in a ballroom in a Beverly Hills hotel. We arrived late, but before midnight, and Dillon pulled me onto the full dance floor by a simple yank of the diamond-flecked leash attached to the thin leather band hugging my slender throat. Then we were dancing, moving together, the rest of the room dissolving from my vision.

I set my head on his shoulder and his arms came tight around me. I could feel his heart beating, thought I could actually hear it over the throbbing of the rhythm section, the staccato tapping of women's heels on the wood floor. Spinning, twirling, the heat of the people around us that I couldn't register, the feel of his arms, tight, then relaxing his grip as he moved a step away and slid the dress over my head and from my body, my trembling body. Dillon always makes me tremble.

Nearly nude, still dancing with him, clad only in a skin-toned garter belt, sheer hose, matching panties, black pumps. Moving against him, so obviously his property, feeling the gaze of other partiers, not shock, but acceptance. It's always that kind of a party.

"You ready, Sarah? You ready, child?"

A nod, a low murmur.

"Come on, then."

And he was leading me to the center of the room, bending me over the punch table, taking off his belt, thrashing me. Just as hard as when we're in private. Just as hard as when we're alone. Harder, if possible. The table shook with each blow, though I tried to absorb it with my body. The punch bowl jogged against the glasses and spilled crimson drops of liquid onto the white linen cloth—drops more watery then the flecks of my blood that came next.

"Hold still. Take it." A hiss, under his breath. People had come in tight to watch. I was the show.

"Don't make me have to tie you."

No...no...that would be bad. That would be unbearable.

My fists were clenched, my wrists crossed and held over my head. My eyes were closed until he ordered, "Look at me," wanting me to open my eyes and stare in the mirror on the wall across the way while he slammed into me with his belt. I obeyed him, frightened when I saw the glow in his dark eyes. "You're gonna break tonight. You're gonna cry. You know it." A whisper. "You know it."

Fear. Can I tell you about fear? It's a cold fist around your heart. It's a metal ball rolling back and forth in the pit of your stomach. It's a space between your ribs that hurts all the time.

All the time.

A different kind of hurt than the blow of a belt. A different kind of pain than a slap or a strapping or a caning or an ass-fucking. Not a good kind of pain at all. Fear doesn't offer a cool-down of pleasure when it's over. It leaves you shivering and cold and turned inside out.

Looking into Dillon's eyes, I felt fear.

And fear is Dillon's favorite game.

("Scared of you, girl, scared of you.")

The belt kept coming, then the buckle. People had moved in even closer. I could see on Lou's face, a blander version of Dillon's, a look of drunken pleasure at my pain. I could see Jimmy, dressed tonight in drag as he is every Halloween, his peony-painted lips turned up in a half smile. "Scared of you, girl..."

The party photographer was snapping away. It was, as I've said, that kind of party. And our magazine, *Mayhem*, is that kind of magazine. Anything goes, if it gets you there. Anything you want. Anything you need.

Dillon's black gabardine slacks were undone now, and as I watched, he motioned for a strawberry blonde in a bunny suit to get down on her knees on the dance floor. "Make it wet," he told her. "Get my cock all sloppy and wet." She beamed at him, happy to be chosen, glad for the opportunity to serve. Dillon brings out that emotion in people. In the mirror, I could see her gossamer curls bouncing as she took him deep in her throat. I started to move, started to push myself up from the table, but Dillon whispered my name, just my name, and I stayed still.

("Scared of you...")

When he saw that I was crying, he roughly shoved her away from him. Never cried. Never cried before. I am the one. The one who can enter a room full of hardcore drug addicts and get them to tell me about their childhood, about their past lives of abuse that the drug-dreams take away. I am the one who has bent over a leather-horse in an S/M club to receive the pain for someone else, someone weaker. I am the one who doesn't cry.

But I was crying.

And then it didn't matter anymore, because he was in me, fucking my ass, his hands wrapped in my dark curls, his features marred, blurred in the mirror with his victory. And my fear.

The people moved in closer. The heat of their bodies was stifling. I heard bits of conversations—"Scared of you..." "Sweet..." "Open your mouth..."—then tighter, closer, the heat overwhelming me, my tears blurring my vision.

You lose it. Do you understand? When you cry, when you break, you lose part of yourself. An important part.

It shatters, cracks into silver glass fragments that are coldly beautiful, like an angel's complexion, but gone. With the tears, as with blood, you lose something that never comes back.

He covered my body with his, bringing his lips to my ear and hissing, "Sarah, are you truly crying? Does it hurt?" fascinated by my pain, by my defeat. Then his mouth slid lower, to my neck, biting me, bringing the blood to the surface. And back to my ear, his lips and tongue wet and dark with my life: "But you like it when it hurts, when it hurts deep inside. It's what you like best."

Then he was up again, fucking me hard. Twin lines of blood dripping down his chin, two deep punctures at the side of my neck. I watched his reflection. His body. Pounding hard and fast. Coming, coming, deep inside my ass. His hands still clenched in my hair. He'd won.

And I'd lost. But that's the way it goes, doesn't it?

That's the way it goes, when you're playing for keeps.

ALL WORK
AND NO PLAY

Anna Mitcham

I click SEND then shut down my PC and prepare to leave the office for the day to meet a few friends in a nearby bar. I hear the beep of my colleague's computer as it tells him he has mail, and I glance up and catch his eye. He holds my gaze a second too long before moving his mouse to his inbox and reading my message. I watch him take a deep breath and slowly shake his head. I'm smiling inwardly as I pick up my coat and stride purposefully behind his desk, making my way toward the door. My colleague turns in his chair as I pass and I can feel his eyes on my retreating figure, taking in my black stiletto boots and short skirt, and I feel a frisson of excitement. I'm well aware that I am playing with fire, bringing my "hobby" into the office, but somehow the risk makes it all the more appealing.

I am only just out of the building when my phone vibrates in my pocket, taking me by surprise. It's a text message.

You can't send an email like that and then fuck off... it says. I scroll down. *I intend to punish you severely.*

I raise my eyebrows at this and immediately reply with a simple, *How?*

In the time it takes me to get to the bar, greet my friends and order a drink, my phone has vibrated once more.

By pinching your nipples between my fingers until you don't know whether you're moaning in pleasure or pain.

I take a sharp intake of breath as I feel my pussy moisten and my nipples become erect. This is no longer the innuendo-laced electronic flirting that I initiated earlier; my colleague has swiftly upped the stakes and I'm surprised and turned on by his brazenness. I press REPLY and type, *Not before I have wrapped my lips around you and taken you deep into my mouth.*

I place my mobile on the chair between my thighs so that the next time a message comes through I feel it vibrate on my clit. When it happens the message reads, *Then I'm then going to flick my tongue over your clitoris before thrusting my throbbing cock deep into your warm, wet pussy.*

Oh my god. I briefly close my eyes as these images dance through my mind, and I feel myself getting wetter. I take a few swigs of my wine and indulge in inane chitchat with one of my friends, all the while feeling my clit pumping between my legs, and I struggle to control the urge to grind my hips against something. I quickly type, *Wish you were fucking me right now,* and then I reluctantly drag my attention back to the story of my friend's latest disastrous blind date. It isn't long before my phone vibrates again.

Antonia. Need you back at office now.

What? I'm taken aback by the message. I thought I was in for an evening of cheeky sexting over drinks with friends before making my excuses, going home and getting to work with my vibrator—my idea of a perfect night! All of a sudden I'm being challenged to follow through with fantasies I never actually intended to act upon—at least, not so soon. And with the only buildup a brief bout of textual titillation. Besides, I barely even know my colleague—I've only worked here a couple of weeks. On the other hand, that kind of makes it more exciting, and I'm intrigued and turned on and not one to run from a challenge. After a few moments I make a decision and quickly tell my friends that I've remembered something my boss wanted me to do, and that I'll be back soon. I grab my bag and make my escape before I can change my mind and chicken out. My friends tut and roll their eyes at each other—work-obsessed Antonia—but let me go without suspicion.

As I walk the short distance back to the office I realize with surprise that I am nervous. I'm always the one in control, in these situations, and am not used to a man giving as good as he gets, let alone taking the reins. *Maybe I've met my match,* I think to myself and a little shiver of excitement runs through me. I quicken my step, desperate to find out what's in store for me back at the office. As I'm running up the stairs—I have far too much nervous energy to take the lift—another message comes through.

I'm waiting, Antonia...

I reach the top floor and enter the open-plan office, my heart pounding with apprehension and anticipation. I can't see my colleague anywhere so I wander in and sit down at my desk, suddenly paranoid that I have been taken for a ride or gotten the wrong end of the stick. I jump as a hand comes firmly down on my shoulder and a gruff voice whispers in my ear, "Time to put your money where your mouth is..."

My colleague swivels my chair around to face him and I see that he has unbuttoned his fly and his cock is standing proudly, level with my face. "This is for distracting me during office hours," he murmurs as he winds his fingers into my long hair and inserts his penis into my mouth, pushing himself deeper and deeper.

My surprise has rapidly turned into blatant desire and I feel myself reacting between my legs. I maneuver myself so that I can grind my hips up against the leg of the desk. My colleague is fully inside my mouth now and I use my tongue to tease the tip of his cock each time he pulls back, before thrusting once more. I run my hands over his tight arse and bring one around to gently massage his balls as he grunts in approval, his cock roughly working in and out.

"Fuck, Antonia," he moans, disengaging himself and hitching me up onto the desk. My head falls back over the edge and I am able to see out of the office's floor-to-ceiling windows into the apartments opposite. A thrill runs through me as I realize how easily we could be caught in the act. I look up at my colleague and see from the slow grin creeping across his face that he's thinking the same thing.

He forces the already-low neckline of my top down over my breasts and releases my nipples from the clutches of my bra. He takes first one, then the other in his mouth, licking and sucking them expertly while rubbing my pussy through my skirt. I fear I may come there and then. I reach up to push his head down between my legs, and he shifts my skirt up around my waist. He lets out a small gasp when he sees that my tights are, in fact, stockings. He slips a finger into the crotch of my knickers and pushes them to one side as he gets to work on me, circling his tongue over my clit while slipping a finger into my pussy. I moan with pleasure and move my hips against him as the rhythm of his tongue gets faster. He reaches up with his free hand and squeezes my nipple between his thumb and forefinger so hard that I cry out in pain. But I don't want him to stop.

Just as I am about to give myself over to the orgasm, something catches my eye and I see that there is a man standing in one of the apartment windows. He is tall and broad and seems to have one hand inside his trousers. In the other he holds a camera, which he is pointing at us. I have never really thought of myself as an exhibitionist but find that the presence of this stranger has increased my desire tenfold. I look straight into the camera as I succumb to my colleague's touch and come loudly and violently.

He raises his head and clocks the man at the window and I notice that he is just as turned on by it as I am. He climbs onto the desk and hovers over me, his cock rock hard and throbbing, and I see a sheen around his mouth—evidence of where he has just been. My skirt is still up around my waist so I slowly unzip it and ease it over my hips, letting it fall to the ground, as my colleague pulls my top over my head and removes his shirt to reveal a ripped physique. I am now naked apart from my pushed-aside G-string, my stockings and my stiletto boots. He reaches his hands beneath my hips and turns me over, so that I am on all fours, facing the camera, and he is behind me. He reaches around with one hand and cups my breast before twisting it in my hair, pulling my head back so that the camera gets a full view of my breasts. He guides himself into me from behind, filling me up as he thrusts deeper each time.

I lower my head slightly so that I can look at the man in the window. He has released his cock from his trousers and is moving his hand vigorously up and down. I am certain that he has zoomed in as much as his camera will allow and I have never before felt so turned on as my colleague reaches his hands around and starts to roughly rub my clitoris. "Play with those nipples," he barks. He pounds himself hard into me, each thrust accompanied by a guttural grunt, and I feel myself matching him as I keep my eyes on the man in the window.

My colleague's grunts are getting louder and his thrusts faster, yet I am taken by surprise when he raises a hand and spanks me sharply. I yelp as the sting rings through me, and my breath is taken away. He strikes me again, and again, and another time. Each time with more force than the time before, while his cock pounds into me. I gasp in shock each time his hand connects with my body and grit my teeth as I await the next smack, but it isn't long before I notice that I am enjoying the sensation and I feel a second orgasm starting to erupt.

My colleague's thrusts and spanks are getting more and more urgent, and as I reach my second climax, he lets himself go and we come together with an intensity and ferocity that I have never felt before. As the orgasm subsides I look out at the apartments and notice the man at the window convulsing as he brings himself to orgasm before turning off the camera and moving away from the window. My colleague withdraws from me and for a few moments we lie side by side on my desk as we catch our breath, laughing, the reality of what we have just done beginning to sink in.

"Antonia!" one of my friends drunkenly calls as I walk back into the bar, and I wonder if my dirty secret is written all over my face. "You work too hard!" she chastises.

Another friend pipes up and teases, "You know what they say, Antonia, all work and no play…"

I take their jests with good humor as I sit down among them, wincing ever so slightly when my bottom connects with the chair. *If only they knew,* I think to myself smugly, as I pour a large glass of merlot. *If only they knew.*

PRISON BITCH

David Wraith

Her."

I had no idea whether that single syllable would unlock one of my greatest fantasies, or just throw a monkey wrench into an already complicated dominant/ submissive relationship. The "her" in question was my one-word answer to Mistress Monika's question, "What do you want for your birthday?" At that point in our history together, I wasn't sure how Mistress Monika would react to me saying I wanted another woman, even jokingly. I was kidding, but I was kidding on the square, and Mistress Monika could tell. I held my breath until she answered, "I'll see what I can do."

Maybe it was meant to be: the timing was too perfect. If Mistress Monika had asked me what I wanted at any other time in any other place, it's not like I would have

had the big brass balls to say, "Iris Crocker," if she
hadn't been walking right toward us.

Iris was a butch lesbian. Mind you, this was 1995,
before the AJ Soprano Lesbians with their backward
baseball caps and pastel tracksuits. Before the Eminem
Lesbians with their platinum-blonde Caesar haircuts.
These were the days of the Elvis Lesbian and the James
Dean Lesbian. I was an Elvis man myself, and Iris
played the Elvis Lesbian to the hilt. That night in the
dungeon, Iris was wearing her jet-black hair, which was
usually in a pompadour, parted in the middle with spit
curls on either side of her forehead. She wore a tight,
white, ribbed tank top with a black lace push-up bra
underneath. From the waist up, she was all cleavage and
broad, bare shoulders. Her dark blue jeans were folded
over at the cuff and her black Doc Marten boots shone
like mirrors. I felt my erection crawling slowly across
my inner thigh as I imagined myself kneeling on the
floor naked, licking those boots so hard she could feel
my tongue through the steel toes.

It was as if she knew she was being discussed. No
sooner had I said "her" than she had pulled a sliver
flask from her pocket and taken a swig as she made her
way over to us. A chain hung from her belt loop that
went to the wallet in her other pocket. The chain wallet
completed the look, like a pocket square on a dapper
gentleman, "What are you two talking about?" Iris
asked. She offered the Mistress her flask and she took
a swig and gave it back. Iris tilted the flask toward me

and looked at the Mistress for permission to offer me some. When the Mistress almost imperceptibly shook her head, back in Iris's pocket the flask went.

"Assume the position."

I just stood there, not quite sure what position she meant. It was Caroline, the statuesque transwoman, who had answered when I knocked on Goddess Evelyn's door. When I didn't move, she grabbed me by the shoulders, spun me around and shoved me up against the wall of Goddess Evelyn's foyer. I braced myself for whatever would come next, scanning the room for any signs of my Mistress. It was the day before my birthday and I had shown up at the Goddess's house as my Mistress had instructed.

Caroline was dressed like a police officer, but in her light-brown button-down shirt and dark-brown pants, she looked more like a sheriff's deputy or a state trooper. An interrogation scene? I pressed my palms to the wall and spread my legs. She patted me down from my ankles to my waist, roughly grabbing my crotch and giving me a light punch in the balls for good measure. "Do you have any concealed weapons?"

"No Ma'am."

"Well, maybe you should, considering who you'll be sharing a cell with." She patted down my chest and pinched my nipples. Her fake nails felt like the serrated edge of a hunting knife.

Sharing a cell? A prison scene? My Mistress had

loaned me to Goddess Evelyn a year and a half ago to help her move into this house. I had seen the secret room in the basement that had a wrought-iron barred door. The Goddess told me her real estate agent had no idea why the room was there, but the moment she'd seen it, she knew this was the home for her. I imagined my Mistress waiting for me in the cell.

"I'm not satisfied with the search." It was my Mistress, walking down the hall with her arms folded, in a pin-striped navy-blue blazer and matching pencil skirt, cream-colored silk blouse, stockings and open-toed stilettos. "Strip him."

"Yes, Warden." Caroline said. If my Mistress was "the Warden," then who the hell was waiting for me in the cell? Before I could ponder any further, Caroline pulled my jacket off, snatched my shirt over my head, undid my pants and yanked them to my ankles. I stepped out of my shoes and my jeans and stood there naked, covering my erection with my hands.

"Remove your hands," the Mistress commanded. "Don't try to cover yourself. Open your mouth and lift your tongue." Caroline looked down my throat. "Lift your ball bag," the Mistress said. "Turn around. Let me see the bottoms of your feet. Now bend over, spread your cheeks and cough."

"Body cavity search, Warden?"

Looking at her upside down, through my legs and past my scrotum, I could still see the smile on the Mistress's face. "I think that will be taken care of soon enough."

The Mistress and Caroline led me to the bathroom
and instructed me to stand in the tub. Caroline handed
me a bar of soap, then picked up the hose that was
crudely attached to the faucet, turned on the spigot and
sprayed me with freezing cold water. I wasn't sure if the
Mistress was speaking to Caroline or to me when she
said, "Don't miss a spot." She instructed me when to
spread my legs, when to turn around and bend over and
when to open wide and "Take the spray" in my mouth.
When I was thoroughly clean and thoroughly humiliated, Caroline took a stiff towel that felt like it had been
sprayed with starch and hung out to dry, and wiped me
down like I was a '78 Oldsmobile with a bad paint job.

Caroline placed a folded orange jumpsuit and a pair
of flip-flops in my arms, and said, "You can dress in your
cell. Follow me." I looked at the Mistress and I think she
could tell I was hoping she'd be coming with me, but her
sympathetic smile let me know I was on my own.

I followed Caroline down wooden steps to the basement. She led me to the back and opened the iron-barred
door. "Good luck."

The cell had been remodeled since I'd helped Goddess
Evelyn move in. Bunk beds, a sink and a toilet had been
put in and the room had been painted a bland, indus-
trial beige. Whoever had done the work was probably
familiar with the county lockup. I was impressed. There
was someone sitting on the bottom bunk, facing away
from me reading the paper, in what looked like nurse's
scrubs, but they were prison orange like my jumpsuit.

"What do you think you're doing?" It was Iris Crocker. She put her paper down and stood up. I was petrified.

"Getting dressed."

"Uh-uh, nobody wears clothes in my cell but me." She took the shoes and jumpsuit and put them on the top bunk. "Besides, you got better things to do; these boots aren't going to shine themselves."

I looked around the mostly empty cell noticing a duffle bag in the corner, "Do you have any polish?"

She grabbed me by my face, so hard I had to stumble to keep my balance. She pressed her thumb and index finger into the hinges of my jaw, forcing my lips apart, then slipped two fingers into my mouth like she was fish-hooking me, "You got all the polish I need, right here."

She sat on the bottom bunk, crossed her arms and waited. I was stunned for a minute and didn't move, "Unless you have a really long tongue, I suggest you get on your knees and get over here." I took a step toward her. "You're not too bright, are you? I said, 'get on your knees and get over here,' not the other way around." I got on all fours and crawled over to her. "See, you're not as dumb as you look."

My dick got hard the moment I wrapped my hands around the ankle of her right boot to lift it to my mouth, but before I could, she planted it in the center of my chest and pushed me off my knees onto my hip. "You try that again and see what happens. My foot is right where it's supposed to be. You don't bring my boot to your mouth; you bring your mouth to my boot." I got all the way down with my belly on the cold cement floor. "Lick harder! I want to feel that tongue through my leather. Yeah, that's what's what I'm talking about." I pressed my tongue into her boot as hard as I could. Looking up for approval, I saw that she had closed her eyes and was stroking her inner thigh. A phallic bulge was visible beneath her hand and the orange fabric of the jumpsuit.

"Get back on your knees," she said. "You know what you can do for me?"

"No, what?" She slapped me across the face, hard. My cheek was hot and vibrating. My jaw hurt. I felt tears welling up, so I bit my bottom lip to keep from crying and stared at her boots to keep from making eye contact.

"I said, 'Do you know what you can do for me?'"

"No *Ma'am*. What can I do for you?"

"*Ma'am*?"

"What can I do for you, *Sir*?"

"That's better. I'll tell you what you can do," she said, as she caressed my hot cheek and whispered in my ear, "You can suck my motherfuckin' dick." She tugged on the drawstring and pulled the pants just low enough to pull out an eight-inch, peach-colored dildo that she was wearing in a white leather harness that looked like a jockstrap. I could tell from the way she stoked it that the dildo was doubled ended. I had never sucked a cock before, natural or synthetic, but the thought of wrapping my mouth around her cock made me want to. I stared at it so hard I was seeing double and was not quite sure which of the two cocks in my face was the real one. I was afraid I'd guess wrong and put my eye out, but before I could choose, she grabbed me by the back of the neck, "Don't look at it; swallow it!" She pulled my head down and shoved her cock in my mouth.

It was colder and stiffer than flesh, but as I pushed down on it with the roof of my mouth, I imagined the other end sinking deeper insider her, pressing against her G-spot. I tried to take it all and when she heard me gag, she said, "Relax," and I did. I pressed my cheek against her inner thigh and moved my head from side to side and imagined the flared base between the two ends stimulating her clit. I looked up and saw her roll her head back on her shoulders, eyes closed. She opened her eyes and saw me looking up at her, "You're lucky you're such a good cocksucker or there's no way I'd let you eyeball-fuck me like that." Part of me wanted to avert my eyes, but I didn't. I didn't even blink. I just stared right into her eyes with my lips wrapped around her cock. "You are a good cocksucker, aren't you?" I just kept sliding my mouth up and down her cock until she hauled off and smacked me upside the jaw, knocking me on my side. "Well, are you a good cocksucker or aren't you?"

I was breathless, "Yes, Sir."

"Yes, Sir, what?"

"Yes, Sir, I am a good cocksucker, Sir." By the time I was back on my knees, she was towering over me.

"You're pretty slow on the uptake, but you're

learning. As you were, then." She grabbed my head again and fucked my mouth. Standing with both hands on my head, there was nothing to hold up her pants, which fell to her knees. I could see the curve of her hips and her big, muscular thighs. She took one hand off my head to pull her shirt up out of my way and I could see her soft, smooth belly, which was undulating with her heavy breathing. I pressed my forehead into her belly, feeling the warmth of her skin and tugging gently on her cock with my lips as she rocked her hips in and out.

I reached for her thighs and just before making contact, I pulled my mouth away from her to ask, "Sir, may I?"

"You may." I gripped the backs of her thighs for balance, and pulled her into me, feeling the muscles in her legs tense and release as I took all of her cock down my throat, her inner thighs pressing into both sides of my face. Now when I breathed in, I inhaled the sweet, earthy scent of her pussy, not just the showroom-silicone smell of the dildo. "Yeah, that's what I'm talking about."

After a few minutes, I felt her shudder like she was about to come, but she stopped me, pulled her pants up and snatched me up by my armpits. "That's enough. Come here." She dragged me over to the foot of the bed, bent me over, and I instinctively grabbed the metal bed rail with both hands. She fished some short lengths of hemp rope from a bag in the corner of the cell and tied my wrists to the railing. She slapped my bare ass and held a fistful of cheek in her right hand, "You know what happens next, don't you?" She stuck her right boot between my ankles and kicked my legs apart.

"Are you going to spank me, Sir?"

"Not quite."

I watched over my shoulder as she went back to the bag in the corner, produced a condom and slid it over the dildo. She put a rubber glove on her left hand and picked up a bottle of lube. I closed my eyes and dropped my head. I was breathing so heavily; it was all I could do to keep from convulsing. My heart was beating like it was trying to escape. I felt her left, gloved hand reaching around me and grabbing my balls. She wrapped her bare hand around my throat and pulled me close. Her breath was warm and wet in my ear as she said, "Are you okay?" Her voice was different. Feminine. Familiar. The Iris that I knew. "If you need to safeword, you can safeword."

"No, Sir."

"Okay, then. Just relax." I didn't hear anything for the next few seconds. I just kept staring at the beige wall at the other end of the room. Then she said, "Take a deep breath," and a lubed-up, latex-covered finger slid in my asshole. I exhaled and she pumped her finger in and out of me. It was nice. Then she pulled away my right asscheek with her right hand and the next time the finger slid out, I felt her cock slide in. It burned and I clenched up against it, but she just rested her hand on my shoulder, saying, "Relax."

Iris worked her cock inside me, slowly, gently. Each time I took it deeper, she backed off and waited for my breath to catch before she went farther. She could feel me giving myself over to her, inch by inch. She just repeated, "Relax," in my ear and took her time. Soon her hips were right up against my ass, and I was taking all of it. Her legs pressed into my legs. She squatted down a bit and bent her knees into the backs of my knees and my legs buckled. I heard her latex glove snap and hit the floor and she wrapped her arms around my chest. She rocked her hips slowly back and forth against my ass, "That's it, just relax. Daddy's got you. You know who you are?"

My eyes were rolling in the back of my head, my words sounded like linen hanging on a clothesline in the wind. "No, Daddy, tell me who I am."

"You're my bitch. Are you my bitch?"

"Yes, Sir. I'm your bitch."

She gave my shoulders a hard shove, doubling me over, then grabbed my hips and pulled me backward, "Then Daddy's gonna fuck you like a bitch." She was holding me in place so that I couldn't move with her. She fucked me hard. There was a sound at the back of my throat, but my mouth was open and nothing was coming out. I gripped the bed rail, dug my feet into the floor and tensed everything but my asshole. My armpits got sticky. I could feel beads of perspiration sliding along my spine and down my asscrack. I wasn't moving, but I was getting drenched with sweat. I tried to ignore the huge cock that was being slammed into me and focus on the oddly comforting feeling of her thighs slapping against my ass with each thrust. "Whose ass is this?" She slapped me across the ass so hard it echoed on the cell walls. "Do I ask rhetorical questions? Whose ass is this?"

"It's yours, Daddy."

She dug her fingers into my shoulders and a rattling breath came out of her. She stood still and her legs shook. She came. Thank god, she came. She let me go and I collapsed over the bed rail, ass in the air.

She went back to the bag and produced a cigar and a Zippo lighter.

"That's enough." Mistress Monika's voice sounded like it was coming from another dimension. "Cut him down." By this time I was on the floor with my wrists still attached to the bed rail, arms splayed out crucifixion style.

Iris got a pair of safety shears from her bag and cut my bonds. I fell into a heap on the concrete, rubbing the ligature marks on my wrists. Iris smiled at Mistress Monika, put the cigar in her mouth, cut the tip of it off with the shears and lit it. She took a puff and through a cloud of smoke said, "This one's nice, you bring him back anytime," and winked at the Mistress. Mistress Monika smiled at Iris and led me away. Before we reached the stairs, Iris called out, "Hey, happy birthday."

THE DAY
I CAME
IN PUBLIC

D. L. King

L isten honey," Marla said, "don't knock it until you've tried it."

At the time, the idea of calling your boyfriend "Sir" and letting him order you around didn't strike me as the sexy romance she made it out to be. "Are you telling me he hits you?" I grabbed her hand across the table. "Marla! Do you have bruises? Has he hurt you?"

"Listen, it's not like that. It isn't abuse," she said. I let her hand go but continued to stare at her over my martini. "Don't jump to conclusions. I want you to make me a promise. I'm gonna give you a book to read. Read it and then we'll talk again. Promise me you'll keep an open mind until then."

She reached into her workbag and pulled out a well-worn paperback. "What is this? Porn? What, you just carry this stuff around with you all the time now? I don't know what's happening to you, Marla. I'm afraid for you."

"I figured you'd be a hard sell, and I wanted to be prepared. Just read it, Libby, then we'll talk."

I looked down at the book on the table. It was the first volume in that fairy tale trilogy. I'd heard about it but hadn't read it. "I don't know what difference you think it'll make, my reading a fairy tale. I'm worried about you, Marla."

"Read the book. We'll meet here next Friday, after work, and we can talk more then. I don't want to discuss it anymore, not till you've read the book."

"But Marla…"

"Nope! What I want to talk about now is Joe and Holly. I walked in on them in the copy room yesterday. I gotta go to the bathroom; order me another drink? I'll be right back."

I was a little concerned but she seemed fine and we got off on another topic. Between the vodka and a long workweek, I couldn't concentrate on anything heavy anyway. I forgot all about Marla's crazy boyfriend and the book until Saturday afternoon, when I remembered I hadn't taken care of my empty lunch container from Friday. I took the Tupperware out of my bag and noticed the book hiding underneath.

I took it out. Pretty cover. I didn't recognize the author's name. I seemed to recall this was written by someone famous, but under an assumed name. It must be pretty dirty for the writer not to want to own up to it. Why the hell would he—she—whatever, want to hide unless they were ashamed? But I remembered hearing that lots of writers, famous ones, published their books under false names, pseudonyms, like Mark Twain. I didn't have time for this anyway. I had laundry and housecleaning to do. I left the book on the coffee table and promptly forgot about it.

When I finally settled down to relax in front of the TV, there was nothing on. I thought about watching a DVD but couldn't get excited about anything in my collection. That's when I noticed the book.

Three hours later, a little out of breath and with drenched underwear shoved tightly between the swollen lips of my pussy, I realized it was after midnight. Holy fuck! I needed to go to bed—but first I needed to find my vibrator.

The end of the week finally came and Marla and I left work at five on the dot to secure a table at our favorite haunt.

"Well?" she said.

"Yeah, okay."

"Yeah okay what?"

"Yeah, okay, I get it."

"And...?" She grinned.

"Yeah, yeah, okay, it was hot," I conceded.

"Can I pick 'em or can I pick 'em?" she asked the ether. Directing her attention to me once more, she said, "I just knew if you understood, you'd get it and be turned on. So?"

"So, what? That stuff isn't real. I mean it's hot, but those things don't happen. No place like that really exists and no one does those kinds of things really. I mean, it's a hot fantasy, but that's all it is."

"Of course that's a fantasy. But you'd be surprised what there really is; what people get up to; what's out there if you look for it. I know you want to know more." And then she proceeded to give me a primer in kinky sex and how to find it.

Once I started looking, I couldn't believe how much there was. All of a sudden I understood the true purpose of the Internet. I researched and researched and couldn't believe what I'd been missing all my life. Who knew? Well, I guess everyone but me. Sometimes I'm slow on the uptake.

I joined lists. I joined chats. I read lots of smut. I watched lots and lots of porn. Finally, I took an online friend up on attending a public meeting at a local diner. I liked him. He was obviously intelligent and seemed to know what he was talking about. He also made me cream my jeans every time I saw his name in my in-box.

He was the domliest of doms. We'd be chatting about art or work or something equally innocuous and he'd write something like, *Pull your pants down to your ankles. Pull your panties down to the top of your pants. Now, sit back down. No touching,* then he'd continue on with whatever we'd been chatting about before.

Just when all the wet was beginning to dry up, he'd refocus my attention to my bare ass and naked pussy.

He seemed to know just when to give me another sexual push to keep me on edge. Sometimes at the end of our correspondence for the evening, he'd take pity on me and give me permission to come but, as often as not, he'd tell me to go straight to bed—that if I couldn't keep my hands off myself, I was only permitted to touch my nipples. Yeah, that would make for some seriously sleepless nights.

I'd find myself thinking of him at odd times. In the middle of my commute to work, his last email would pop into my head and completely carry me away from reality. I'd be sure the people on the bus could smell me. Or worse, I'd be in a sales meeting and the same thing would happen. I'd have to fight to keep focused. So, of course, the idea of finally meeting him in the flesh, as it were, was exciting, and a little scary.

It was scary because I didn't know how I'd act around him. I had my idea of what he looked like, but what if I was wrong? All I knew for sure was that he had dark hair and was physically fit. What if I wasn't attracted to him? What if I was? God, what if he wasn't attracted to me? Scary.

I was definitely attracted to the personality I knew online. He was my ideal, I suppose. He wasn't the "On your knees, slave; lick my balls" kind of dom. I'd met plenty of them online and I couldn't take those guys seriously. I mean, really! No, he was someone who wanted the same things I wanted; someone I could believe in; someone I could take seriously because he took both

me, and himself, seriously. I could tell this guy wasn't
playing, even when he was playing.

"Libby?"

I must have looked totally lost. I'm not all that
outgoing under normal circumstances, but here I was,
standing by the door of the back room of a diner,
looking at ten or fifteen total strangers, all of whom
were into kinky sex to one degree or another. A woman
was making her way toward me with a welcoming look
just as I heard the masculine voice behind me.

"Libby?" I turned and he smiled. "Hi. I'm Chris. I'm
glad you made it."

My mind was on autopilot as he introduced me to
all the people. All these thoughts swam through my
consciousness: *Chris... Wow, he's short... Great voice...
Gee, I didn't know he wore glasses... Nice ass; yeah, he
is pretty fit... Look at those eyes... That voice, god, that
voice... He's hot—I think he's hot—he's...look at those
hands. He's talking about buffalo wings and I'm getting
wet...*

Finally, things started wrapping up and people
began to leave. "Shall we go somewhere and chat?" he
suggested.

We went to a quiet pub and talked until they closed,
then made plans to meet at the diner the following
Saturday. We'd go to a private S/M club so that I could
watch people play; watch him play. He wanted to take
things slowly.

The week seemed to crawl by. I met Marla at the bar on Friday, as usual, and she asked how the meeting went. I told her all about it and about how I was going to the Mansion on Saturday.

"Ooh, I love that place. Hey, maybe I'll see you there. Are you going to play?"

"In public? I don't think so! I could never get naked in public—um, do people really get naked there?"

"Sure. Sometimes. Sometimes they leave on some stuff. It depends. But if you aren't going to play, why are you going?"

"Chris wants me to watch. He said it would be good for me to see what it's like, to watch the doms and see the reactions of the people on the receiving end. He said he wanted me to watch him play with someone before I made a decision about allowing him to play with me. He wants to make sure I'm comfortable with everything. He doesn't like to jump into things."

An email was waiting for me when I got home.

We'll meet at the diner at 8:00 tomorrow evening. From there I will escort you to the Mansion. Wear a skirt, something short and flouncy, not black. Wear a feminine blouse that buttons in the front. If you feel you must wear stockings, no panty hose. You may either wear thigh-high stockings or stockings with a garter belt. I'll leave the choice of shoes up to you, however, my preference would be heels

*that lengthen your legs and show off your
calves. Oh yes, no panties or bra.*

Chris

I had to go shopping. I didn't own most of that stuff.
I seldom wore skirts, and when I did, they were only
slightly above the knee, and straight. Most of my clothes
were black, or at least dark. I'm a New Yorker, after all!
I needed to buy stockings. I decided to go for thigh-high
stay-ups, rather than a garter belt. A garter belt sounded
really hot, but it also sounded like a lot of trouble, especially if this never happened again. I had a closet full of
shoes; they were the one thing I wouldn't have to buy
for this date. Was this a date?

I became more and more nervous, preparing for my
evening with Chris. I wondered about everything. Would
he like the smell of my soap and shampoo? Should I wear
perfume, and if so, what fragrance would he prefer? I
worried about my hair; should I wear it up or down?
Should I try to curl it or leave it straight? Everything had
to be just right.

I worried he wouldn't like the outfit I'd chosen,
a ruffled miniskirt with little flowers on a blue background. I'd bought a darker blue silk blouse to go with
it. While I might never wear the skirt again, at least the
blouse would be a keeper. I decided on platinum strappy
sandals with a four-inch spike heel and hoped I wouldn't
have to do much walking.

As I fussed with my makeup, I became more aware of the missing panties. It was an odd sensation. Depending on how careful I was when I sat, I often found my bare bottom making contact with the chair. At least the full-ness of the skirt draped well over my thighs, and with my legs together no one would be able to see my pussy. As that thought entered my consciousness, I felt the first hints of moisture. This could be bad! Just before leaving, I put on the stockings and shoes. Somehow, the stay-up stockings made me feel even more naked than I had before. The silicone material at the tops, which caused them to stay up without garters, hugged my thighs and made me even more conscious of my missing panties.

I arrived at the diner fifteen minutes early and waited outside for Chris. As I saw him round the corner at precisely 8:00 my heart sped. He wore black leather pants, which fit him perfectly, not too loose and not too tight, a charcoal, long-sleeved shirt and black leather boots. Somehow, he no longer looked short; in fact he looked rather imposing. I hadn't noticed how sexy his Hugh Grant hair was before, and his glasses somehow added to his air of control.

"You look lovely," he said, ushering me into the restaurant.

"So do you," I murmured.

Over salads and sandwiches he talked about the club and answered my questions. "Even though you won't be playing tonight, I want you to do exactly as I say. Afterward, with your permission, I'll take you home and we'll chat about your experiences and feelings.

"I like your choice of outfit," he said. I felt his hand on my leg, stroking the nylon of my stocking. He moved it up to the stocking top and ran his finger along the edge briefly. My breath caught as his fingers worked their way past the stocking top and up to the fold of my thigh. He slowly shifted direction until his hand cupped my uncovered sex. "Good girl," he said, taking his hand away. He picked up his napkin and blotted his mouth. "Shall we?"

Silk may not have been the best choice for my blouse. My nipples felt like they would poke straight through the material, and his brushing the back of his hand against one while we stood at the cash register didn't help. Thankfully, he hailed a cab and I scooted into the back and did my best to sit on my skirt, squeezing my legs closed.

As it was still early, there weren't many patrons at the Mansion when we arrived. Most people seemed to know him, and they said hello. He chatted with a few, who either smiled at me or scrutinized me. Not once did he introduce me or mention me, but he kept his hand on the small of my back the whole time.

Using his hand, like a dancer, he directed me through the entire club, showing me all the different rooms, explaining what each was for and drawing my attention to different pieces of equipment and furniture. I was sure juices were dripping down my legs by the time the tour was over. We moved to the bar and he ordered me a bottle of water. "Wait here for a minute. Don't talk to anyone. I'll be right back."

One guy in jeans and a black leather vest blatantly stared at me but didn't come over. A woman in a tight black rubber dress smiled and made her way to the bar. "Hi, lovey," she said. "Is this your first time here? My name's Hennie, short for Henrietta. You're a sweet little thing. I'm sure I would have remembered if I'd seen you before." As she reached over, Chris returned.

"Hi, Hennie, she's with me."

"Sure, Chris, no problem. Anyway honey, you get tired of this guy, you just remember Hennie."

Chris brought me to another room, with a raised platform and benches lining the walls. He led me to a bench directly across from a man and woman. "George has graciously given me permission to play with his girl. You sit here," he said. "You'll get the best view and I'll be able to watch you as well. George'll be watching, and other people may come in to watch too; you never know." He sat me down in the middle of the bench, which was only about ten feet from the stage. "I'll play with Becca for about an hour, and then we'll leave."

I straightened my skirt over my thighs and made sure my legs were together. The bench was low, so with my heels on, my knees were higher than my thighs. I took great pains to keep them glued to each other so I wouldn't be exposed.

"One last thing," Chris said. "Stand up." He lifted the back of my skirt and had me place my bare bottom on the bench. "I want you to keep your legs open the entire time you're watching." He put his hands on my knees and moved my legs about a foot apart, putting me on display for George or anyone else who happened to look.

"But Chris, I..."

He put a finger to my lips. "Remember our agreement? No one will bother you; they all know you're with me. Would you rather I took you home instead?"

I felt on the edge of tears. "No, Chris."

"Good girl. The room lights will be turned down and there will be spotlights on the stage. No one will see you, or even know to look, but me. Now remember, even if you get excited and want to squeeze your legs together, don't. We'll each be able to gauge your reaction better this way. Don't move until I come for you. Clear?"

"Yes, Chris." I couldn't believe I was acting like this, but I simply couldn't react any other way. It was as if I had no choice, and had lost the willpower to do anything other than what Chris wished. It was both scary and hot and I felt wetness seeping out of me. God, but I wanted to squeeze my legs closed.

The room lights went down, the stage lights came up and Becca appeared. He had her take off her clothes and then he fastened her wrists to chains attached to the ceiling, suspending them above shoulder level. He put cuffs on her ankles and had her spread her legs. There were eyebolts in the floor to which he fastened her ankle cuffs.

He started by stroking her body: long, gentle strokes with his hands. I couldn't believe she could be there, so naked and open, in public like that, but as she began to react to his touch, that thought went out of my mind and I could only think of the sensations she must be feeling—and the sensations I was feeling.

Chris began squeezing her breasts, gently at first, but then harder, until she cried out. He squeezed and pulled her nipples, elongating them, and then attached clamps to them. It looked painful, and I saw her wince. He attached weights to the clamps. They were heavy enough to pull her nipples in a downward stretch. He brushed his hands against the weights, setting them swinging. I could see her nipples being pulled from side to side by the clamps as the weights swung. Her breasts were large, larger than mine. I wondered what that would feel like. My nipples weren't overly sensitive, but they *were* sensitive.

As I mused about my nipples, Chris added the same type of clamp and weight arrangement to her pussy lips, but this time the weights looked heavier, stretching them far from her opening. By now, a constant trickle of moisture had begun to leak from my open pussy. It tickled and itched and fought for my attention.

Chris attached a delicate clip, with a bell on the end, to Becca's clit. It looked something like a bobby pin. He played with the bell on the end, making it ring. With each flick of his fingers, the girl moaned and I gushed. My god, I felt like I was sitting in a puddle.

Next, he moved behind her and used a thin cane on her bottom. He seemed to strike her lightly, almost gently, but she winced or moaned with each strike. It made me wonder what that would feel like on *my* bum. After a while, the bell began to ring and he stopped. He gently stroked her ass, where the cane had just fallen, and whispered something to her. She sighed and closed her eyes and I imagined being in her place and must have closed my eyes too.

I heard a smack and my eyes flew open. He stood in front of her again, this time with a riding crop. She hung from her chains, leaning slightly forward. Chris used the crop to smack the sides of each breast, causing the weights to swing in ever-widening arcs, until she released tiny, high-pitched screams. At that point, he used his hands to steady the weights and whispered to her again.

He used the flat of the crop against her shaved mound, just above where the clip hung. I hadn't noticed until then that she was shaved. I think her smooth, hairless flesh made the smack from the crop sound louder than it would have otherwise. All I know is that shortly after he began hitting her there, the bell began to ring intermittently, until, after a while, its clear tone rang out continuously. He continued until her hips began to thrash back and forth.

He put down the crop, cupped the weights and clamps in his hand and gently removed them, first from one lip, then from the other. Leaving the clit clip on, he gently massaged the area while he spoke to her. When she nodded her head, he stopped the massage and slowly removed the weights from her nipple clamps. With the removal of each weight, her clit bell jingled. My clit felt like it was three times its normal size.

He whispered something else and she shook her head, no. He spoke to her again, and again she shook her head. Using his bare hand, he spanked her ass. Based on the sound his hand made, I'd guess it was pretty hard. Again, he spoke to her and this time she nodded in the affirmative. He gently removed the clamps from her nipples and she screamed. Quickly, he used his hands to massage them and then he used his mouth on them.

When he took his hands away, I could see the deep impressions the clamps had left in her skin and how red her nipples were. More liquid gushed from my sopping cunt. He removed the clit bell and unfastened her ankles. He helped her bring her feet to a more normal stance and George came over to hold her while Chris undid her wrist cuffs.

As the room lights came up, I looked around. Somehow, without my noticing, the room had filled with people. They slowly got up and began to file out as Chris came over to me. He put a box down on the bench, leaned down and put his hands on my knees.

"I see you were not unaffected by the performance," he said, looking at the puddle of wet I was sitting in. All I could do was moan.

"Lean your head against my chest," he whispered,

"and grind that nasty fuckin' cunt into the bench. Do it now. There's no way you'll be able to walk out of here otherwise."

God help me, I did it. I shoved my naked, wet cunt against a hard bench in a room with strangers walking in and out. I rocked against that bench until I shook with release, and what was possibly the most intense sexual itch I'd ever had began to subside. Chris handed me the box of wet wipes. I looked up at him.

"Clean the bench too. Then I'll take you home. It's still early, you know."

A CHANGE IN THE LEATHER

Rob Rosen

G lenn let me borrow his apartment while I was in town on business and he was away on vacation. Then my meeting got extended, which meant that I had to stay in San Francisco for the weekend. All in all, it could've been a lot worse—I could've been stuck in, say, Boise. The drawback, however, was that I'd only brought my work clothes.

So that Saturday night, I searched my friend's wardrobe for an alternative. There were mostly jeans and T-shirts and sneakers. Glenn had mastered this look back in his late twenties and was fairly locked in that mode.

Or so I thought.

As I began to take out a pair of Levi's and a crisp white tee, I spotted something on the very last hanger to the far right of his closet. The overhead light reflected on the matte black, instantly catching my eye.

I reached in and removed the articles. "Well now," I said to myself, with a low, appraising whistle. "What do we have here?"

Glenn, it seemed, had mastered yet another style. Go figure.

Leather. One full outfit of it. And from the look and feel, expensive leather at that. Still, I put the ensemble away and pulled the original jeans and tee back out. Secret safe. No harm, no foul.

Glumly, I looked at my prior selection as it dangled blandly from the two hangers—the black leather remained in my line of vision, calling to me like an ebony beacon. A smile spread across my face, wicked and gleeful. What was one more secret? And who would know, anyway? Again, no harm, no foul. Besides, when in Rome...

I removed the leather, carefully arranging it on the bed behind me: one pair of leather pants, one leather vest, two armbands, one eye mask, and a black hankie. My cock swelled in my boxers at the mere sight of it all. Oh sure, I'd seen my share of leather before, but, up until that point, I'd never worn any. Like Glenn, I'd found my style and stuck with it; there was safety, after all, in the familiar.

That trend, however, was about to be bucked.

I slid out of my boxers and stood there naked, my prick jutting out and slightly up, clearly eager for what I had in store for it. I grabbed for the pants first, sliding my feet into the soft legs. The fit was tight, as I supposed it was meant to be. I stood back up and yanked on the material, bunching it up around my thighs and hips before smoothing it all out. It fit like a glove, encasing me, leaving nothing to the imagination—as was evident by the outline of my rock-solid cock.

The vest was next. It buttoned down the front and could be tightened on the sides. Again, the glove analogy worked well. In fact, there was no room for one extra ounce of flesh. Still, it was, if nothing else, comfortable. The quality was excellent, and the material bent and flexed like a second layer of skin as I walked to the mirror to check myself out.

And damn if I didn't look good, too. The outfit looked like it had been made for me, accentuating all my attributes, especially the still-rigid one, smack-dab in the center. I snapped my fingers as I noticed the remaining items on the bed. I retrieved the armbands and slid them up my arms. They rested loosely against my biceps before I tightened them with a pull on their straps. Then came the eye mask. The leather was thin, sensuous, instantly warm against my face.

Again I looked at myself in the mirror, my outfit now complete. An intoxicating stranger stared back at me, decked out all in black. My stomach tightened as a bolt of adrenaline shot up my spine and rumbled through my crotch. I rubbed my cock through the leather. The feeling was almost indescribable, warm and tight and perfect. I inhaled deeply, filling my sinus cavity with the heady aroma of leather.

"This could work out nicely," I quipped, with a mischievous grin, as I spotted the black boots that rested on the floor of the closet. I slid them on. "Oh yeah, very nicely." Then, like a cherry on an ice-cream sundae, I stuck the black hankie in my left, rear pocket.

A cab picked me up moments later. "Where to?"

I pondered my options. "The Eagle," I responded, figuring my look would go over well enough there. My cock pulsed at the thought of what I was getting myself into.

The cab dropped me off and I paused, took a deep breath and walked into the sparsely populated bar. Quickly, I ordered a scotch to calm my rattled nerves. Already I could sense my entrance did not go unnoticed. I squelched a grin and downed half my drink. It was then that I spotted the outdoor area to my right.

Newly emboldened, that's where I headed. The patio was already half full. Most guys were dressed in denim and T-shirts. A few were clad in leather, like myself. Still, I stood out. I could feel the dozens of sets of eyes boring into me. Was it because I was fresh meat, or did I really look that good? Not that the answer mattered all that much, as the effect was the same: I was the hot new kid on the block and was now in total control of the situation.

I stared down at the obvious bulge in my crotch, as did half the bar. Then I leaned on a wooden pole and waited for the inevitable. The masses trooped by, one by one. I stared at them, incognito, from behind my mask, nodding at those who made eye contact. My lungs expanded, stretching the tight leather to its limits.

Then I caught the stare of spectacular blue eyes from across the patio. He was lean, in denim shorts, and shirt-less, revealing a tight hairy chest and defined abs. His sinewy legs and calves were equally hairy. He wore his hair short with long sideburns and a pointy goatee that snaked off his chin. But it was those eyes, those brilliant sapphire orbs, which held me there, riveted.

He grinned when he noticed that he'd made a connec-tion. I looked away, watching the crowd as it grew. There was no use in being so obvious. He was already mine for the taking; of that I was certain. I figured I'd make him work for it. When I looked again, he was gone, only to reappear at my side a moment later.

I glanced over at him, locking eyes. He smiled. I remained stone-faced. Instead, I ran my hand appre-ciatively across his chest and slowly, deliberately, down his taut belly. He twitched, and I noticed goose bumps forming along his defined arms. He reached over to put his hand in my vest. I stopped him, grabbing with a vise-tight hold on his wrist.

"Ask first," I whispered into his ear, forcing my voice to stay even.

"May I touch your chest?" he asked, his head slightly bent down, subserviently. I squinted at him and leaned farther in until my breath mixed with his. "Sir," he quickly added.

The word sent an eddy of pleasure through my

stomach, and my prick jolted like one of those famed San Francisco earthquakes. "No, you can't," I replied, with just barely a smile, enough to give him an ounce of hope. Still holding his wrist, I positioned him in front of me, his back leaning into me, my hard cock pressing snug against his denim-covered ass. He wriggled and moved in closer. The smell of his sweat, his shampoo and my leather now permeated the air around us. "Good boy," I whispered in his ear, biting down on his lobe as I wrapped my hands around his narrow waist.

He moaned softly as I let my hands roam over his hirsute torso, stopping intermittently to tweak his already rigid, eraser-tipped nipples. My mouth worked his neck and my stubble ran rampant across his shoulders. All the while he stood there, his hands resting on my thighs, bumping and grinding his ass into my crotch. The crowd appraised the scene, jealous, it seemed, that they had obviously been beaten to the punch.

I rested my chin to the side of his cheek and stared down hungrily at the bulge in his shorts. Behind the mask, I knew I could tell him to do as I wished. "Show me your dick, boy," I commanded.

Without hesitation, he pulled his shorts out an inch or so. He was going commando, his thick cock jutting to the right, crammed inside the denim, eager for release. I groaned in his ear. "Nice. It's mine now."

"Yours, Sir," he whispered back, turning his head slightly so that his lips could meet my own. I grabbed his goatee and pulled him in toward my face and our eyes locked. His lips were soft. I parted his mouth and swirled my tongue around his. He trembled as I tugged on his nipple, jamming his mouth hard, harder against my own.

I detected the hush of the crowd around us as they witnessed the spectacle. I decided to give them an encore before the final curtain, turning the man around and positioning him in between my legs.

I patted his belly, then slapped it. This I repeated on his pecs. His eyes closed in rapt delight with each spank, the sound echoing out in all directions. My hands had only ever known how to caress; now they appreciated the force and the sting. I leaned in to kiss him again. Tentatively, he reached into my vest. This time, I allowed his entry. Slowly, he unbuttoned the garment and removed it, sliding it down my back. I opened my eyes. The crowd was staring. I moved my mouth to his ear. "Show's over, boy. Take me home. *Now*." The last word came out deep and serious, almost a moan.

He looked into my eyes and lustfully smiled in return. "Yes, Sir," he replied, grabbing my hand and leading me through the now-dense mob. All eyes turned to watch us exit. When we made it to the deserted sidewalk outside, the air was already turning San Francisco nippy, so I quickly slipped my vest back on. I reached for my prize and held him tightly in my arms. His bluer than blue eyes sparkled beneath the lamppost light. My hand slid down his back and inside his shorts, cupping the hairy, firm cheeks within. He smiled and planted a warm, wet kiss on my waiting lips.

"Ready, Sir?" he asked.

"Are *you*?" I replied, with a mischievous smirk. He unzipped his fly and removed his fat cock. The head shone brightly, slick with precome. "I'll take that as a yes," I said.

He nodded and led me down the sidewalk. My hand stayed in his shorts, splaying his crack as my index finger ran rings around his hair-rimmed hole. My mind raced at the thought of what lay ahead. I was, after all, in uncharted territory.

Ten minutes later, we arrived at his flat. He held my hand and walked me inside. A long flight of stairs led upward to his second-story unit. "Wait," I said, stopping him from going up. "Take the shorts off."

He paused and then obeyed, unbuttoning, unzipping and then sliding the shorts over his black boots. He stood there waiting for my next command, his cock mostly soft but growing rapidly as I intently watched. As it thickened, gradually making its rise out and up, it curved to the side. He was a good six-plus inches, thick as a sausage, with a fat, wide, helmeted head. My mouth practically drooled at the sight of him. "Kneel on the stairs, boy," I told him.

He did as I said, turning around so that his ass now faced me, whiter than the rest of him, though equally hairy and defined. I crouched down for a closer look, spanking each cheek several times until a faint crimson flush appeared. "Show me your asshole, boy."

"Yes, Sir." He reached behind with his hands and spread his cheeks wide for me. His pink, puckered hole winked back. I spit on two of my fingers and glided them inside of him—no warning, no preamble, just brute entry. He sucked in his breath, but quickly relaxed and allowed me to navigate up and in and deep, deep back.

"Push your prick through your legs," I said, and he did. I grabbed it with my free hand and ran my tongue around the salty head before engulfing it whole. I added a third finger up his tight hole as I sucked him off from the rear. He moaned, loudly, and bucked his rump into my hand.

"You like that ass worked, boy?" I asked, in between hungry slurps.

"Yes, Sir. Fuck me, Sir," he begged, the sound of his pleading voice running up and down my spine like a runaway freight car.

"Trust me, I will," I replied, pulling my hand out of his ass and releasing his pulsing cock. "Now, up the stairs." He stood and walked up, stopping each time I spanked his ass. When we reached the top of the landing, I grabbed his hand and told him to get on his back with his legs apart and in the air. Again he did as he was told. I lay down on the last few stairs, my face to his hairy hole, and told him to finger-fuck himself while I watched. Two of his fingers instantly went inside. I grabbed for his massive nut sac, pulling hard at his heavy, hairy balls. He fingered himself with fury as I yanked and tugged and jerked.

"You like that, boy?"

"Yes, Sir. Harder please, Sir."

I obliged, also slapping at his dick and his belly. His moans filled the stairwell. "*Yeaaah*," he rasped. "Spank that meat, Sir." And so I did, holding it at the base as I sent my palm flying out against the shaft and the head, which leaked copious amounts of sticky spunk that dribbled out and down. I craned my neck up and sucked it off.

Behind the mask and stuffed into all that warm leather, I'd suddenly become brutal. The more he begged for the abuse, the more I wanted to offer it.

"Stand up," I told him. He stood up. "Hands behind your back." They disappeared in an instant. I stood and faced him and again our eyes locked. His drew me in like a magnet until our mouths were meshed as one. All the while, I patted his cock from the underside with one hand. The other roamed around his body, feeling the muscle and tufts of fine hair that covered him. He was mine to do with as I pleased; and what I pleased was to please him with tender cruelty.

As we stood there, our mouths locked, our eyes open, watching and waiting for what was to come next, he again removed my vest as I unbuttoned and slid down the leather pants. Our cocks were now grinding against each other. His hands roamed my body with abandon. Mine tortured his nipples, causing his legs to intermittently buckle.

"Suck it, boy," I finally said, grabbing my thick seven inches in my fist.

He sank to his knees. I slapped my meat on his cheeks, his nose, and his waiting lips, which he parted to allow access. Greedily, he sucked on my cock, taking it to the hilt and gagging in delight. I grabbed the back of his head and pumped my prick down his throat. He stared up at me, grateful for the abuse, his blue eyes shining in rapturous satisfaction.

I tilted my head back and groaned, filling the stairway with the sound. I reached down and grabbed his shoulders, yanking him back to his feet, then removed my boots and pants, before saying, "Bedroom. Now."

Quickly, he led me through the front door and into his bedroom. "You want to be fucked, boy?" I growled.

"Yes, Sir. Please. Fuck me," he pled, flinging himself on his bed and raising his legs up in the air as he tossed me a rubber and some lube from his nightstand.

I watched this stranger from behind my mask, the only leather I still had on besides my armbands. Like Sampson's hair, it was the apparent source of my strength.

I hopped into bed with him and slid the rubber on before resting his legs over my shoulders and pressing the head of my now-lubed-up cock up against his asshole. I looked down at him with a smirk and slapped his chest and roughly tugged on a nipple. He closed his eyes and moaned. And then I entered him, slowly, inch by inch by thick, meaty inch. He sighed, long and low and deep, as I filled his hole up with my cock.

When I reached the hilt, I bent down and kissed him

with the full force of my mouth. Our tongues thrashed as I withdrew my prick and then slid it home again. In and out it went, at first slowly, then lightning fast. I grabbed his cock and matched the rhythm of my thrusts.

"Close, Sir," he groaned as his asshole clenched tightly down and around the length of my dick, sucking me inside of him like a Hoover. I rammed his already solid prostate one final time just as he shot. His moans filled the room as ounce after white, sticky ounce of hot come exploded from his dick and splattered on his stomach, his chest and his chin. The sight of it sent my ass bucking into overdrive, and then, loudly, I too came, filling the rubber with a thick, heavy load.

Exhausted and spent, I collapsed on top of him. Tenderly I kissed him while I plucked his nipples. And then I began to laugh, a soft chuckle that rumbled through my chest.

"What's so funny, Sir?" he asked, with a toothy grin, running his hands through my hair.

"I just fucked you silly and I don't even know your name. Not unless it really is *boy*."

He pondered this, still staring at me with delight and apparent interest. "It is whatever you want it to be, Sir," he finally said.

Again I laughed. "I'll be back in town in a month. How about I let you know then?"

He kissed me and then whispered into my ear, "Will you be wearing the leather then?"

I turned around and stared at the crumpled pants

and boots that lay in the hallway, then I looked back down into his eyes, my cock growing hard again, still buried deep inside of him. "Not the same outfit. A better one next time. Maybe with gloves and some chaps. Maybe some handcuffs and a cock ring and some nipple clamps for you. And then we'll see about a name for you, boy."

I could feel his cock pulse beneath my stomach. "And the mask, Sir. Don't forget the mask."

"And the mask, boy. There's no forgetting the mask."

After all, look what happened to Sampson when he lost all that glorious hair.

MAKE MINE RARE

Kristina Wright

Neighborhood barbecue. Not a phrase I ever thought I'd become familiar with. But here I was, a decade into marriage, two kids and an SUV in the driveway. Who knew the wild girl who was going to see the world would settle down and have a family? My wildness didn't disappear, though. I just play things a little closer to the vest.

Damon, my ever-adoring husband, knows the wild me. And loves the wild girl he married who recognized his submissive streak before he was even ready to acknowledge it. The wild girl who proposed to him (oh yes, I did!) and whisked him off to Miami. The wild girl who throws the perfect dinner party or barbecue, who still rocks a little black dress even after two pregnancies and who, whenever the mood strikes, can wield a crop like nobody's business.

And there, amidst our friends and families at an Independence Day cookout, the mood was striking. Pun fully intended.

Damon was at the grill, my introverted man doing what he does best—taking care of other people. I sidled up to him and leaned my head on his shoulder.

"What's the ETA on the steaks?"

The answer was irrelevant. I'd only come over so I could sneak a feel. I slipped my hand under his KING OF THE GRILL apron and gave his cock a squeeze. He never missed a beat in his steak-flipping routine, but I did get a smile.

"About five minutes, Ma'am," he said.

The "Ma'am" sounded like a cute little nickname—and it was—but it also took on a whole other meaning when I had his quickly hardening cock in the palm of my hand.

"Good. That'll give your cock enough time to calm down. When you get off grill duty, you're on husband duty."

His eyebrows went up. "Now? That's bad form, don't you think, slipping away from our own party?"

I gave his erection a squeeze. "You let me worry about form, okay?"

It was a rhetorical question. My tone said it all—*obey me and I'll make it work.*

And I did.

Ten minutes later, the hungry crowd had food in front of them, our kids were being entertained by

Damon's father and I was tipping my hand to Melissa, my next-door neighbor and closest friend. But I only tipped it a little—as close as Melissa and I are, I'm a firm believer that what happens in the bedroom stays in the bedroom.

"Hey, would you keep everyone occupied for a little while? I have a wicked tension headache and Damon is going to give me a massage and see if it helps."

The tension part was right, but it wasn't in my head.

Melissa gave me a practiced look—she's a public school teacher and can smell a lie a mile away—and nodded. "Headache, huh? And he's going to give you a massage."

"You don't have to put air quotes around *massage*," I laughed. "But yes, that."

"Okay, if you say so," she said. "I'll keep everyone outside while you get massaged." She barely restrained herself from air-quoting again.

"Thanks." I kissed her cheek and beckoned for Damon to follow me. "I owe you one."

She gave Damon an appraising gaze as he came toward us (no sign of an erection tenting his apron) and I have to say, even in that ridiculous apron, he cut quite a profile. "I'll keep that in mind," she murmured.

I'd have to address that flirtation sometime, I thought as I followed Damon into the house. The idea of my best friend and husband together had a peculiar effect on me—and no, it wasn't jealousy.

Once we were in the kitchen, Damon looked to me for direction.

"Upstairs," I said. "Our bathroom."

"Going to make me clean it, huh? That's kinky."

I slapped his ass. "Watch the sarcasm, or I really will make you clean it and leave you with blue balls."

"That's a myth, you know," he said as he went up the stairs.

"Maybe. But I bet if I tied them up they'd turn blue."

That stilled him. "Huh. You're probably right."

Another thing to add to our sexual bucket list, I thought. But I was getting too far ahead of myself. I gave him another encouraging smack, hardly anything through layers of cloth, but that got him moving again. We had time, but not enough to be bantering about blue balls.

Once in our bathroom, I closed and locked the door. We live in relatively new construction, which means our bathroom is roughly the size of a typical studio apartment in New York City, complete with a jetted tub, separate shower, double-sink vanity and a nook for the commode and a heated towel rack.

I shimmied out of my shorts and panties and hopped up on the counter. "Come here," I said, beckoning him.

He had that amused smirk he always has when we start playing. I knew it would be quickly replaced by a look of pure concentration. "Yes, Ma'am."

I reached under his apron and unfastened his shorts. "Take them off. But leave the apron on."

"Am I going to be grilling something?" He smirked even harder, but in a moment he was naked below the waist except for the apron. "Because I left my tools outside."

"The only tool I'm interested in is the one between your legs," I said, giving his erection a smack through the apron and enjoying the look of shock that crossed his face. "And I like my meat rare."

"Yes, Ma'am." No trace of smirk or snark this time. Good.

"Turn around."

He obeyed, and I admired his ass for a moment. My favorite part of his body, besides his magnificent cock, is his arms—so strong and muscular and yet the skin on the inside of his forearms is so soft—but his ass is a close second. I used my nails on his cheeks, scratching him lightly until red marks appeared on his lily-white bottom. The skin here was as soft as the inside of his arms, and I thrilled to watch it blush under my touch. He squirmed, and I smacked him hard.

"Stay still."

"Yes, Ma'am."

I picked up my hairbrush and used it, bristle side down, to smack him again. He yelped and the sound echoed in the bathroom. "Quiet now," I said. "You don't want everyone rushing up here to find out what's going on."

"No, I definitely don't," he said through gritted teeth. "Sorry."

"It's okay. I'll just take it out on your ass."

My bright tone was in direct contrast to the threat. I wield a mean hairbrush, and Damon knows it. A few smacks later and he was literally panting with the effort of remaining quiet. But he didn't move, and he didn't yelp.

"Good boy," I said soothingly, rubbing the palms of my hands over the inflamed cheeks of his ass. I knew he'd have a hard time sitting down to his steak. Of course, I didn't intend to let him sit down. I slapped his ass, with my hand this time. "Turn around."

He obeyed, his face flushed and beads of sweat popping out on his forehead. He looked like he'd just run a couple of miles. I knew the exertion required to handle the sting and stay still and silent—once in a while I let him play the dom. Not often, though. Both of us preferred it when I called the shots.

"Had enough?"

He hazarded a smile. "Not until you say so."

"Good answer."

"You're a good teacher. And I love you."

"I love you, too, but you're not getting off the hook that easily." I balled up his apron in my hand and tugged him down by the neck. "On your knees. Get me off."

"Oh yes, Ma'am," he said enthusiastically, slipping to his knees on the tile floor.

I spread my legs on the counter, sliding around a bit as my juices slicked up the marble. This was the part I loved best. Inflicting pain gave me a thrill, mostly because I knew how hard it made him and how eager he was to make me happy, but being able to get exactly what I wanted when I wanted it gave me a rush like nothing else. And right now I wanted my pussy eaten well and thoroughly.

He used his fingers to spread me open, and I smacked his face lightly. "No hands. Just your mouth, bad boy."

He looked up from his position on the floor. "Sorry, Ma'am."

And that was the last thing he said for a few minutes. I rested my head against the mirror and hooked my legs over his shoulders as his tongue dipped into my wetness and moved up to circle my clit. Then back down, plunging into my pussy in a way that was softer than his cock, and not nearly as filling. I squirmed on the counter and arched my back, desperate for release. I could smell my own sweat and musk, feel the beads of perspiration trickling down to the small of my back. Now it was my turn to stay silent, and I wasn't nearly as good at it as he was.

I dug my hands into his thick hair, twisting and tugging to make him go faster, then slower, moving him where I wanted him, giving him a sharp tap on the back of the head when he slowed down to tease me.

"Don't play with me," I said. "Make me come."

He mumbled something and went to work in earnest, sucking on my clit with the kind of focused attention he knew would do the job. And it did. Within moments I was gasping and coming, holding his head to my crotch as I grinded against him and he tried to take my entire pussy into his mouth.

I finally released him, tugging at his hair to pull him away. He seemed quite content to continue eating me out, though I knew he was enjoying my discomfort as my oversensitive clit thrummed with every additional stroke of his tongue. The countertop, not to mention my thighs and ass, was soaked from my juices and my stomach muscles were still quivering with the aftershocks of my orgasm. I felt like I'd had the best workout of my life.

"Very nice," I said. "You can get up."

He groaned—in the not-good kind of pain this time—as he stood. "I'm getting too old to be on my knees."

"We'll put a towel down next time," I assured him. "You'll never be too old to be on your knees for me."

"True enough," he acquiesced. "Thank you for letting me serve you, Ma'am."

I was still leaning back against the mirror, feeling warm and relaxed and disinclined to move. But I knew we couldn't linger much longer. "That was very nice, but I'd guess we'd better get back outside."

"Thank you, Ma'am," he said again, then cleared his throat. "Might I do something about this?" He gestured to his cock peeking from around the bunched-up apron.

I considered leaving him to suffer, but that seemed cruel. He'd gotten me off in record time, and we probably still had a few minutes before someone came looking for us. I nodded.

"You have exactly three minutes," I said, tapping my watch. Then I added, "To jerk off."

He groaned at being denied intercourse, but he knew better than to complain. "Yes, Ma'am."

"Go."

He took his erection in his hand and began stroking it slowly. I knew that wouldn't last long and I was right; soon his hand was a blur as it worked over his shaft, coaxing it. There was a time when he couldn't masturbate in front of me. It took a while—and a couple of weeks of orgasm denial—but now he could get off while I watched anyplace, anytime, as long as I demanded it. Now I demanded it at least once or twice a week—not as a punishment, though sometimes it was, but because I so enjoyed watching him pleasure himself. The sheer concentration on his face, the veins popping out in his forearm as he milked his cock, the slow, languid final strokes to coax the come from his shaft. I loved it all. And now, watching him, I could feel myself becoming aroused all over again.

"Yes, yes, that's it," I murmured, only vaguely aware I was talking.

He had told me before that my encouragement made him that much hotter, made him come even faster. And now we didn't have time to waste. I'd said three minutes and I meant it, but I would be as disappointed as he was if he didn't finish.

"Do it for me," I said. Then, more firmly, "Come for me. Right now. Come for me, Damon."

"Yes, Ma'am," he said through gritted teeth. "Yes!"

I glanced up from his cock and saw that he wasn't

looking at himself, he was looking at me. And at that moment, with our eyes locked, I felt the first hot spurt of ejaculate streak my thigh. He moaned softly, his jaw clenched. I put my hand out and felt the wetness leaking from him, the white ropes of come across my belly, my thighs, my pussy. I rubbed the last of his come across the slippery head of his cock and then brought my thumb to my mouth and sucked the wetness from it, tasting him. He jerked as if it was him I was sucking, never breaking eye contact with me.

"Thank you," he said. "God, I love you."

I leaned forward and kissed him, letting him taste himself on my lips. "And I love you. Now, we really have to get back outside. I'm *starving*."

We laughed all the way downstairs.

A HOLE

Lillian Douglas

Paul cinched the last strap around my left ankle and slipped the blindfold down over my eyes. I tested the restraints binding my wrists and ankles to the four posts of our bed, and found them secure. I suppressed a wave of panic—I was now completely out of my own control.

The doorbell rang. Paul put on some Charlie Parker to mask any identifying sounds before leaving to greet the first of our guests.

I love making love, enjoy sex that is sweet, wholesome, unifying. I love knowing that I'm valued for who I am, for my intelligence, wit, experience, personality. I love having a man like Paul who caters to my needs, cares about my pleasure, works to please me.

But sometimes I want something else. Not to make

love, but to be *fucked*. Not to be valued as a whole person, but simply as a *hole*. A slippery, warm place for a man to use as he wants. For my enjoyment to be disregarded, beside the point. To be someone's toy.

In school, I had heard a good definition of social or political power: the ability to make someone do something, *no matter what they want*. I wanted to be subject to that kind of sexual power. To be temporarily free from choice.

I'd acted on this urge only slightly: a rough hand from Paul, when I could convince him; some hot, chaotic gropings in certain sorts of clubs; but I wanted more. I had mustered up the courage to tell Paul my fantasy, and now he was making it come true.

The doorbell rang again. That made two—of how many that Paul had invited? A murmur of conversation from the living room, subdued laughter. The clink of glasses: a little liquid courage? Where was mine? I strained against the cords, suddenly parched. Considered calling down to Paul for a drink.

But a *hole* doesn't ask for favors, and if she does they're not forthcoming. A *hole* doesn't get to choose what fills it. I swallowed, my throat still dry but a certain other orifice distinctly less so. I could feel the moisture pooling in my cunt, my decidedly less-than-arid lips open between my forcibly spread legs.

The doorbell rang again. And again. And again. And again. The conversation downstairs amplified, grew jollier, more sophomoric. I couldn't hear their words, but the tone wafting up to me was quintessential locker room: boasts and bluster.

Then, suddenly, silence. Just Charlie's warm sax upstairs with me. An extinguishing of sound as complete as a candle blown out. Then feet on the stairs. Quiet—no shoes. But the padding of more feet than I felt I could bear.

A quiet click and the susurrus moved into the room with me. I imagined a many-legged, many-eyed beast, its twenty hands groping for its ten cocks, staring at my body. No speaking, not even whispers. The electric zing of zippers, the rustles of bodies emerging from clothing. I forced myself to breathe.

Through the knot of sound pierced a single strange electronic beep I could not place.

A weight on the bed, between my legs, compressed the mattress springs, upsetting my equilibrium. I began to sweat, considered our safeword, rolling it around in my mouth like a marble: *Kumquat*. Deliberately silly, jarringly out of context. A word to make cocks shrivel back into their everyday, pliable shapes to be packed back in jeans for the lonely drive home. I considered sending them all away with a word, clung to that last shred of power left to me. The capacity to make them do what they certainly did *not* want, in that moment.

I imagined what they saw in the low light of our bedroom. They wouldn't notice the spotless floors that had taken me so much time to polish that afternoon. Rather, their eyes would be drawn to my naked body on our clean white sheets, the dark blindfold across my eyes, the tight nylon straps around my wrists and ankles, the aroused pucker of my dark nipples atop the goose-pimpled flesh of my breasts. Could they see the glisten between my legs?

Warm hands on my thighs, roving up to my hips, over my pubic hair and down to my open labia. A fingertip explored my recesses for a moment, finding the wetness there. A satisfied grunt, and then more weight on me. A hard body pressing me into the mattress. Relief for a moment as he situated his cock at the entrance to my sex.

Here it comes, I thought, with a thrill of excitement tinged with fear. What if he had some sort of disease? There was definitely no condom between us. I had to trust that Paul had done his research thoroughly, that he would only invite safe men into our bed, into my body.

He slid into me effortlessly. His cock was a revelation, the bringer of a stretching, aching satisfaction. I groaned loudly, and that seemed to impel him. Men can be so quick to trigger, when they give themselves permission. He fucked me silently, starting fast and getting faster with every stroke, his weight crushing me with every thrust, his breath on my neck and stubble scraping my skin. I continued to moan, encouraging him to use me to completion.

A raw, throaty grunt, and his weight left me. In his place, a constellation of searing points lit my belly and breasts. The mattress eased back up into its prior state as he withdrew, his semen cooling on my skin, beginning to drip down my sides.

The next man had already undressed, it seemed, because he took his comrade's place within seconds. He avoided bringing his chest in contact with mine—an aversion to another man's spend?—but sort of lifted my bottom from the bed and knelt between my thighs, impaling me on his cock and moving my hips up and down in his own preferred rhythm. I cried out with each thrust, when the head of his cock pressed against my G-spot. I could feel his pubic hair tickle my clit, and the two sensations combined into one large, awkward glob of longing.

He lasted longer than the first man had, taking his time to enjoy the clutch of my pussy. He began at a more leisurely pace, a trot at most. But urged on by the ragged sounds he was forcing from my throat, he sped to his culmination. At the last moment, he pulled out of me and treated the room to a tortured-sounding sigh as he disgorged a torrent of heat onto my left inner thigh, and then he was gone.

A moment later, the mattress sank in an unexpected way: not between my legs, as I'd come to expect (new habits are so easy to form), but beside me, up nearer to my head. The third man crawled to me, straddled my left arm. An unexpected, blunt warmth nudged my mouth. I opened my lips and welcomed his cock inside, swirling my tongue beneath his foreskin. This was not something I'd counted on; I realized I was not *a* hole, but *several* holes. And I loved it, sucking him with relish. He graced me with sighs and subtle moans when I did something he especially liked.

After a few minutes, when his cock reached its full potential—a fragment of smooth stone—he took it away from me. I bit back a whine—a *hole* doesn't get to choose how it is filled—and waited for his next move. He slipped between my legs and slid into my pussy. Knowing his dimensions as well as I did at that moment, the specific shape and volume of his cock, somehow translated the vague, less-defined but more pleasurable sensations from my cunt into a better mental image. I could see, in my mind's eye, exactly how his cock fit inside me. He fucked me dutifully, clearly preferring my mouth—no little sounds of pleasure—propping his body up above mine on his elbows.

He buried his face in my throat, his lips and teeth finding the spots on my neck and ears that make shivers wash down my spine. Then he did something strange, something I had never considered in my fantasies: he kissed me. I tasted whiskey on his tongue, which he pushed into my mouth as roughly as he had his cock, exploring in a different, more active way. Could he taste himself, I wondered?

Whether he could or not, the kiss got him close. He pulled out of my quim and scrambled up my body, heedless of the rivulets of cooling come on my skin, to place his cock before my lips. I opened my mouth like a baby bird, squealing in delight and anticipation and need. I thrust my tongue out to taste the tip, finding the commingled flavors of my salt brine and his subtle musk. I felt his body shudder above me, and my mouth was flooded with foam, a tide of salty-bittersweet. I closed my mouth to swallow—finally getting that wished-for drink—and the second and subsequent cascades littered my lips, chin, nose and cheeks. I spluttered, a reflex to wipe my face jerking my restrained right hand against its bonds futilely. His deposit made, the third man rolled away from me and was gone.

The fourth made himself first known by his hands. He caressed my thighs, my belly, and paid special attention to my breasts. He smoothed the rills of his predecessors' seed into a single sticky sheen that mixed with my sweat and left me feeling unbelievably dirty. His cock nestled into my cunt gently—I got the impression that he was not quite as substantial as the others had been. As he fucked me, his hands never left my breasts, tweaking and pinching my nipples and gripping the soft flesh until it was almost painful. He carefully knelt above my chest when he was close and jerked off onto my tits, which he held together with his free hand.

The come on my face streaked down my throat, down to my earlobes, back into the hair at the nape of my neck. Cooling, almost chilly, and puckering my skin with every waft of air.

The fifth man began oddly, rubbing and then kissing each of my bound, useless feet. Then he slowly slid what I assumed must have been his cock, from the warmth and smoothness of it, over my soles and heels and toes. I accommodated to the extent I could—how does one act sexy with one's feet?

He finally put aside this specialized interest and followed the others into the space between my splayed legs. He grunted with every thrust into my pussy, his hands to either side of my come-tattooed face, keeping his distance from my body with everything but his cock. He bolted away before he had come, and I wondered what he was doing. The answer came in the form of a shockingly unexpected torrent of warmth on the ball of my left foot and onto and between my toes, which quickly coursed like lava down my arch and the top of my foot. I suppressed a giggle, and he faded into the anonymous dark.

The sixth man eschewed my pussy altogether. He crept slowly between my legs, a wet, smacking sound revealing some sort of lubrication that my body had not produced. Like the second man, he lifted my ass off of the bed and set it on his knees. But he rotated my hips so that my quim was aimed directly at the ceiling, confusing me for a moment before I felt the head of his cock press against his true purpose: the chaste pucker of my asshole. I squirmed, and very nearly cried out "no," something that would have done nothing, other than to make me seem pathetic. Again I felt *kumquat* on the tip of my tongue, waiting like a rapier in a scabbard.

His hands were firm on my hips; I wasn't going

anywhere. His cock, with equal stubbornness, nudged and pressed against my anus. I gave up trying to bar his entrance, and began to try to relax enough to allow it. Together, we coaxed the torus of muscle open enough for his head to pop inside. I cried out against a wave of pain mixed with the uniquely intense pleasure that can only be found in this unintended use of this specialized orifice. The pain subsided, and he very slowly, very gently slid deeper inside me. I reveled in how *used* I felt: a different cock in every hole, a sticky river of come literally from my head to my feet...

He began to move, and again I had to fight through twinges of discomfort. But the intensity of the pleasure didn't fade, and soon my groans changed meaning.

He never fucked me very hard or very quickly, taking great care with my fragile insides. But soon he began to gasp and tremble, his cock palpably quivering inside me. At last, I felt a gush of warmth in my ass and his body arched and shook above me. Taking great care, he withdrew from me and out of the bed.

I was paradoxically exhausted and frantic for my own climax. I tried to remember how many times the doorbell had rung earlier. Was I finished? Would Paul let me free now, to rub my own relief out in peace?

No. Number seven took up his position between my legs. No nonsense, no foreplay, nothing out of the ordinary, he just *fucked* me. Good and hard, his pelvis grinding into my clit. He didn't interact with the other men's come, but didn't avoid it either. His skin pressed against my sticky flesh, his hands finding purchase on my shoulders.

He fucked me for quite a while, and I got closer and closer. I transitioned from urging him on because I wanted his pleasure to doing so because I wanted *mine*. I almost never come just from fucking, but I could feel my orgasm in the subterranean parts of myself, building, growing distinct, gathering itself.

But with a ragged grunt, he pulled out of me. I gnashed my teeth for a moment at the loss of sensation, before he replaced it with another: a searing gush cascaded down my clit, over my inner lips. Another surge joined the first, drenching me in heat. It felt like my clit had been struck by lightning. Suddenly my orgasm was very close.

I imagined myself from their perspective. My pussy wide and red and glistening. A steady trickle of come leaking from my ass. A wash of semen across my torso, and drizzles drying on my face, my foot, my breasts, my thigh. And now the *coup de grâce*, a waterfall of come slathering the center of my need, those raw, red lips that had welcomed in so many and that hard, lonely nubbin of flesh twitching and trembling for the touch that would send me over. *I must be so beautiful*, I thought.

A subtle pressure between my legs. Not a body—no, I'd come to know exactly how the bed moved when a man's full weight depressed it. Only *part* of a body. Confusion and hope vied within me.

Hope won out. A breath on my thigh revealed a face.

The wiry hair of a beard against my outer lips identified the face as Paul's.

"Oh god," I gasped, the first words I'd spoken.

Two of his fingers slid inside me and pressed expertly up against my G-spot as he sucked my come-drenched clit into his mouth. His tongue immediately snuck up under my hood and began to lick my head. After such a long wait, the attention was almost too much, but I gritted my teeth and broke through the over-intensity to a narrow, sub-orgasmic plateau. I could see my orgasm approach like a train on a flat plain, the onrushing glimmer of lights.

I thought of his face, down between my legs, the taste of another man's come in his mouth. All the pleasure I had given as an object, a slippery *hole* to fuck. I had been disintegrated, atomized into a pair of breasts, a mouth, a pussy, a face, a foot, an asshole, a thigh. A canvas of skin to decorate, to paint with the wet manifestation of pleasure. Not a person, not myself, not even a woman. A concatenation of *things*, disconnected from context and self. Three holes to fuck.

Now, abruptly, hands reached out of the dark to shower those disassembled parts of me with caring caresses. A hand rubbed the arch of my foot. A mouth kissed mine. Fingertips gently rubbed my sticky nipples. Palms swept up and down my thighs, pressed on my belly. A single narrow finger navigated around Paul's busy face and hand to find the asterisk of my asshole and wriggle its way inside.

I began to shout, to scream, to bellow. Not from up in my head, or even in my chest, but from deep in my belly, perhaps even deeper still. I felt the deep reservoir of liquid pleasure that they had built up one drop at a time surge against the dam holding it back, and the dam give way. I flooded Paul's face with a tsunami of my own, and the room with a torrent of sound.

Like those trust-building exercises in which one is carried by many hands, my lovers gently set me back on the bed, and one by one the hands winked out of existence. I breathed in the dark, alone, until a hand clasped one of mine, still in its restraints. I recognized it as Paul's. The room sounded like a forest, all shuffles and rustles, until one by one our guests padded downstairs and let themselves out into the night.

Finally, after what felt like an eternity, Paul undid the straps on my ankles, then my wrists. At the last, he carefully removed the blindfold.

In the corner, a camera gaped its Cyclops eye in my direction. I searched Paul's face for an answer. "In case you ever want to know who they were," he explained gently. "Let's get you into the shower."

BIG BOTTOM

Rachel Kramer Bussel

Gemma could tell from the way the women at the play party were circling around Kevin—hungrily, greedily—that they wanted him, or rather, wanted something from him. Even if they hadn't had those predatory looks on their faces, she'd have been able to tell. She recognized that desire written across their slick lips, their bodies angling forward, eyes clocking his every move, hungry for the kind of recognition only an innately dominant man could give them. She understood it, too, because when her tall, husky hulk of a man strode across a room, he did so like he owned it, and made women—and men—want him to own them as well. He could have easily owned almost anyone in the room, if that's what he was after, but Kevin wasn't made that way. He looked the part, but he had far more in common with those quivering, quaking, hungry-to-please women than he did with the doms they dreamed of.

Gemma regularly thanked her lucky stars that was the case, because she was perhaps the only one there who *didn't* want to be owned by him—not like that, anyway. Beholden, beloved, besotted she'd cotton to, but actual ownership went in the other direction in their household. In her own way, Gemma appreciated the fact that her man was an object of attention, lust and desire, but she also knew things about him that these kinky women never would, and she liked that just as much as having a popular man to parade around. She was an exhibitionist in a sense, but appreciated their private power play more than anything she would ever show her kinky friends. Even when she did reveal clues to their inner workings, nobody at these parties would ever know Kevin like she did, from the inside out, his every fierce longing laid bare whenever she so much as asked.

This was a new crowd, one that hadn't seen the two of them in action before. *Watch and learn*, Gemma's silent look said as she locked eyes with a brooding blonde, lustrous hair gleaming all the way down to her rounded ass encased in a skimpy red thong that hugged her cheeks, bejeweled nipples twinkling. She was the type who dressed for success—if success meant being bound, gagged and beaten.

Gemma had been forewarned that this particular play party tended to attract more women than men, and

most of them were looking for tops, doms, masters—
sadistic men to tie them up, spank them, humiliate them,
show them off, make them do all manner of things in the
name of submission. She'd wanted to check it out, to get
outside their usual scene, and was willing to drive three
hours to do so, amusing herself with periodic forays into
Kevin's lap, her hand searching for the hardness she'd
secured there, before they left, with a cock ring she'd
purchased just for him. Hearing his groans, seeing the
drool glide from his lips as she pulled up to a red light,
and feeling him twitch beneath her fingers made the
drive seem like nothing. Sure, she could've easily made
him drive, but giving him nothing to do but sit patiently
and await her touch was more than enough reward for
behind-the-wheel duty.

For the most part, these achingly eager submissive
types amused her, perhaps because when she had first
gotten into the scene, Gemma had been one herself.
Gemma would never forget donning a corset that turned
her already large breasts into gigantic, over-the-top,
practically inhuman globes threatening to pop out of
their trappings, and a skirt so short that her coat fell
several inches below it. It was the first time she'd ever
left the house without underwear, the first time she'd
dared show her face at a party designed for people like
her—kinky people.

That night, soon after graduating and securing her
first real job, reveling in finally escaping her college town
for the big city, she was heady with excitement. She'd

attended a few munches and mixers back in school, but everyone had been too timid to do more than issue a few stray smacks. Timidity isn't becoming on anyone, especially the kinky, she'd decided, making do with a rotating cast of well-hung vanilla boys who she could occasionally get to hold her down and fuck her hard, but that was as far as it went.

On that fateful night, she'd figured she'd just watch, and gave herself permission to leave the moment anything or anyone become uncomfortable or off-putting. No sooner had she stepped through the basement door, though, and taken off her coat, than she felt herself let out a breath she hadn't realized she'd been holding. These were indeed her people—people who loved pain, people who loved power, people who wanted to crawl around on all fours, be bitten, beaten, humiliated, slapped and tormented, people who loved to hear their loud cries echo through the room, their mouths occasionally saying "no" but their bodies saying extremely loud yeses as they writhed against all manner of exquisite tortures. Gemma spent the first hour watching, sipping a tepid soda in a plastic cup as her heart raced, her lower lips bursting with arousal at the ever-wilder scenes before her.

Eventually, her curiosity had gotten the best of her and she'd volunteered to get flogged on her back, which had led to the whip striking her ass, then her upper thighs, each lash making her wetter and wetter. She hadn't even known that the guy about her age had handed the flogger over to one at least double her age, but when she'd turned around, she found out. She wouldn't have pegged Sam, the older guy, as her type, but that didn't stop her from wanting more from him. She'd let him lead her with a strong hand around her neck into a far corner of the party, where he sat on a chair while she straddled him, her bare pussy against his pant leg as they kissed, only pausing when he grabbed her by the hair and bent her head back to lick or bite or kiss her neck.

"Now you're ready for your spanking," he'd said after she'd been "forced" to come from grinding against him. His words contained no question, just as there was no question that Gemma wanted that spanking more than she'd wanted anything else in her young life. When she told him she'd just turned twenty-two, he gave her that many smacks, all of them hard, powerful, on the edge of mean. She didn't know that first night exactly what he was doing, only that she loved every second of it and had to get off again in the bathroom before she left. She'd exchanged contact info with Sam, and gone home with a sore ass and a newfound pride in herself. Subsequent dates in the privacy of his home had shown her exactly how kinky she could be, as bare-handed spankings turned into paddlings, whippings and, a few times, caning. Sam would photograph her ass and threaten to show his friends, order her over at odd hours to suck him off, give a beating and then push her out the door, generally driving her mad with desire. They saw each other for a year before each of them moved on to new partners.

Over the years, though, Gemma had found that she was actually more of a top than a bottom. It was an awareness that had gradually caught up with her the more she played at parties, trying her hand at delivering a spanking, teasing a naked man with a feather duster as his wife looked on, attaching nipple clamps to a very eager sub who looked like Justin Bieber and begged to lick her pussy (a request she denied simply because she could). She moved on to full-fledged domination, ordering whatever man she was seeing to crawl around for her, wear butt plugs for her, hold off on orgasming for her (when she did finally let them come, it was like watching a fountain explode, a sight she'd never get tired of).

The power alone made her pussy wet, but it was more than that—it was the look on a true submissive's face when she captured him in her gaze, in her command. As a sub, she'd gotten off on the pain and obedience, but she'd never glowed from within the way, say, the guy she'd made lick his come off her breasts did. How could she resist someone grateful and boyish and beautiful like the Bieber lookalike, whose name was Paul and who was, in fact, twenty-nine? He was the type who would probably look boyish and get carded into his fifties, and when he let her bind his hands behind his back and put a cock ring on him, she just wanted to smother him in kisses, before smothering him with her pussy. She took turns doing both.

When she'd met Kevin, all those instincts had kicked

in, and, due to his natural servitude, his eagerness to do everything from rub her feet to bend over and get spanked, his intuition and sensitivity that still managed to surprise her, given his size and height and looks—all muscles and tattoos and fierceness—they'd joined forces to become a kinky power couple. Unlike the others, who'd been fun and hot but with whom the spark dimmed a bit outside the bedroom, she and Kevin were perfect complements. He didn't mind cooking the bulk of their meals, booking their travel and generally taking care of business, nor was he put off if she simply wanted him to run her a bath and give her an evening of solo fun. Ironically, he spent his days in his tattoo shop, delivering a different kind of pain, but that was the only pain he was interested in administering, and in fact, he'd had to get over his fears of hurting others when his passion for art had taken a turn for the human canvas.

She loved the fact that Kevin could protect her as a chivalrous gentleman should, that he was a strong, beefy man, given to his own macho proclivities like watching—not to mention playing—football, but at play parties and in their bedroom, he wanted to cater to her. He loved it when she tied him to the headboard and straddled his face, and she loved settling her petite form over him, controlling him not with her heft but with her need, equal to his. There were nights when she simply had him suck and bite her nipples while she pressed her favorite vibrator against her pussy, directing him to use his teeth, or twist her nubs with his fingers.

Even when she was getting some form of pain, she was always controlling him, and he knew it.

In public they made quite a pair, him topping out at just over six feet and weighing almost three hundred pounds, while she was five foot three, with most of her weight in her very large natural breasts. That she could get this beast of a man to whimper and blubber and sometimes even cry for her, to open himself up in every way, still amazed her after almost five years together. She called him her "big bottom," its dual meaning one she cherished. The longer they were together, the deeper their dominance and submission took them. They played at parties, but what she could never convey in those scenes was how devoted Kevin proved himself to be at all hours of the day and night. He sought to please her sexually and otherwise, beaming when she praised him, verging on tears when she scolded him. Sure, he had his own career, but every part of him was ultimately hers to control.

So when she saw the metal talons in the store, she knew they'd be the perfect anniversary gift. One for each finger, five for each year of their partnership, five sharp pieces of silver to attach to her digits and dig into his skin. Slipping them on made her feel taller, bigger, stronger. She'd waited until the party to debut them. "Are you ready for your anniversary present?" she whispered the not-really-a-question. By nature of the formal agreement they'd signed, Kevin's "answer" was a foregone conclusion. Technically, yes, he could balk at the prospect of the talons, or anything else, but in all their years together, even when she'd seen fear or nervousness on his face, he'd never denied her. He wanted her to choose, trusted her to know what lines were okay to cross.

When the blonde crossed their path again and locked eyes with Gemma, she beckoned her over. "Like what you see, honey?" Gemma asked, running her hands up and down Kevin's burly body. The blonde was taller than Gemma, her gleaming bright hair glinting with the room's light.

"Yes, Ma'am," she said, which earned her a smile from Gemma. She couldn't stand the losers who assumed that Gemma bottomed to Kevin simply because she was smaller, and didn't bother wasting time with them. "Then why don't you do me the favor of undressing him? No gratuitous touching, though, just do what you need to take his clothes off."

Gemma rarely let other women get near Kevin, and she knew the blonde's nearness would practically have him coming in his pants. He didn't always go for the prototypical "hot blonde" but he was a heterosexual man, after all, and the woman was barely clothed. Gemma smiled as she watched the blonde strip her husband down, proud that he was the object of such blatant lust—Gemma couldn't have missed the blonde's intake of breath when his jeans eased down to reveal a very hard cock, one that his heft couldn't hide. When he was completely naked, Gemma surveyed the pair, taking pity on the woman. "Can you take his weight on top of you?" she asked the blonde, teasing a pointy red nail along the gold ring adorning her right nipple.

"Definitely, Ma'am."

"Then take off your panties, lie down and spread those pretty legs, darling—and keep your heels on," Gemma said directly into her ear. Using her smarmiest tone made her wet, as did the view when the blonde followed the command, giving Gemma her tiny red thong before she offered up a view of her sex.

"Beautiful, isn't she?" Gemma murmured to Kevin.

"Not as beautiful as you," he replied—they were long past the point of formalities with each other.

"No kissing and no fucking—do you understand? You will take what I give you, no more, no less." Gemma pressed her fingers into his cheeks and made sure Kevin was looking right at her.

"Of course."

Gemma smiled. "Good. Now get on top of her." She knew Kevin would have to be careful to make sure his cock didn't slide into a forbidden zone. Outside this scene, she wouldn't have minded—but this was about teasing him, taunting him, letting him get as close as he could be to another woman, but no farther. She'd let him fuck for her before, but this was about him taking his beating fully while holding back. The idea that their anonymous blonde's body would also be almost ready to explode didn't escape her.

Gemma smiled at the crowd that had formed to watch the three of them. Kevin nestled his head against the side of the blonde's neck, while she beamed a beatific smile. Before she began, Gemma leaned down to whisper in their ears. "If either of you needs to stop, say 'jagged.'" She liked the image that formed when she said the word—the jagged edge of a knife, something rough and uneven. She liked to get Kevin to a point where he was no longer sleek and smooth, but jagged in his own way, tumbling, tipping over, uncertain but clinging to that uncertainty because he always knew she'd take care of him. This was not their usual safeword, but a spontaneous one she gifted to them, a souvenir mouthful to ponder as she took her place.

Gemma started with her hand, which she always treated like the most delicate of instruments. She made sure her hands were soft to the touch, covering them at night with a special moisturizer and gloves. She paid meticulous attention to her manicure, needing her sharp red nails to signal to Kevin and the world just what kind of woman she was. She knelt down and found the most comfortable position with which to deliver her first smack. When she found it, she waited, counting silently to ten. She knew too many tops who rushed their scenes, so intent on their own dominant desires they forgot that keeping a sub at their mercy is a torment in itself. Plus, making Kevin rest his hefty body on top of the blonde dreamboat gave her more time to admire the view. She could stare at his ass all day—forget bubble butts, give Gemma a solid, hairy and, best of all, eager bottom like Kevin's any day. There was more to smack and stroke and squeeze and pinch, though she was well aware it would take some pretty firm smacks to jostle him against the blonde. She was up to the task.

When Gemma sensed that Kevin had started to relax an infinitesimal amount, she let loose with the first blow, digging her nails into his skin at the end for an added treat. "Thank you," he murmured against the blonde's neck, but the sound was drowned out by the next blow. Gemma heard whispers from the onlookers between smacks as she covered each cheek with successively harder blows.

When her hand started to sting, Gemma decided to give Kevin his anniversary present—or rather, give Kevin's back the gift of her using his anniversary present on him. "Your ass is going to get a break now," she said to him. "But there's more in store for it soon. I have something else planned for you. Are you both ready?"

Of course it was an unfair question. How could they be ready for something when they didn't know what to expect? But they were subs, and good subs are always ready for anything, as long as they trust the person they've let control their fate. After getting a chorus of confirmation, Gemma took out the talons and allowed an eager boi from the crowd to place them on her dominant hand, her right.

"This is your present, Kevin," she announced loud enough for everyone to hear. "Even when my nails are at their longest and sharpest, you seem to want more, so here's more." She dragged her now-spiky digits along his back, from his shoulder down. That first pass was more about the sensation, getting him used to it. "You can tell your blonde friend what it feels like."

Gemma couldn't catch his exact words, but saw the ripple pass from the blonde to Kevin after he'd spoken. She dug in more sharply, smiling as he writhed in response. Soon Kevin's wide, hairy back was scored with streaks of red and pink—and she'd only just begun. But they'd have plenty of opportunities to explore how much pressure of the claws Kevin could take. His ass was calling out to her once again. She allowed the same boi to help her remove the claws and place them back in their velvet pouch, in return granting him a kiss on top of his head that made him blush.

Next she called out to the assembled crowd for some audience participation. "Does anyone have a really good paddle I could use?" Immediately, an array of kinky tools were proffered—made of wood, PVC, leather and in a variety of colors. She smiled at the almost dizzying array of toys, but chose one, after a quick inspection and whispered assurance of its extreme usefulness, that was different from any paddle she'd ever held. It was a glass paddle, and featured a handle swirled with red that felt pleasing to the touch.

"I know—glass, right?" the tall, elegant olive-skinned woman who handed it to her whispered in her ear, giving Gemma a delicious chill. "But it works. Maybe too well. I only use it on my greediest subs, but he seems like he can take it."

"Oh, he definitely can," she replied with a wink, for a moment wondering just what it would be like to bend over herself and have this woman spank her. *I'll ponder that later*, Gemma promised herself, before returning to Kevin.

"Get ready," she said so fast he couldn't possibly do the two words justice, before she made his lightly pink ass a much deeper, more beautiful shade of red. She smiled as he screamed—"Aahh!"—the sounds welcome because he was usually much more stoic in the face of a beating. The rush of being on display and the pain she was causing had to be a challenge. She didn't make Kevin take too many strokes of the glass, just enough to ensure his bottom was on fire.

"Very good—both of you," Gemma said to Kevin and the blonde after she'd handed the paddle back to its owner. "Roll over onto your back," she instructed Kevin and then lifted the blonde by her hair. "How was that, honey?"

She stared at Gemma with a lustful glaze in her eyes. "Amazing."

"I think you deserve a spanking too, sweetheart, but you'll have to earn it. You jerk Kevin off and I'll spank you. When you want me to stop, you make him come." She had a feeling this would involve a prolonged hand job for her big bottom—and she was right. Gemma placed a large pillow beneath the blonde's hips, raising her ass in the air so she could lean against one arm, while the other was free to touch and tease Gemma's man.

Kevin's cock looked ready to explode, but the blonde knew what she was doing. Gemma sat on the floor next to the blonde so she could see each handprint blooming on her bottom while also taking in the view of her hand around Kevin's dick. Both of them made ecstatic noises. Gemma wished she had a butt plug to stick between the blonde's beautiful cheeks.

Seeing and sensing how eager the blonde was, Gemma smacked her harder than she'd smacked Kevin, almost at full capacity. She grunted, and Gemma couldn't help but notice the twisting motion she was using on Kevin's cock. In moments, just as her spanking escalated to its most vicious, Kevin was erupting all over her hand.

"That was beautiful," Gemma praised them. "Now I want you to sit on his face and get what's coming to you." She curled a finger toward the glass paddle's owner. "You take her left nipple, and I'll take her right." Together, Gemma, Kevin and her fellow domme got the blonde off—three times, no less. It was hard to say who was the bigger bottom—the blonde or Kevin—but it wasn't a contest. At least, not tonight. Gemma could make them battle it out next time.

SIGHT
READING

Alison Winchester

By midafternoon, the hallways are thankfully cleared of the children and their parents who come in for the community education classes. The only sounds he hears as he makes his way down the last few stairs to the basement level are the hiss of the steam through the pipes and the muted sounds of students practicing: brass and strings blending in a dulled cacophony. The lone computer lab on this floor is near silent, with only the shuffling of papers and occasional clatter of typing to reveal its occupants.

He knows exactly where she'll be. Her favored practice area is a cramped little space just before the wide hallway narrows into twists and turns that lead past offices assigned to unfortunate adjuncts and the unten-ured, and finally to the elevator up to the concert hall and the classrooms. How she stands it with the sweltering heat of the pipes is anyone's guess, but she told him once she felt cozy in there: just her and her cello, and the bonus of no loud trumpets or wallowing French horns on both sides of her.

Through the door, he can hear her going over a particularly tricky section, and he pauses for a moment, not wanting to interrupt her until she's worked out the kinks. She plays through the measure seven, eight, nine times before it meets her standards and she moves on to the next. He takes a deep breath, needing to steady himself and get into the right mindset, before he opens the door. He knows exactly what he'll find once he does. She'll have stripped down to a camisole and one of her long peasant skirts by now. Her short blonde hair will be spiking in all directions from where she's wiped sweat off her brow with her arm, not wanting to use either of her hands and risk contaminating either her bow or the cello strings. The taste of salt on her neck will be irresistible.

But he's here to encourage her to take a break. To get some lunch. To relax. Not to simply screw her in a practice room like some horny undergrad.

He adjusts himself before he opens the door, hoping the smile on his face will disguise the overwhelming want.

To her credit, she's grown so used to interruptions of all kinds that she continues playing without so much as a hesitation when he enters the room. It bodes well for her audition that her nerves are that steady, even if he does find himself a bit jealous of her cello these days.

"I'm still not entirely sure about the Bantock," he says.

She doesn't miss a beat as she answers, "Neither am I, but every last cellist there will be doing Bach, and I don't need to be compared to Yo-Yo Ma on top of all the other candidates. If nothing else, maybe they'll give me points for balls in making them look him up on Wikipedia."

He snorts.

"Truth time, though: do you think it sounds too stark without the piano? That's my biggest concern."

He listens for a few measures more before offering his opinion.

"No. I think you've made the right adjustments. You can probably afford to go bigger in a few spots, but from what I hear, it's sounding great. How are you feeling about it?"

She makes a noncommittal noise and keeps playing.

He clears his throat, and the music stops immediately.

"Did you need something?" she asks.

He waits.

Laughter bubbles under her voice, but she manages a calm, "Did you need something...Sir?"

He crosses to her in three steps and stands beside her, waiting. Her clothes are shed with a soft rustle, and her

cello makes a dull thud as she sets it down. He asks if
she doesn't want to store it in its case.

"I don't want to keep you waiting, Sir."

He lets himself smile when she's in position. This is
so second nature to her that she makes no sound when
she moves. But her cheek resting against his leg is a reas-
suring pressure, and the damp heat that radiates off her
is an invitation to touch, to stroke, to lick. On her knees
with her head bowed, she can't see his face.

A gentle caress of her hair, and she moves to stand in
front of him. He loves that, for the most part, they don't
even need words. It's like a smooth tango at this point,
just two people moving in choreographed synchronicity.

"Is the door locked?" she asks.

He unbuckles his belt.

"Sir, I'm sorry, Sir. I know you think of my needs
always."

"Pick your cello up. No sitting."

The endpin scrapes as she adjusts the cello for standing
height, and she begins to play. Not the Bantock, no, but
Gossec's Gavotte.

"A Suzuki piece? That is going to be five extra. And
don't miss a note."

He cracks the belt once between his hands, knowing
the harsh snap will put her on edge. He can feel the
anticipation as it seeps out of her skin, as she waits for
the first strike, which he places with careful precision
right at the top of her ass.

She hisses, but hits every note. There may have been

a method to her madness in picking such an easy piece to play. No matter. His goal is to make her miss.

Three more swings, each one so perfectly under the one before that he's sure he could measure the strikes with a ruler. He knows, because she's actually done it. Practice is everything. Practice is...

He clears his mind. There is no room here to think about anything but her. Four more strikes and she moans, but still manages to hit the pizzicato notes perfectly, and that simply won't do.

Seven left. Does he mete them out one at a time or quickly, to match the notes that dance from under her fingers? Slowly, he thinks. Off-tempo. Adagio to her allegretto. Seven strikes like dripping syrup and still she plays perfectly, even as she begins a repeat.

He drops the belt and presses himself against her back, sliding a hand along her arm, brushing the side of her breast, tickling the inside of her elbow.

She plays on.

His fingers glance across her belly—too thin, he thinks—along her slightly jutting hip bone, and then dip between her soft, bare lips.

"You're so wet for me, aren't you, Petunia? I've barely even touched you, and I can feel you all over my fingers. I wonder...?" He trails off and she hesitates, just for a moment. But that moment is enough for him to take her bow.

"Don't let go of that cello," he orders, holding her bow in rest position.

"*Pizzicato*," he whispers into her ear, plucking first one erect nipple, then the other in quick succession, keeping perfect time.

She makes a sound—a quiet moan—and he increases the tempo of his fingers.

"I want to hear you," he says.

"Some—someone will hear."

"No one will hear. And if they do, they'll think you're an opera student doing a very unique, and very sexy, warm-up."

With that, he takes the bow in hand and whispers again. "I'll pay to have the bow rehaired. Now spread your legs a bit more."

That's the only warning he gives her before drawing it slowly—and so very gently—along her inner thigh.

"Please, Sir."

He ignores her, running the bow against one leg, then the other, playing a song he can only hear in his mind. He taunts her, moving his playing upward, almost to the point where she thought he'd finally allow the bow to touch where she wanted it most, before moving downward again.

She whimpers like a breathy flute descant over the music he hears in his mind. *The Bantock*, he thinks, and begins to slip the bow closer to where she wants him. He follows the precise rhythm of the piece, playing solely from memory. The bow skims over her wetness as he makes full use of her body as the fingerboard: her plush lips, her ballet-dancer throat, her taut nipples, her ticklish ribs. She squirms, trying to work the bow to speed her orgasm, but she doesn't let go of the cello.

"Do you think you can still hang on?" he asks.

She nods, and moans with a quick, begging glissando at the end.

He shoves the bow into her hand and unfastens his fly, stroking her breast with his other hand before sliding it down to her hip. With the slightest pressure, he pulls her with him as he takes first one and then a second step backward. He can feel the tension in her arms as she holds the cello out from her, and with another gentle push of his fingers on the back of her neck, she bends forward.

He wants to be slow. Wants to take his time with her. Wants to splay her out and bury his face in her pussy and flog her until her skin burns under his hands. But she has practice, and someone could conceivably walk by and hear them and he needs to move things along.

With one last sweep of his fingers, he revels in the evidence of how much she wants him right now. One finger slips inside her and she grunts, the first sound she's made that offends his ear.

"Petunia—" he warns.

"Sorry, Sir. Please, Sir," she breathes.

His hand forces her lower back into a graceful bend, mimicking the curves of her cello. In a simple, practiced move, he lines himself up and thrusts inside her, burying himself until he can no longer tell where she ends and he begins. For just a moment, he is still, then he gives her a single order, issued in a near whisper.

"Count."

He begins thrusting, altering his rhythm as she struggles to meet his demand. She tightens and releases around his cock once, twice, three times before she manages the first answer:

"Three-quarter."

He alters his rhythm to keep her guessing the time signature of his thrusts as the heat of the room begins to overwhelm him. Sweat slides down his forehead to trail alongside the planes of his cheekbones, and his grip on her hips begins to falter.

"Common time."

"There's nothing common about you, Petunia."

She pants between answers, her breath urging him faster and faster.

"Are you close, Petunia?"

"So. Unh. Close, Sir."

"What do you want then? Tell me. Conduct."

"*Alla breve. Presto. Prestissimo.*"

He obeys, speeding his hips as if he's adjusted the weight on a metronome. Slide the weight down and increase tempo. He's first chair, following his conductor to the climax. Whatever she asks for, he'll give her.

His breathing sounds too loud in his ears, the slapping of their sweaty bodies obscene. He wonders how anyone in the building can escape hearing them.

"*Con brio,*" she says. "*Con fuoco.*"

He'd laugh if he didn't think it would set off his orgasm. She tightens around him as she barks her commands. Vigor? That he has. But she is the fire.

The orgasm he's chasing is so close it consumes him. Every muscle is wrought iron, holding him back until she goes over. He's sloppy, out of rhythm, and the tell-tale scrape of the cello's endpin on the floor tells him she's losing control as well.

"So close," she moans, then repeats.

He lets go of one hip to slide his hand over her clit. In less than three passes of his finger, slipping her wetness over her, she's coming: A below middle C, sliding to a staccato F-sharp, slipping to a breathy but sustained E-flat.

He doesn't let go until he feels her tight clench release and flutter around him, thrusting deep, wanting to come, but more, wanting it to never end. As he pours into her, he hears her soft sigh and feels her muscles finally go lax.

After pulling her up so she's standing, he kisses the back of her neck and her shoulders, darting his tongue out to taste the salty sweat. He helps her balance when she wavers, seeing to his jeans only after she's steady on her feet.

She sets the cello on the floor and turns into his arms, pressing her lips to his neck, then finally greets him with a kiss, her tongue softly dancing over his lips before dipping inside. He gets lost in her, but she pulls away.

"Scene over?" she asks.

"Yes."

"You were sneaky," she says. "No cane. I'd have heard you coming. Been more prepared."

He laughs as he reaches into his back pocket for the collapsible cane. "It jabbed me in the kidneys a few times, but I think it was worth it, don't you?"

She wraps herself around him, tucking her head under his chin. Her hair is damp with sweat, but she feels so relaxed in his arms. The tension that had filled the room when he arrived has dissipated.

He strokes his fingers down her back. "More relaxed now?"

"Yes," she says. "Are you?"

He knows what she's asking for, knows what she wants, but it's beyond him.

"It's fire."

"So you won't blindfold me."

"It's too dangerous."

"I'll be watching."

"You can't do that and reach subspace."

"Baby," she says. "You did this. You came in here and gave me exactly what I needed in a strange room—well, at least a little strange. We can practice. Like we did with everything else. You can play piano and strings and how many other instruments? Half your students don't even realize you're blind. The candles are just one more thing. I trust you. You need to trust me, too."

He drops his lips to her forehead.

"I want to give you everything," he says.

"You do. Now let me go back to practicing. I'll be home later."

He kisses her softly and makes her check to make sure he's not too rumpled before unfolding his cane and heading reluctantly out of the room. His cane scratches softly along the carpeted hallway as he winds his way back. His gait is faster now, not as worried about keeping his steps even to count them. Lockers ping softly until he reaches the softer click of the marble stairs, and he makes his way up to his office, the sound of Bantock a faint whisper in the background.

CORPORATE COMPLIANCE

David Wellwood

The box sat on her desk, pure white with a scarlet-red bow. What had he sent her this time? He'd told her to expect a delivery, instructed her to leave it closed until their scheduled meeting. She bit her lip; she had kinda broken that order already. The brown box had been sitting on her desk when she arrived. For half an hour, she had tried to ignore it, forget it existed, but the bloody thing was a magnet for her eyes.

She'd tried hiding the box in her desk drawer. That hadn't helped and the question burned in her mind. She couldn't concentrate; by ten thirty she had given up and ripped it open. Inside she'd found the white box, the scarlet bow gleaming, and a card. A simple statement, written by him, thrilled her—*I told you not to open the box*. She was in a little bit of trouble already.

Her foot turned lazy circles, unable to sit still. Checking her watch for the thousandth time, she saw she had five minutes left. She shivered, excited.

Time. She stood, walking to her open door. "Lucy, I'm going into conference with the Ellison account, no calls and no interruptions please." Lucy nodded.

She shut the door to her office, closed her eyes and prepared herself for the meeting. She walked back to her chair, waiting for him to appear online. Her computer pinged, announcing his arrival.

"Hi, you. Did the package arrive?" His voice was distorted by the speaker.

She paused, wondering if she should lie about opening the box. "Yes...though I've been a little naughty; I opened the brown box."

"I thought I'd been clear about that."

"Well yes...I couldn't help myself."

"I guessed you wouldn't follow instructions. I hope the card stopped you." He laughed.

"Yes, I was good, honest."

"Hmm, I'll be the judge of that. Are you ready to turn your cam on?"

"Yes, I'm ready."

"Then let's begin."

She clicked on the camera, pushing her chair back from the desk, her body filling the shot, waiting for his instructions. Upright, legs together, hands clasped in her lap, ready to follow his every command.

"Unbutton your blouse."

Her hands oozed up her torso, pausing to cup her breasts before she began to unbutton her white blouse. Taking her time with each button, revealing her lace bra beneath, she pulled the front out of her skirt, the blouse falling open, her hands resuming their place in her lap.

"Good choice, the lace hides practically nothing. Stroke your breasts."

A coy smile played over her lips; she'd picked her outfit with care. The sheer lace panels practically see-through, darker patterns obscuring her nipples beneath the fabric. She began to stroke them, pushing them together, the flesh threatening to escape from the cups, forming the massive cleavage he liked to have his cock between. She circled her fingers around her nipples. They stiffened, sending the first waves of pleasure through her body.

"Pinch your nipples."

She complied, taking them between a finger and thumb, squeezing them, pinching them hard, pulling them toward the camera. She suppressed a moan, heat rising throughout her. She pinched harder, rolling them, spikes of pain increasing her arousal.

"Pull your breasts out."

She scooped her breasts out of her bra, eager to expose them to his gaze; the urge to push them toward her mouth and lick her stiff nipples was hard to resist. She dropped her hands back to her lap, breasts hanging free over her bra.

"Pull your skirt up."

This order sounded simple, yet there were rules. She grasped the hem of her skirt and began to inch it up over her thighs; she mustn't let her legs part and flash him a glimpse of her sex. Every wiggle of her hips and pull of her skirt caused her breasts to sway. It was entirely for his pleasure and this excited her further, the desire aching in her soul. Her skirt finally sat bunched at her waist, the wide lace bands on the black hold-up stockings he demanded she wear fully on show.

"Did you complete your preparations? You may answer."

A shiver ran through her thinking about the preparation for their meetings. The night before, she was to shave her pussy smooth; forty-five minutes before the start, remove her panties; spend five minutes fingering her pussy; devote a further five minutes to teasing her clit, to assure her pussy would be good and wet; stuff her panties into her pussy and leave them inside for two minutes; extract then and seal them into a Ziplock bag. Normally they were Fed-Ex'd next-day delivery, but he hadn't sent an address this time, so they sat in her desk drawer.

"Yes, Sir, I have followed your instructions."

"Show me your pussy."

Such a casual request. Her body chilled, legs parting and opening wide, heels on the ground, toes pointing out. Totally exposed, she sat behind her desk, webcam broadcasting, tits hanging out, bare pussy fully on show. She loved it: very wrong and yet so right. Her pussy began to twitch, lips slick, begging for attention.

"Pull you lips apart."

Her hands moved to her pussy, eagerly pulling her lips apart, exposing the hot, pink, wet inner folds. She brushed her hard clit and a stab of electric pleasure shocked her. Looking directly at the camera, she smiled, totally exposed to his gaze.

"You may have one minute to do as you please."

He must be happy, she thought. One hand grabbed a breast, pinching the nipple hard; her middle finger began to grind on her clit. She wanted to moan, needed the release, but the rules said otherwise. She threw back her head, eyes closed. The pleasure and pain washed over her in equal measure as her pussy glistened for the camera.

"Enough."

She stopped. Panting, she moved her hands to rest on the lace bands of her stockings, her legs spread wide once again. Her clit pulsed, pleading for her to continue, to drive on to the orgasm it demanded. She mustn't, she couldn't. Her reward would come when he allowed. Her breathing settled, ready for his next instruction.

"Is your pussy good and wet? Show me."

She thrust two fingers deep inside, muscles clamping hard onto them, desperate to have them thrust in and out. She withdrew them, and learning forward, held her slick fingers up to the camera.

"Time for your present. Take the box and sit back down, legs closed."

She grabbed the box and sat down, pressing her legs together harder than before, crushing her clit and feeling the throb. The box felt oddly cold on her bare thighs. She was desperate to see what was inside.

"Open it."

She pulled the bow, discarding the lid. Inside was a glass dildo. Slightly curved, it had a bulbous head and blue ridges spiraling down the outside. It was quite fat, and her pussy pulsed, ready to have it thrust deep inside. She'd never had a glass toy before, but she'd heard they were fantastic.

"It's going to be cold. Tease your nipples. Show me your pussy again."

She touched the dildo and the coldness shocked her despite his warning. Her brow knitted, how had he kept it this cold? She wanted to ask him, the question almost escaping her lips before she caught herself.

"Tease your nipples and show me your pussy now," he said again, snapping her back to the present.

She lifted the dildo from the box. She opened her legs, spreading them wider than before, pussy lips parting, juices oozing from within. The ache between her legs was becoming unbearable. The dildo tip touched her nipple; she cried out, the cold touch biting. Her nipple was now harder than ever before. She circled it and the stinging coldness felt fantastic. She moved to the other nipple, savoring the bite of the cold for a second time. Her fingers holding the dildo were becoming numb to the cold. This was better than ice!

"You'll find lube in the box. Cover the ridges."

She bent to find the box and the small bottle of lube inside. She was puzzled, as she'd never had need for lube on her other toys. How different was this glass cock? The ridges did stick out quite far, and maybe the cold would have an effect. She pumped three beads of lube onto the dildo. Taking it in her hand like she did his cock, she began stroking up and down, circling the tip with her thumb, hoping all the while he was mimicking her actions. The ridges felt strange in her hand, and she wanted to know how they would feel deep in her pussy.

"Put it into your pussy now, nice and slow—all the way in and stop."

She placed the glass cock against her entrance, biting her lip; the shocking cold stung her hot pussy. She pushed the head onward, opening her pussy, inching the dildo inside. It was unlike anything she had used before—the biting cold of the dildo, the ridges teasing parts of her never touched at the same time before, the unforgiving hardness of the glass. After what seemed like an age, she could push no more, her pussy numb, full of freezing-cold, hard glass. She began to clamp and release her muscles, pleasure washing through her, her clit throbbing hard, nipples tingling, crying out for attention, pleading to be the trigger to her building orgasm.

"Fuck yourself with the dildo. Take your time. I want this to last."

She eased the glass out, heat prickling deep inside

when the cold dildo withdrew. She paused with the tip
at her entrance and eased it back deep inside. She built to
a steady rhythm, hot and cold, the sublime caress of the
ridges, the fat hardness of the glass filling her pussy. She
felt faint, every part of her body screaming for release,
mini-orgasms breaking inside her with every thrust.

"Stroke your clit. Do not come."

Was he fucking joking? How was she supposed not
to come!

Her finger found her clit and she circled it, unable to
risk direct touch. She closed her eyes, mouth clamped
tight to hold back the screams of pleasure. She felt as if
she would explode; she had to come soon.

She heard the sound of the door clicking, beginning
to open, and her eyes flew open. Her hands stilled where
they were. She was about to be discovered—marketing
director found in office, tits hanging from bra, glass dildo
stuffed in pussy, broadcasting live to one of their key
clients! Her body froze, the chill of the dildo forgotten.

He stepped through the narrow opening, closing the
door behind him with a shit-eating grin on his face.

"You bastard!" she spat.

"We haven't finished," he said, the grin gone, his
gray eyes staring hard, "and I never said to stop. Fuck
your pussy. You may come."

Her cheeks were on fire, emotions running wild, but
she had to obey. She began to thrust the dildo harder
into her pussy, finger circling her clit directly now.

He strode across her office and leaned against her

desk, eyes locked on the dildo flashing in and out of her sodden pussy. The fire returned to wipe away the cold shock, and her pussy throbbed in time with her finger's movements. Her hips thrust desperately; she closed her eyes, only moments left.

His hands grabbed her breasts, pulling hard on her nipples, and her orgasm exploded. She kept her mouth clamped shut as the orgasm ripped through her, pulsing out from her pussy and clit, washing through her body, shaking her legs. Once spent, she slumped back into the chair, panting hard, stars swirling behind her eyes. She'd never had an orgasm quite so intense before.

He pushed her hand away and pulled the dildo from her pussy. She stared into his flint-gray eyes, thinking she'd never want another toy again.

"You have a dirty mouth, and trouble with instructions."

She gulped, her heart beginning to beat at a normal rate, her pussy aching, missing the hardness already. She said nothing. Regaining her composure, she sat up straight, placed her hands on the lace of her stockings and spread her legs once more.

"That's better, but transgressions have consequences. Take off your blouse."

She tossed her blouse aside, hands returning to the lace. Consequences, oh yes, she hoped so.

He reached into his pocket, withdrawing a chain with nipple clamps at each end. He fastened them onto her still-hard nipples, tightening them to the limit of what she could bear. Her nipples throbbed with delicious, heavenly pain.

"Bend over your desk, palms flat."

She stood and did as she was told, her arse high in the air, legs spread, her pussy completely exposed and at his mercy.

He pushed the chair away, moving to stand directly behind her. He grabbed her buttocks, squeezing them roughly. The first smack came from nowhere, hard on her right cheek. Tingling pain shot through her and she was sure the skin blushed red.

"That was for opening the box before you were told." Another smack fell on her left cheek. "That was for not following instructions." A third smack fell, harder this time and deliciously painful. "That is for having a dirty mouth." A final smack landed, evening out the stinging across her arse. "And that one is for stopping without being told. You are a bad girl. What are you? Answer."

"I'm a bad girl." The words thrilled her.

"And should bad girls get taught a lesson? Answer."

"Yes, Sir, this bad girl must be taught a lesson." Boy did she need a lesson; her pussy was aching to be full.

His belt rattled as he unfastened the buckle, his zipper growled open and then his cock was pressing against the entrance to her pussy. She braced herself. His thrust was brutal, as he forced himself deep inside in one firm push, filling her up. The heat of his flesh was welcome after the chill of the dildo; she tensed, his cock throbbing as she clasped him tight.

He grasped her arse, reigniting the pain from the smacks, and she welcomed it. He spread her cheeks, exposing her anus. She felt cold liquid dropped onto it and a finger teasing around the dark entrance, spreading the lube, pushing gently inside. She clenched instinctively, forcing herself to relax and accept the finger penetrating her. In and out, each thrust easier to take than the first. It withdrew, replaced by two, his cock pressed hard into her pussy. More lube and a third finger slid into her arse, spreading her wider still, pushing deep. A small orgasm shook her, her cunt pulsing against his rock-hard flesh, both arse and pussy delightfully stuffed.

"Time for the naughty girl's lesson. Does she deserve one? Answer."

"This naughty girl wants her lesson, Sir." The words tumbled from her mouth.

She felt the fingers leave her and then the tip of the dildo penetrated her arse, still cold, fat and hard. She savored the stabs of pain as it slid relentlessly into her, both holes full now. She felt the cold, hard dildo in her arse, his hot cock in her pussy, her nipples pulsing in their clamps; she couldn't tell which was the most pleasurable.

He withdrew his cock, the tip teasing her entrance before pushing back inside, again and again. Time began to blur. She closed her eyes, the pleasure intense as he fucked her. A hand grasped her hips, his pace increasing, pushing harder and deeper with every stroke, keeping the dildo shoved tight in her arse with his other hand.

She responded, pushing her hips back to match him, the noise of their fucking getting louder and louder, flesh clashing with every thrust. His fingers found her clit, stroking hard and fast, her orgasm built, pussy pulsing, ready to explode. His finger slowed on her clit, bringing her back from the brink only to resume the frantic teasing seconds later, keeping her on the verge of orgasm for what seemed an age.

"Does the bad girl want to come? Does she promise to be a good girl in future? Answer."

"Fuck yes, the bad girl wants to come, yes she promises to be good. Please, Sir, fuck your good girl." She clamped her pussy hard around his cock, his finger pressing hard on her clit, cock slamming deep inside her, pressing the dildo in her arse down. Her whole body shook with the force of her orgasm. She felt her legs shake, threatening to give way, as the fire burnt through her. He grunted and came inside her as he continued to thrust.

Finally, their breathing slowed and their bodies stilled. He eased the dildo from her stretched arse, released the clamps on her nipples and slipped from her raw pussy.

"Clean me."

She turned around and knelt before him, greedily licking his cock, savoring the taste of her pussy and his spunk. She pulled his foreskin back, tongue licking fast, taking him deep in her mouth and swallowing every drop.

"Stand up."

She stood, legs spread. He knelt between her legs and gently licked the wet trail leaking from her pussy, tracing up her thigh to the source. "Spread your lips." She complied, pulling her lips open wide as he kissed her pussy, thrusting his tongue deep inside, seeking to clean her with each thrust. Finished, his tongue flicked wickedly at her clit, sending one small orgasm spiraling through her.

Standing again, he kissed her, tongue pushing against hers, sharing the taste of their fucking, and then he pulled her into his arms, their session over.

"I'm a bastard am I?" he said, his words softer than before.

"I thought Ted was walking in on me! You could have hinted you were nearby."

"Oh, I'd pay to see that, the CEO finding his marketing director fucking a dildo!"

"John!" She hugged him, broke the embrace. Walking to her desk she opened the drawer and threw her wet knickers to him. "Yours, I think."

He opened the bag, removing the panties, sniffing at the crotch. "Hmmm, much better when they're fresh, aren't they? But you can't beat the real thing." He held them out to her, "Wear them; I like the smell on you."

She ignored the offered panties and pulled the cups of her bra up while he recovered his pants. Walking to a hidden closet, she took out a fresh blouse and skirt.

"Do you want to have the meeting here or over lunch?" She finished buttoning her blouse, picking up the white box and putting the dildo inside. "And where did you find the dildo?"

"Let's eat. Then later I'll eat you." He winked. "I found the toy on the Internet, You like it?"

"It was fantastic, so cold and hard. Thank you." She kissed him, "Let's get out of here."

He held the door for her as they left. She turned to her secretary, "Lucy, I'm gone for the day. Mr. Ellison and I will conduct the meeting out. I'll check my messages later."

"Yes Ms. Walters." Lucy resumed typing on her computer.

She headed for the lift, a delicious idea forming. "Oh, Lucy, I'm going to need you here at eight tomorrow morning, I have something special for you."

"Yes, Ms. Walters, I'll be here on time, ready for you."

She nodded and turned back to him, waiting for the lift.

"Lucy is a good girl, isn't she?" he said.

She smiled back at him as the lift arrived. "Oh yes, she's a very good girl."

NO BURN NIGHT

Valerie Alexander

An icy rain was pelting my windshield as I waited in my driveway for the garage door to go up. My car was full of firewood, flowers, wine and artichokes—the final items I needed for tonight's party. Our daughter was off at her grandmother's for the night, my husband had been cleaning the house all week and I had a slutty new dress that would be safe enough for our work friends and sexy enough for our poly-kinkster friends. Then I pulled into the garage and the rain cut off and in the silence I started thinking about Nick again.

Nick, my husband's ex-boyfriend who was coming tonight. Who'd broken his heart in college eleven years ago and then resurfaced in our city, as handsome and smoldering as ever. Their freshmen relationship on the college lacrosse team had been intense and disastrous, ending when Ian went home with Nick on spring break and Nick's father caught them in bed, Ian hog-tied while Nick cock-slapped his face and jerked him off. Nick had insisted Ian pressured him into it, his father had almost punched Ian and somehow the whole incident had gotten Ian kicked off the lacrosse team back at school. My husband had long since forgiven Nick, but I hadn't.

Even though I enjoyed hearing some of the details of their relationship—like Nick fucking Ian's face in the locker-room shower or cuffing him to his dorm-room bed, I didn't enjoy Nick being in our lives. You could say my resentment was just one alpha wolf holding another at bay. Nick had been the first person to dominate Ian, which rankled the territorial domme in me. But really Nick himself bothered me. The qualities that could make for hot and twisted jerking off—Nick's black hair and strong jaw, those pale deadly eyes and his devious personality—made me guarded and brittle around him in real life. I didn't like that he'd moved to our city two years ago, or that he had become the hottest, most well-known dom in town. Nick might not be blaming other boys these days for his tendency to enslave and debase them, but he was still seducing and discarding them like tissues. Not that it was held against him. He was so good-looking that it had become an honor to be used by him.

"You were Nick's sub in college?" gasped my husband's date a few months ago. "What was he like? Do you have pictures of him?"

Nick's legend had seemed to erase Ian at that moment, which was another crime to hold against him. My beautiful blond husband belonged in no one's shadow. But that's how it had been ever since Nick had moved here. He made a splash when Ian took him to the local clubs and play parties and soon everyone was referring to my husband, who'd lived here all his life, as Nick's friend. Everyone was blinded by that megawatt dominance he radiated—part sun god, part animal magnetism. He seemed born to turn heads and make people weak with just a smile. Which was, of course, the real reason I detested him.

Simply put, I didn't think my husband could resist him.

I put the bags on the counter just as Ian walked into the kitchen. "I cleaned all afternoon," he said. "You don't have to do anything, Veronica."

I kissed him. "I still want to take a bath, and then I have to get the fire going."

This would be our first real party since we bought this house. It had to be perfect. The food had to be exquisite and the wine had to be sophisticated and most importantly I wanted a grand fire to roar in the enormous stone fireplace that was my favorite feature of the house. Yet at the same time, it was important to differentiate from the kind of parties our parents used to throw. It was important our kinkster friends knew that just because Ian and I got married, had a kid and moved to the suburbs, we hadn't gone dull. We were still radical, still deviant. We just had a backyard garden and three bedrooms to be radical and deviant in.

I took the flowers and artichokes out of the bags.

"I love watching you get ready for this party," Ian said. "You're like a kinky Mrs. Dalloway."

"I feel more like a second-rate Martha Stewart." Then I saw a tension in his jaw. *Nick*, was my first thought. "What's wrong?"

"I know you wanted a fire tonight. But the county just announced a pollution warning—it's a no burn night."

My first reaction was relief. No Nick drama tonight. Then I realized what my husband was saying. Due to unhealthy air quality, the county had put out a notice against burning wood. We couldn't build that grand, roaring fire I'd envisioned. Our massive stone fireplace would stay cold and dark.

"Goddammit." It was a sign.

"Come on, Veronica. It'll still be a great party. We'll light candles."

"Candles are banal," I said bitterly.

Ian gathered up my long dark hair, then kissed the back of my neck. He knew my investment in this party bordered on the neurotic. That I wanted to show all our friends that we weren't boring suburban sellouts. And of course he knew that I wanted to show Nick what a blissful domestic existence Ian and I enjoyed—that his conquistador's life of seducing submissive boys was shallow compared to our domestic lair of family love and femdom.

"Go soak in the tub," Ian said. "I'll bring you a drink. And don't worry, I'll take care of everything."

True to his word, he did. My husband was kind of perfect like that. But the cold and empty fireplace taunted me every time I passed through the living room that night, and it made me irrationally tense. I was thinking of how mesmerizing the ambience would have been with a fire when the doorbell rang and Nick came through the foyer archway, looking debonair in a black overcoat.

His pale eyes locked with mine and he came straight for me. "You look beautiful," he said, kissing my cheek. "That dark red color really suits you."

"Thank you." I deliberately failed to return the compliment because Nick already had enough people telling him how handsome he was.

My husband's blond head sailed past me as he went into Nick's arms—and although it was just a friendly hug, jealousy rose in me like a firework. I smiled past my gritted teeth. Ian and I had been nonmonogamous forever, and it was rare for me to feel threatened by anyone, but Nick was an exception. Maybe it was because they looked so sexy together, one fair and one dark, both so tall. Or maybe it was the way Nick held his arm too long as he asked after Ian's latest architectural project. Anyone could see they were ex-lovers. Guilt, lust, memories of an adolescent spring love—of course Nick still carried a torch for him. And the fact that I'd issued a firm veto on them having any kind of scene had to stoke his fire even hotter.

"Veronica, you look distracted," he said.

Our gazes locked again. I wanted to tell him that I wasn't some infatuated sub in awe of him. That I knew all his dom mind tricks because I was a skilled domme myself, and I would never be charmed or won over by him.

Instead I smiled. "Let me take your coat."

In the spare bedroom I found three people tangling together on the pile of coats. As soon as I kicked them out, the sound of smashing glass brought me to the kitchen; my friend Becca had dropped a bottle of beer on the tiles. "I'm so sorry! Don't be mad!" she begged drunkenly. When she looked over my shoulder, she melted into a lascivious smile and I knew who it was even before I turned.

Nick looked very serious. "Veronica, I know it's off limits tonight, but is there any way I can use the master bath? Apparently someone's been locked in your powder room for twenty minutes now and there's a line for the other bathroom. I'm sorry."

The last thing I wanted was Nick in our bedroom. Goddamn whoever was hooking up in the guest bathroom. "Fine, go ahead," I said ungraciously.

"Thank you so much," he said with that same serious politeness.

That bastard. I wouldn't put it past him to steal some

of Ian's hair from his brush for a love spell—or some of mine for a hex. I checked the other rooms, making sure no fourways or spanking scenes were brewing—why did I ever think throwing a party with both our poly-kinkster friends and our work friends was a smart idea?—and rousted the couple having sex in the powder room. Ian was on the living room sofa, talking to his drunken boss, while people I didn't recognize were making drinks in my blender. But all I could think about was that it had been seventeen minutes now and Nick was still in our bedroom.

I went upstairs to find Nick going through our bureau drawers.

Paranoia confirmed. He was so in love with my husband that he was going to steal his underwear. "You nosy little fuck," I said bitterly.

He glanced back at me way too casually. Oddly he was rummaging in my drawer, not Ian's. "You have beautiful corsets," he said. "I wasn't sure if you were the kind of domme who dressed up or not. You're hard to read."

"Maybe because it's none of your business?"

He sat on the bed and looked up at me. It had a queer and tremendous effect on me, my rival and husband's ex-dom sitting on my marital bed.

"I never could have given him all this," he said.

"Definitely not all of it," I said somewhat meanly.

His lips twisted. "I don't just mean your daughter. I used to sketch out houses…think about the life we would have…"

"You were only eighteen," I said.

"I was in love with him."

My heart began to hammer. "Well, you'd better be over it now."

He looked around the bedroom again. "You and I are a lot alike, you know."

"Because I'm married with a toddler, and you're seducing a different busboy every weekend?"

He smiled. "Fair enough." He looked up at me. "Maybe it's not that I want to be you; it's that I want to have you."

It was the most bizarre thing he could have said. Yet it didn't take me by surprise. "Shut up," I said harshly.

"I know," he said, leaning back on his elbows as if our California king bed was his to sprawl on. "You can't stand me. Tell me about it."

"I despise you," I said immediately. "You're smug and you're arrogant and you don't give a shit about anyone but yourself."

He shrugged. "More or less. But that's not why you don't like me."

"Oh, please. I'm not jealous, if that's what you're implying."

Nick unzipped his pants and liberated his cock. Somehow it also wasn't surprising that he was hard. He was probably perverse enough to get off on his weird trip through my lingerie drawer. "You know he still wants this."

I stepped up and slapped his cock. A soft grunt

escaped him and he grinned and thrust his hips forward
as if he were offering it to me. I slapped it again, trying
not to admire what a thick, beautiful cock he had.

His eyes glittered with calculation. "Come on. Get
it out of your system. You've hated me for years, so let
me have it."

I was on the bed a second later, pinning him down
and giving that smug and handsome face a good slap.
His grin widened and he grabbed my hand and kissed it.
"I knew you'd be a tiger," he said. "Ian wouldn't have
married anything else."

"Fuck you and what you think you know about Ian."
I pinned him again, aware that he was letting me, and
annoyed by his obvious strength advantage. My dress
was hiked up around my thighs and he was positioning
me over his crotch, I realized—moving me with his hips. It
pissed me off. There was no way I was letting Nick control
this situation. I reached back and grabbed his cock. As
expected, he sighed and immediately submitted.

"The things I would do to you if you were my sub,"
I said.

"Tell me," he muttered, trying to shift his cock in my
hand.

"For starters, I'd degrade you ruthlessly until you
dropped that cocky expression. And then I'd lock *this*
into a good chastity device." I squeezed his cock hard,
but he just smiled dreamily. I pushed up his shirt and
pinched his nipples. "And yes, you have beautiful pecs—
but I'd scratch *V*s into them for Veronica, so everyone

would know who owned you as soon as you took your shirt off. Go on and smirk—you wouldn't like it. I'd dress you up like my own personal maid-whore and if you missed just one spot cleaning the house, I'd get out the paddle until you begged for my forgiveness. Oh, and your cock would be my toy. I'd use you whenever I felt like it and if you ever let me down, it wouldn't be the paddle—it'd be the whip."

His cock was spilling precum all over my fingers. "Keep going," he murmured. "I can take it."

"I decide what you can take. Not you." I played with his cock and another moan escaped him. Arching his back, he looked like any sub boy begging for more, but it wasn't any sub boy sprawled on my bed—it was Nick, my husband's ex and the most gorgeous, heartless dom in town, and he was apparently signing himself over to me to do with as I pleased. I knew I should stop but a complicated brew of jealousy and lust blotted out all logic and I reached for the chains attached to our bed. Around his wrists I wound them, the click of the padlock zinging in my clit.

I reached into our nightstand and pulled out the thickest toy we had, a shiny black silicone cock.

Nick went still. "Uh, hold on," he said. "I'm a top through and through, and I don't…"

"It's not for your ass." I slid it neatly into his mouth, enjoying the way he obediently opened his jaws to accommodate it, and his full lips closed around the silicone.

His pale eyes stayed locked on my face as I roughly took his pants all the way down to his ankles. He was a beautiful and hard-muscled animal, his quads flexing under my fingertips and spreading to show off his balls; I could entirely appreciate what all his smitten pet boys saw in him, and I could have spent hours studying every part of him and making plans for canings, for welts, for arm binders and photo shoots. But it was critical not to lose control. Nick was chained and naked on my bed, his mouth gagged by an enormous dildo, and a feral new rush was hitting me like a drug. To hide how intoxicated I felt, I moved down to his swollen, blood-darkened cock. I licked off the pearly strand of precum on his stomach, taking my time, moving my tongue through the light hair on his navel, until he groaned through the gag. Then I sucked his cock into my mouth, torturing him until he was twisting around on the bed like a madman. He was making frantic noises around the dildo and even though I knew he could have pushed it out himself, I pulled it out and let him talk.

"Please," he said hoarsely.

"Please what? Be detailed, Nick."

"I need to come. Please let me come."

"Not yet. Grovel for me first."

"I'm nothing compared to you. I'm a worthless slut—you can do anything to me—"

"Promise to serve me."

"I'll do anything you want. I am at your command."

I pulled my dress off and straddled him, then pretended to fiddle with my bra. "Don't stop," he urged hoarsely.

That earned his mouth another slap. "You really need some training," I said. But I pulled it off and pushed my breasts in his face, forcing him to suck one nipple, then the other.

He did it. He did it well, too, and his tongue on my tits felt so nice that I didn't notice his hips shifting beneath me until his cock was pressing against my leg. His whole body was shaking and straining against his chains and I wondered dizzily just how far we were going to take this. I'd only heard of him dominating pretty blond boys, but his stiff cock was straining toward the naked brunette on top of him, and before I lost my nerve, I retrieved a condom from the nightstand.

"Do it," he whispered. I was too nervous to admonish him for giving an order. Instead I mounted him like he was any sub squirming beneath me, even though my heart was hammering madly and my legs were shaking as his thick cock pushed inside me. If I came too fast, it would be the ultimate humiliation, a statement of just how completely he had claimed my pussy. I clenched my jaw, a trick I'd always used to stay in control when I was riding a new sub and didn't want to go off like a bomb on top of him.

But a smug joy stretched across Nick's face, as if he knew how intensely I was swooning inside. He arched his back, showing off his hard stomach, and began driving his hips upward in one forceful thrust after another. We were really fucking now, as fast and seamless as if we'd fucked a thousand times before. I was riding my husband's first dom and my greatest rival. And if we were scratching a bizarre and forbidden itch, we were also competing to see who could strip the other psychologically bare the fastest and leave him or her naked and humbled.

Then my mind melted, because his dick felt so good inside me and my entire body was a buzzing, wet crucible of lust. Nick dug his heels into the bed and pushed himself up toward the edge, bringing me with him until he had more slack in the chain. Then he brought his bound wrists down and held them against my clit, letting me push against his hand as I rode him. My skin was electric, my pussy a wet storm of heat, and when Nick groaned in defeat and began to come, I followed, imploding in one drenching wave after another.

I couldn't meet his eyes as I fell on the bed next to him. My long, dark hair was a heavy mess and I moved it off my neck, fanning myself before I looked for the padlock key. It hurt to unlock him—Nick looked so beautiful in chains, his damp hair tousled and his wet skin flushed. After shaking his wrists, he leaned over and we kissed for the first time, his tongue unexpectedly sweet. We kissed for a long time actually, until I remembered I had a houseful of guests downstairs. Then I realized someone was in the room with us.

"I've been waiting for you two to get this out of your system," Ian said. "But of all nights to pick…"

He smiled, letting me know he was okay with this. I knew I should have checked with him first and the magnanimous gesture of his acceptance prodded me into making one of my own.

"Come join us," I said. The words weren't easy to get out, but I forced myself to pat the bed in invitation. Ian looked hesitantly at me, I nodded, and he began to undress. Nick picked up my hand and kissed it. That old hellfire of jealousy ate at my stomach for just a moment as I accepted that my husband and his ex were about to have the reunion I'd always dreaded. But as Ian crawled naked on top of us, I understood that this was something different because it was the three of us. A wave of hunger and anticipation obliterated my jealousy and with that, a new era began.

THE STORY OF HOW WE MET

Iseult Reage

The evening started off well; my hair was up in a messy chignon, my "bitch" glasses were sitting comfortably on the tip of my nose and my chandelier earrings were grazing the nape of my neck. I was ready for the game; I was ready to play.

Wearing my satin corset with the hummingbird embroidery, my skintight, knee-length, lucky black skirt and my alligator five-inch stiletto heels, I was ready to sound the horn and start the chase.

I had a plan: to continue the flirtation I had started these last months with the man whose party I was attending. The last event had ended with him handing me his business card with his number underlined. On the back of the card he had written *Call Me*.

I hadn't.

And so the stage was set. I was lounging comfortably on a couch when I saw him at the bar, chatting away with his guests. He looked at me from across the room and we locked eyes; the electricity that passed between us was instant and definitive. I was His.

Slowly and seductively, I smiled and waved. In return, he bowed his head, smiled and walked over.

"Well hello again."

I rose from my seat to greet him; he leaned in close to kiss me and I coyly turned my head and presented my cheek, upon which he planted a most delicious kiss. He kissed my neck all the way down, stopping to bite at the fleshy part where my neck and my collarbone met. He slid his hands over the silk of my corset and planted his eyes on mine. He kissed me, deeply, his hand squeezing the back of my neck while he pressed his body into mine. He complimented my choice of corset. I thanked him and told him with a mischievous smile that it needed to be relaced, knowing that he would jump at the opportunity to do so.

He offered his help.

I walked over to an exposed support beam and grabbed onto its edges, pushing my derriere toward him, arching my back this way and that way to let him see how tightly he could pull the laces and tie me in. He slowly started to unlace my corset, sliding his hands all over my upper body, discovering my curves and soft flesh with the tips of his fingers. Then he proceeded to relace me into the corset, first from the bottom up, then from the top down, and finally he pulled on the lacing in the middle of my back as hard as he could, constricting my waist, trapping my ribs and restricting my breathing. With his right knee pressing down hard at the small of my back, he whispered in my ear as I struggled to stay upright and breathe, "What exactly are you trying to accomplish here?"

"*Moi*? *Rien*, I just want this corset to stay up properly."

He pressed his knee into me again, harder, and then declared his work finished. I turned to thank him, curtsied and walked away.

I left the bar area and returned to sit on the couch, quietly taking in the night's unfolding events. Suddenly I felt something cold and wet land on my shoulder blade, something coming from behind me. I turned to find that the culprit was my corset lacer, throwing water at me.

He winked and with a smile asked me if I would like a drink. Before I had time to reply that I would, he handed me a gin and tonic. (How he found out about my favorite drink, I do not know.)

Having handed me the drink he knelt at my feet, took the right one in his hand and placed a gentle kiss atop it. He caressed my leg with his free hand, running his fingers lightly up and down my flesh, leaving tiny goose bumps along the way. He straightened up for a moment before sitting on the armrest of the couch upon which I was ensconced, giving him a good foot above me and ensuring I had to look up to see him. Bluntly, he asked me the question I had been hoping he would ask since the start of the game:

"What *are* you?"

Tilting my head slightly to the left, I looked at him and replied, "I'm sorry; I don't understand. Whatever do you mean?" I knew full well what he meant.

He looked down on me tenderly, cupped my face with his hands, tilted my chin up, making sure I could not break eye contact with him, and said, "Are you a top. Or are you a bottom?"

He had served the first ball. It was up to me to return it. I sat up straight, pushed my shoulders back and my breasts out, lowered my eyes and my voice. I looked at him from underneath my eyelashes and whispered, "A bottom; a slave, actually. Always."

This was the moment I had been waiting for—the very one I had engineered. My planning and preparation had paid off. The look on his face quickly went from stunned to sadistic glee. My words had the desired effect: he was interested. Finally, to complete the moment, I added, with big, innocent doe eyes looking up at him, "And you, what are you?"

I knew what he was.

As if to reinforce his point, and to show me that he had already picked up on my little game, he suddenly, rather brutally and harshly, drove his steel-toed boot down into my knee, hard. As he pushed his boot deeper and deeper into my knee, my bones starting to shudder under the pressure, he asked me with a cold and detached smile, "What do you think I am?"

Shivers ran through my body; the more he pushed down on my knee the more it cracked and the more aroused I got. The sexual tension that passed between us in that moment reminded me that I hadn't played in months and that it would take very little to bring me to the brink. I excused myself and headed to the wash-room to regroup and catch my breath. Once I was sitting comfortably in a stall, I started counting back from sixty, hoping that by the time I reached zero I would have regained some of the composure I had lost from even a brief interaction with this man.

There was a knock at my stall. I chalked it up to some girl too impatient to wait and continued with my countdown: thirty-six, thirty-five, thirty-four. The knocking continued while I reached ten then nine and at that point I said, quite annoyed with the person on the other side, who was still knocking, "It's taken, clearly it's taken, there is someone using this stall so obviously it's taken! TAKEN!"

I gave up on finishing my countdown, stood and went to the door. Unlocking it, I opened it a bit—just enough to see who this impatient woman was.

"Yes, what is—"

He barged through, pinned me against the wall and locked the door behind him. He crushed my mouth under his. His tongue attacked mine, his kisses deep and dark. And then he growled in my ear, "Have you ever fucked your shoes, baby? Have you? Have you ever fucked your shoes, little girl?"

He drove into me again. I couldn't stand, couldn't breathe; I was getting wet and excited, his words waking up the beast buried deep within me.

"Yes. Yes, I have."

He growled and bit down on my neck so hard that I felt the sharpness of his teeth pierce my skin.

"Really, baby? You've fucked your heels? You've fucked your heels and you liked it?"

His hands were all over me, pinching and pulling at my breasts, twisting and slapping my nipples. He scratched and bit at whatever piece of skin he could expose. His mouth was devouring my face, biting at my ears and neck.

"Yes," I said. "Yes I like fucking my heels."

He stopped kissing me and bit down on my shoulder—the thick, fleshy part—until I bled, my blood coating his mustache and staining his teeth. He pulled on my hair until I stood on my tiptoes. Calmly he said, "Repeat after me: Yes, yes I like fucking my heels, *SIR*."

In pain from my position and the bite on my shoulder, but excited by his words and presence, I repeated slowly, "Yes I like fucking my heels, Sir!"

He let go of my hair and had me spread my legs wide as he started to play with my pussy. He shoved a finger inside of me, exploring my folds, discovering my wetness, making me moan. He inserted a second finger, then a third, stretching me out, widening his grip inside of me, fucking me hard with his fingers, overloading my senses until I moaned and begged for him to please fuck me, to please stick his cock into me.

"No."

He crushed me under his weight and inserted another finger in my pussy, the width of his hand stretching me, his knuckles scraping at my insides, making my body shiver and my pussy throb. I pushed back into him, rocking my cunt back and forth on his hand, wanting to feel all of him inside of me. He fucked me like that, with his hand, for what seemed like an excruciatingly long time, my head spinning from the pleasure and the pain.

As I began to come, he pulled his hand from me, knelt down and covered my pussy with his lips. He licked and lapped at my opening while I rode out my orgasm. He bit at my folds and darted his tongue in and out of me, going deeper and deeper, exploring me. I screamed and bucked under his wet touch. I clawed at the wall behind me, trying to hold myself up from under the weight of my powerful climax. I shook over and over as I rode the last of my orgasm, slowly returning to the land of the clearheaded. He stood up, kissed me again and looked deeply into my eyes. "I wanted you to understand where my mind is at."

And with that, he stood and walked out of the bathroom stall, leaving me disheveled and out of breath— half-naked and sticky with my own come.

The game had begun.

A HEALTHY DOSE

Andrea Dale

I stand at the window with Professor Vondergraft. His office is on the third floor, and we have an excellent view of the gardens, mature and well manicured.

It is a far cry from the dull and sterile medical offices in which I have been serving my internship. I've been sent to learn more about this place, determine whether their methods are scientific and safe.

It's spring, and not just the roses are blushing.

"Many of the women come here of their own will," he's saying. "Generally the older ones, frustrated by what they've experienced so far. They want to claim their sexuality, learn what joy their bodies can give them. Some are...encouraged to sign up for the program by their husbands. Others—the younger ones—are sent by their mothers." He tugs on his mustache, thoughtful. "Never the fathers," he murmurs. "Always the mothers."

"Hm," I say, a noncommittal answer. My mind whirls at what he's telling me, even as it skips away from the truth of it.

"Pleasure," he continues. "We show them the true meaning of the word. In a variety of ways, with a variety of...aids...we help them reach the pinnacle." He chuckles. "Over and over again."

"Aids," I repeat, not quite a question, but offering him an opening to elaborate.

"We also have at our disposal the latest technologies. Plus, the men and women who work here are trained in various theories of eroticism and use that knowledge to the fullest extent. We've determined what works best for each woman, but most learn the same thing about themselves: that they have a deeply submissive nature and find a delightful level of joy in experiencing erotic pain. Plus, there's nothing like a healthy dose of humiliation to heighten their pleasure, eh?" he asks jovially.

I say nothing, pretending not to understand.

"For example," he says, "you see that girl down there?"

I cannot deny that I do, although I cannot see her features well. She wears a maid's costume, black with a frilled white apron and cap. The skirt is extremely short, revealing shapely legs and even the barest hint of high, rounded bottom.

She's carrying a tea tray with a cut-glass tumbler on it. Whiskey, probably. There's a gentleman sitting at a garden table, enjoying the sun and grounds as he peruses the daily paper. The girl bends to set down the tray, but just before she does, she suddenly stiffens. Her hands jerk, and the drink sloshes out of the glass.

She manages to get the tray safely on the table, but the gentleman is on his feet in an instant. I cannot hear what he says to her, but she puts her hands behind her back and arranges her stance, her face down. The instantaneousness of her submissive pose intrigues me.

Professor Vondergraft opens his hand, and I see the remote-control device he holds. I can no longer hide behind the lie of not understanding. My prick understands, and responds accordingly.

"With this, I control the level of her pleasure," he says. "I gave her that little jolt so she'd require chastisement, which that gentleman will happily provide. See, now?"

The girl is bent over, her hands gripping the edge of the garden table. The gentleman has flipped up her flounced skirt. She wears no undergarments, and her bottom is pale and, as I suspected, firm and high, with a lovely curve. He reaches into a satchel by his chair and pulls out a glove, which he slips on, and then retrieves something I can't see. I realize quickly that it's some sort of lubricant, as he begins sawing his finger in and out of her bottom. Her back arches, thrusting her curvy rump in the air.

That she enjoys this invasion is curiously fascinating. I knew that men did, but women? It is a revelation.

When the gentleman is obviously satisfied, he gives
me another surprise by reaching over the maid to his
drink. It takes me a moment, at this distance, to parse
what he's doing. He slides one ice cube, then another,
into her proffered bottom.

I discover my mouth is hanging open.

The girl dances on her toes at this ignominious invasion and, no doubt, the frigid, shocking sensations the
ice causes, but otherwise she remains in position, dutiful
and meek.

I find myself eager to see more.

The gentleman removes his glove, reaches back into
the satchel and produces a wooden paddle.

When the implement first crashes down—for the
gentleman does not check his hand or otherwise seek to
begin gently—the young woman's head jerks up. At the
next blow, she shakes her head, slowly, and lets it sink
closer to the table again.

As the punishment continues, she raises one foot,
then the other, in what looks to be an excruciatingly
slow, sensual dance. I wonder if she's even aware of her
own movements.

My mouth has gone dry. Oh, that she would deliver
to me a tumbler of whiskey...

Throughout the spanking, Professor Vondergraft
works the remote control, explaining as he does that he
is repeatedly bringing her close to climax, but not giving
her a final release.

"This teaches her to associate the pleasure of arousal

with the pain of the spanking. She's been an excellent student thus far; I imagine if I hadn't caused her to spill the drink, she might have done it herself, just to earn the spanking." He smiles like a proud parent. "The public display is also a new excitement for her; she finds it horribly embarrassing to know that people could be watching. I'm sure some are watching now, downstairs, on the patio—she would have seen them as she went out. As I understand it, her greatest humiliation—and greatest joy—is knowing someone else controls her orgasm...and that others are witness to her helplessness."

I watch, my hands in my pockets to hide their trembling. I understand that she hates this and craves it in equal measure.

The gentleman below finishes the spanking. As he puts the paddle away, I can see, even from this distance, the bright-red flush on her tender, exposed flesh.

I find it intoxicating, and wish I could see it more closely. I want to lay my hand against the sweet curve of her cheek and feel the heat radiate into my palm.

Unbidden, the thought rises: I want to be the cause of that heat, that rosy, swollen evidence of pleasurable pain.

Other parts of her will be swollen, too, I realize. Her nipples, her cunt...

"Here." Professor Vondergraft's voice startles me back to the room. He hands me the remote device. "Toy with her all you like. Just be sure to make her come, though—it's imperative to their health that they have frequent orgasms." He chuckles again. "Ah, yes, that's another use of the device, making them come and come again until they beg for mercy—but that's for another time."

My hands are clumsy, and I don't know the controls well enough to have much finesse. But I enjoy watching her writhe, her hands still gripping the table, her hips undulating as if in a slow-motion fuck against the air. I wonder what she's thinking, whether she cares who manipulates the device pressed against her clit, whether her desperation for release outweighs her humiliation at orgasming, helplessly, in front of so many watching eyes.

Finally I take pity on her and twist the dial to the maximum.

Her reaction is spectacular. Once again, for a moment she freezes. Then her entire body judders before her hips simply go mad with motion. She remains in position as her thrusts become faster, more frantic....

She thrashes, her head flung back, and even from this height I can hear her high-pitched, keening wail. Her movement jostles the table, causes the drink to spill again, and I wonder if she knows she'll be held accountable, that another punishment is in her future. And I wonder if knowing that makes her orgasm stronger.

I'm surprised at my own nature, as I wait before turning off the device for a long minute after she's come, guessing how excruciating that is against her sensitive nub. I see her take a deep, shuddering breath.

Then she straightens, steps away from the table and sinks to her knees as the gentleman unfastens his trousers and pulls out his stiff prick. Before she takes him in her mouth, however, she looks over her shoulder, directly at the window at which we stand, and smiles her gratitude.

My own prick surges with heat and need as again my mouth drops open.

It's my fiancée, Trudie.

Did her mother send her? Or did she choose to come here, to put herself in these people's hands?

The questions make my cock throb, impossibly hard, in my trousers.

"Well done, my man," Professor Vondergraft says heartily. "You have a knack for this, most certainly. I might just have to hire you away from your current position."

Before I can craft a response to his unexpected suggestion, he continues.

"At any rate, you seem to have taken a shine to this girl—would you like me to have her sent to your room later? As part of her training, of course."

"Yes," I hear myself say, "that would be absolutely lovely. Thank you ever so much."

DON'T LET
ME WIN

Athena Marie

This was dangerous. My heart knew it and my head knew it, but my body didn't care. Seeing his name in my in-box had been a shock. We hadn't communicated in years. But he was still there in the back of my mind. Always, I was haunted by the memory of his face, his words—an obsession that had nearly destroyed me. He was like a bruise that just wouldn't fade.

I'd cried for weeks when he disappeared. But I wouldn't cry today. I swore it to myself for the tenth time. I would fuck him and leave him…because I wanted to. Because despite all those tears, and the passage of over three years, I still wanted him. And because, for some reason I still hadn't put my finger on, he made me hotter, wetter and hornier than any man I'd ever met.

Of course, we'd never actually met. Perhaps that's

the reason it had been so intense. Carrying on an affair through the safety of email and the distance of thousands of miles, it's easy to mistake lust for love. It's easy to turn a fantasy into truth.

I glanced back down the hotel hallway. There was no going back. I took a deep breath. It didn't help. With a shaking hand I knocked on the door. A rush of panic swept through me. Maybe he wouldn't answer. Fuck. Maybe he would.

The door swung open, and it was like a slow-motion punch in the gut. He was just as I'd imagined, dark and handsome, dressed in black slacks, a white dress shirt, and a red tie loose around his neck. But it was his energy, not his physical appearance, that turned me inside out. Sensuality seemed to drip from him, just as it had from his words.

"You came." His voice was deep, with a trace of an accent I couldn't place.

I walked into the middle of the room, set my purse on the chair and turned to face him. "I came."

The door clicked shut. He looked me up and down, then smiled. "You're beautiful."

I laughed. I don't know why. I *was* beautiful. But I was relieved to hear him say it. Photographs could be so misleading.

"Would you like a glass of wine?" He reached for the bottle on the desk. I thought I saw his fingers tremble.

"No."

He turned to face me and clasped his hands in front

of him. Smug. Stoic. But I knew exactly what he was thinking. He had hurt me once before and now he saw me as delicate. He was afraid of hurting me again. He wanted to take it slow. Well, I didn't. And I didn't want this watered-down version of him. I didn't want to be handled with kid gloves. I wasn't broken anymore.

I unzipped my dress and let it fall to the floor, revealing a shelf bra and garter belt ensemble, complete with matching panties and silk stockings. His eyes darkened as they swept over my body. He reached out and pulled me against him. His kisses were deep and possessive, and his hands gripped my arms so hard it hurt. Soon our hands were everywhere, rubbing and touching in desperate exploration, both of us vying for control. A control I prayed I wouldn't get.

I pulled away and leaned against the wall, cold against my heated skin. He was breathing heavily and his erection strained against his slacks. Staring into his eyes I pulled aside my drenched panties and lifted one foot onto the nightstand.

"Lick my pussy." Even as I said the words my thoughts betrayed me.

Please don't let me win.

A flicker of surprise crossed his face before he arched his eyebrows in defiance. He leaned in close, brushed his lips against mine, then slipped his fingers between my legs.

"What, no please?" He rubbed my wetness over my swollen pussy lips, then thrust two fingers inside me, curling them forward to stroke the inner wall of my cunt, hitting that perfect spot. My foot fell off the nightstand, and I shamelessly pushed myself against his hand.

"Do you know what I think?" He smiled, nuzzling his face against my neck. He smelled like cinnamon and aftershave. "I think you're a liar."

"I think you're an asshole."

He chuckled and pulled his hand away. I couldn't help but whimper for the loss. "I may be an asshole..." He raised his fingers to his nostrils and inhaled deeply. "But I know what you want, babe." He stepped closer, securing me between him and the wall. "And it isn't to have this sopping cunt licked. You want to be on your knees with my big cock in your mouth. Isn't that right?"

"No." I shoved my hands against his chest.

"Liar." Suddenly he had my wrists pinned against the wall above my head. I struggled against him, testing his will. "Suck my dick you little slut." Holding me immobile with one hand, he unzipped his pants and his prick sprang free. It was just like I remembered in the pictures—thick and long, with a head that was the loveliest shade of pink. He pushed me down to my knees. But he didn't force it into my mouth as I'd expected. Instead he let me touch him, explore him, slowly lick the length of him. Up then down I licked as I cradled his balls in one hand and gripped the base in my other. I rubbed the head against my lips over and over, savoring the smoothness, the smell and the taste of him.

Finally, with a moan he grabbed my hair in his hands and shoved my mouth down around him. I opened the back of my throat and took him deep, reminding myself of how long I'd wanted this. There was something about it—being a mouth for his pleasure—that I both loved and despised. Of course, that had always been the theme with us hadn't it? I reached my hands up and under his dress shirt, scraping my long nails across his chest as he fucked my mouth.

"You're still my dirty little slut, aren't you?" he growled above me. "You still belong to me. You always have and you always will. Because you love how I use you, don't you?"

His cock slipped from my mouth, and he yanked my head back to look at him. I wanted to sob with the vision—his face finally above me, so handsome and so filled with domination and desire.

"Answer me. Don't you?" He slapped my face. Gentle enough not to cross a line, but hard enough to make me feel utterly owned.

"Yes."

He twisted my hair painfully in his hand. "Yes, what?"

"Yes, Sir. I love how you use me." Like he always promised he would.

"And why is that?" He was whispering now, one hand tangled in my long hair as he gently stroked my stinging cheek with the end of his tie. I turned my head toward his hand, and he cradled my face in his palm.

"Because I'm a slut."

He ran his fingertips over my lips, then slipped them inside of my mouth. I could taste myself on him.

"You're my slut."

I nodded and spoke as best I could with his fingers stroking my tongue. "I'm your slut."

"Good girl. Take off your panties and lie on the bed."

I hadn't noticed the bindings on the headboard until he was strapping them around my wrists. Sitting back on his heels he looked me up and down hungrily, then began running his hands slowly over my body, exploring his conquest with firm but gentle caresses.

"Such nice, big tits...pretty belly...mmmm, and look at this pussy." I moaned as he spread the lips of my labia, leaned down and licked me from asshole to clit. One teasing stroke.

"Oh god, yes." I tilted my pelvis and spread my legs.

He sat up, shook his head, and slapped me right where his mouth had just been. I cried out, tugging against my restraints. "That was always your problem, baby. You're so fucking impatient."

I knew he was right. I had been impatient for him. I'd wanted more than he could give, and it had driven him away. I turned my head, burying my face in the pillow.

"Don't worry, baby. I'll eat that hot little snatch before the night is out. But first I'm going to teach you a lesson in patience."

Slowly he pulled his leather belt from his pants and looped it around my neck. There was no hesitation in his movements, no lack of confidence, and as he began to pull, a dark glimmer in his eyes, a trickle of fear ran through me. I was propelled back to the days of our affair. To the days when his words had made me realize exactly the kind of woman I wanted to be.

His words. They'd always been so damn perfect. And now, the way he was touching me...it was the same. A part of me had hoped he would disappoint me. It would have been easy to let him go if he had. It would have been easy to say, "game over." But he wasn't disappointing me...and this game was just beginning.

Stealing the breath from my lungs, he leaned down to kiss me. He kissed me gently and slowly, swirling his tongue deep inside my mouth as my world started to grow dark around the edges. Finally he released his grip on the belt as he exhaled into my gasping mouth.

"Please..." I didn't recognize my own voice.

He stared down at me almost lovingly as he traced a fingertip down my cheek. "Please, what?"

"Fuck me."

"Oh, I'll fuck you. I'm going to fuck you all night, baby." He squeezed my breasts roughly as he spoke. "But not yet."

He kneeled between my legs and stroked his cock, letting the head just barely brush against my soaked, swollen lips. My hair was in my face and the bindings were digging into my wrists, but all I could feel was the emptiness that needed to be filled. He started stroking himself faster, sliding his cock up and down my slit, slipping the knob inside my cunt then pulling back out. It was torture. I spread my legs wider, inviting him in.

"You want me to fuck you, baby? You want me to pound this hot little hole till you beg for mercy?" I whimpered in assent. And then he was rubbing his dick against my clit. There was nothing but friction, heat and him. "Well I'm not going to. Not yet. Do you know why?"

"Be-because you're an asshole."

His eyes narrowed. "That's right. I'm the big, bad, asshole that broke your heart." He grabbed the end of the belt and pulled it tight around my throat once again. "And yet here you are—still begging for it like the cockhungry slut you are."

He was right. And I didn't care. The pressure of the belt and the steady rubbing of his dick against my clit were too much. My orgasm was building. Breathless, I screamed his name, just like I used to do, alone in my bed and dreaming of him. But this time I wasn't alone. This time he came with me, his warm cum splattering over my pussy and belly.

As I lay there, his body slumped over mine, I realized how ironic it was; we were finally together...but I was still waiting. He unfastened my restraints in silence, then sat on the edge of the bed, his head in his hands. I yearned to speak, to ask him the hundreds of questions that had been burning inside of me for the past three years. I swallowed the questions along with the tears.

Finally he broke the silence with a question of his own. "Why did you have to fall in love?"

I considered it a moment, even though I didn't have to. "Because you don't let me win." I used the edge of the sheet to wipe his cum off of me, then stood up and slipped on my dress.

"Where are you going?" First confusion, then panic, flashed across his face. But it was quickly replaced by a confident smirk. "I'm not done with you yet."

"That's a shame, because I'm done with you." I returned his smirk, grabbed my purse and turned toward the door. But there was hesitation in my steps and a single thought kept repeating: *Please don't let me win.*

MADAME
TUESDAY

Zoe Amos

I'm a nine to fiver, a district supervisor at a water supply company overseeing the managers at our six satellite offices. On Saturday afternoons, I like to relax in a most unconventional way. What works for me isn't on the radar screen for your average woman. I may look like your next-door neighbor: five feet four, twenty-five pounds overweight, pasty skin and dyed hair to cover the gray, with a closet full of black suits and low-heeled shoes. Appearances can be deceptive. You don't know the real me. I'm guessing the woman next door to you doesn't visit Madame Tuesday.

In my street clothes, you wouldn't have noticed me standing in front of a nondescript brick building with blacked-out windows and peeling green trim, and you never would have suspected something unusual was about to go on. There was no need for me to check the address—it's not posted above the door and it wasn't my first visit. I knew the routine, pressed the buzzer two shorts and a long, and was buzzed in.

I hiked up the flight of stairs. "Hey, Gert," I said to the woman sitting behind the desk. "Looking good." Her ample girth hid her chair from view and it groaned as she leaned forward.

"Save your flirting, honey. We have new forms. Here." She thrust a clipboard at me. "Fill this out."

"What's this? A health survey?"

"New government regs starting today. Check all the boxes that apply. On page two, fill out the services you want."

Gert never was one for conversation, not that her demeanor invited it. I sat down and filled out the first page, a health history similar to one given to me the last time I had a massage, silently acknowledging the prevalence of regulatory "protections." At least they hadn't shut down the salon. On page two was a new list of services with categories and subcategories where one could check off preferred lubricants, sex toys, penile enhancers, bondage props, et cetera, and of course, the activities of choice that Madame Tuesday would inflict upon the client, as well as the price, which per usual would be paid in advance—cash only.

"This is ridiculous," I said. "I have no idea which brands we use. Madame Tuesday knows what I want." Gert glared at me through narrowed eyes. I thought about buttering her up. *Your mole looks especially menacing today, Gert*, I thought. *You should see a doctor before animal control comes and fines you for harboring a weasel.*

Dutifully, I started on the form. "Really? You're charging extra for hair pulling? And why is it more for paddling than spanking?"

"Paddles break."

"*Tsk!* Unbelievable. You can be sure I'll tell Madame what I think about this." I added up the cost and jotted down the total. "And you raised your prices. Nice." I pulled out my wallet and fingered through the bills.

Gert double-checked the amount on her calculator. "You didn't add in for the golden shower."

"I don't want a golden shower, and I didn't ask for one."

Gert examined the form. "Well, whaddya know." She scratched her fingernail against the paper. "It looks like you checked the box, but it's a stray mark printed on here." She flipped through the stack of new forms and saw they all had the same mark. "Guess that explains those strange comments I got earlier today. Ha!" It was the first time I'd ever heard her laugh.

"Gloria!"

"Madame Tuesday! Thank goodness. Please say you're ready for me."

She appeared like a fairy godmother, without warning and right on cue. She looked marvelous in her short shorts and strappy, pink-sparkle stilettos with

clear heels. Her open midriff revealed taut abs, and her
stretchy, pink glitter top held her breasts in a way that
would make any man or woman jealous. A perfect spray
tan covered the rest of her exposed skin, setting off her
highlighted, blonde hair held in place with a matching
pink, sequined headband.

"Where do you get your clothes?" I gasped. The sight
of her thrilled me. Had I been a publisher, I would have
created a magazine solely to feature her photograph. I'd
call it *Modern Dominatrix* or *Fab Fetish Fashionista*.

Madame Tuesday extended her hand toward Gert,
showing off her manicured fingers with squared-off
pink-sparkle tips. Gert handed her my forms, and she
gave them a cursory glance.

Madame and I walked down the hall and into the
room I had come to love. Stepping over the threshold
was good for my soul. I saw familiar items hanging on
the walls: the leather masks, collars, leashes, whips, latex
bondage gear, costumes and such arranged around the
room. Lining the tabletops were implements of pleasure:
lubricants, dildos, cock rings, anal penetration plugs
and more, with dozens of others stowed in drawers and
closets. Positioned on the floor in their usual places were
the vault, the rack, the chair and the platform, as well as
the ceiling swing hanging from chains. The room smelled
of cedar-sage disinfectant with an undertone of sweat.
She closed the door with the sole of her shoe, pitched the
paperwork to the floor, and I breathed a sigh of relief.

"Forms, humph," she said. Her pink lips looked juicy

and newly puffed, and I wondered if it was injections or something more recent involving a customer.

I tossed my bag into a corner. "Yeah, what's up with that?" I removed my earrings, placed them on a side table and began to get ready.

"Necessary evil."

"Am I paying for that too," I winked.

"Shut up, bitch, and get moving."

"Yes, Madame. You're the boss." I folded my slacks, hung up my top and shimmied out of my underthings. Time was wasting.

She opened a closet and pulled out the harness, a contraption of thick, black leather straps held together with brass rivets, and threw it at my feet. Heavy, stainless steel O-rings were strategically placed at various intervals, as were various buckles and Velcro fasteners. There were two openings that circled the thighs and a split at the crotch; I stepped into the leg holes, placed my arms through the correct parts and buckled myself in, taking care to separate my cleavage to accommodate the vertical supporting strap. Once everything was in place, Madame Tuesday came around my backside to finish the job.

My body was on autopilot, and I could feel my cunt respond as she tugged on the harness. Its snug fit felt good against my body and made me feel nurtured. I could feel my excitement level rise. "This is going to be awesome!"

She grabbed my hair in her fist and pulled. "Good

job, Gloria. Shut up and let's get you hooked up." She pushed off as she let go of my hair. Oh, how I loved these moments.

"Lie down," she commanded and I obeyed by resting facedown on the floor.

The chains attached to the hanging swing wrapped around a tumbler fastened near the ceiling that Madame could operate with a flick of a wall switch. The rotating tumbler raised or lowered the chains to the desired height. Each link was about three inches long and an inch wide, the type used to secure a motorcycle to a trailer. At the lower ends of each chain were two separate lighter-duty chains. These attached to the four corners of the swing, or in my case would be attached to the two O-rings at my shoulder blades and the two at my lower back near hip level. Madame lowered the swing to the padded floor, unclipped it from the chains and then kicked the rubber swing aside. I could hear as she clipped into the harness O-rings and felt her tug on the four connections. At one point her heels came dangerously close to my face and I could smell the pleasant muskiness of her foot.

"Excellent," she said as she pressed one of her sharp heels into my butt. "You are a good student, but a bad girl."

"Yes, Madame. Very bad."

She walked to the wall switch and pressed upward. The harness grabbed at my body as I was lifted off the floor an inch at a time. In moments, I was suspended several feet off the ground. My arms dangled and my feet hung closer to the floor, but my body was held horizontally. Madame walked back.

"Something's not right, is it?" she asked. "The cuffs."

I gasped. Madame hadn't laid them out, and I had forgotten about them.

"We forgot the cuffs!" I echoed.

"We?" Madame went into the closet, pulled out the leather wrist cuffs and slapped them on me, securing the straps as tight as she could get them. She yanked my arms behind my back and clipped the cuffs together. The tension was uncomfortable to say the least. It was much better to put them on beforehand, but I got what I deserved.

"For that," she said, "you must be punished—something new."

"I've already paid," I said.

"Fine! In that case, anything I add will be on the house. Here's a treat I know I'll enjoy."

She uncapped a tube and rolled a light gel over my nipples.

"That reminds me," I said.

"Shut up!"

The tingling began as soon as the gel touched my skin, and within a minute the temperature rose until it felt like my nipples would burst into flames.

"Yeesh! Whoa, ow! Ow!"

"I'm so glad you like that." She gave a slight touch with her finger on my arm, and I spun to the side. She went to the counter and picked up an anal plug. I could hear her fiddling around with lubricant. Using one hand, she parted my crack. I felt the item slide in my ass past the first rounded ball. She pushed a little, then a little more, and I felt it move into the second position. "Hold on tight," she said. "Be good, or I'll push it in another notch."

"Yes, Madame," I said through stifled breath. It was easy to clench my ass and my cunt at the same time, to work the muscles together. My nipples burned in a spectacular fiery sensation, and I could feel my body tense in anticipation of the delights to come. "I remembered what I was going to say earlier," I gasped.

"*Shut the fuck up!*" Madame Tuesday slapped my ass hard and I swung forward. "What's the matter with you? You haven't stopped talking since you got here." She stopped my movement as I swung back toward her, and she shoved the anal plug in one more notch.

My legs tensed outward with the surge in diameter. I couldn't remember her ever pushing it in so far before. "I had an energy drink before I left the house. Do you think its working?"

"Enough!" Madame Tuesday marched to the closet and pulled out a mouth plug.

"Madame, please let me tell you something important. There are red plastic clothespins in my bag for my nips!" I raced to get out the words before she fit the appliance over my head. She pushed the rubber ball past my teeth and into my mouth. It was worth it.

Madame grasped my chin with her finger. "And you

didn't want to miss out, did you?" She pushed on my chin and my body swung back and forth.

She squatted next to my bag in search of the clothespins I had snagged before leaving the house. I discovered they were a tiny bit tighter than the ones Madame uses. My heart fluttered at the thought she might not find them. The sight of her butt pressing next to her high heels made me shiver. I could see the tattoo on her lower back, dark geometric curls and the top edge of a colorful hibiscus flower that enticed and disappeared into her shorts.

Having found the desired items, she unpinched the clothespins and put one, then the other, over my nips. The intensity made me tighten my twat harder than ever. Madame placed them to fit perfectly. The pinching combined with the tingling heat made my whole body warm, as if sauna heat rolled through me. I definitely felt ready and Madame Tuesday could tell by the pace of my breath. She wasted no time adjusting the strap-on over her shorts.

Again, I heard her messing around with the lubricant. The first thing I felt was the tip of the slippery dildo. She played it around my slit. I didn't know how she could tell, but I was at the perfect height off the floor. I was ready and open for business, but made sure I had a firm grip on the anal plug. It wasn't easy to keep it in place, but the tension of the moment helped me do it. I felt so wet, I imagined I might be dripping onto the floor.

She gripped the straps near the top of my ass and

started moving into me little by little. I never know what
size she's going to use. I had seen two possibilities lying
on the counter, and I guessed she had picked the fatter
one. I felt a little stretched and focused on the anal plug
to keep things tight. She moved slowly and established
a rhythm until I took in the full length. She added a
squirt of lube to the dildo to get it to move easier. It
felt nice and full. I moaned and she moved quicker as
if she were keeping time to a faster song in her head. I
wasn't thinking anything except how my whole body
was quivering with excitement. The next thing I knew,
she pumped into me like a piston engine, and I grunted
through the hole in my mouthpiece.

"Ungh! Ungh! Ungh! Ungh!" It was amazing!

"You are a fucking bitch. You know that?" she said
as she pumped away. "F-u-c-k-i-n-g, fucking bitch!" She
spelled out the letters in time to her thrusts.

She rode me hard and long. I don't know how
Madame Tuesday stays in shape when she's not working
at the salon. Maybe she goes to a gym, but right then
I knew she was getting a workout just like I was. The
tension from the straps ate into my shoulders and my
wrist cuffs were rubbing a spot raw on my back. Through
it all, I could feel the edges of her curled nails digging
into me. I started to sweat and could feel the difference
in the leather as it clung to my skin. My cunt was as
tight as it could get around that fat dildo. My nips were
still on fire, burning sweetly, and the friction on my cunt
was enough to make it spontaneously combust. I could

picture steam wafting off my body. My whole body felt moist, but not as moist as my cunt. I didn't think I could last much longer, though I tried to hold out as long as I could.

"*UhnnNGH!*" A strong, rippling orgasm coursed through me with a jolt and my anal plug dislodged.

"*OW! Shit! My eye!*" Madame Tuesday let go of my straps. "Fucking-A! Your fucking plug hit me in the eye! *Fuck!*" She pulled out and I let out a prizewinning pussy fart. I could hear her knock around behind me, cursing as she kicked the counter. My panting morphed into a convulsion of laughter and tears formed at the corners of my eyes.

"What are you laughing at, bitch?"

She picked up a paddle and pounded me on the ass before she hurled it to the floor. She stomped over to the mirror above the sink and carefully dabbed at her eye.

"This better not bruise," she said.

My laughter through the mouthpiece sounded like a horse whinny. Spittle oozed out the sides of my mouth. My nose ran and my eyes watered. She walked over to me with her strap-on bouncing with each step, and without regard she removed the apparatus from my head, hurled it aside and slapped me across the face.

I laughed out loud, knowing next time my punishment would be severe and all the more delicious. "I'm sorry!" I snorted. "I can't help it. And I can't wait to see you Tuesday." A red welt was forming beneath her left eye at the top of her cheekbone.

"I can't wait to see you! Bitch. You're really going to get it."

"No, I mean I'll see you on Tuesday."

"You mean next Saturday." She walked to the wall switch and pushed the lever down, lowering me gently until I found my footing and sat cross-legged on the floor.

"No, on Tuesday. We have a manager's meeting in the District One conference room. We're bringing in lunch. Did you forget?"

"Oh shit!"

She released the clip on the wrist cuffs. I moved my arms in front of me, took off the cuffs, and rubbed my wrists and shoulders. Reluctantly, I removed the red clothespins. Our session was over. I sat for a moment feeling the wonderful sensations that ached throughout my body. Madame Tuesday brought over the wet wipes and a couple of extra paper towels. I sighed, happy for our time together, and cleaned up.

"That was better than I expected," I said, trying not to sound too cheery. "You're the best."

"Well, tell your friends."

"Not likely. Besides, if I do that, you might quit your day job and then I'd have to find another manager who can keep those junior account reps in line."

"Not my problem," Madame Tuesday said.

I tipped her fifty. "See you Tuesday, Tuesday."

"Yeah, Gloria," she said. "You're the boss."

THE WORK

Andrea Zanin

I knew it the second I laid eyes on him. That energy. That vibe. It's hot and it's dangerous. And it rarely shows up for me with men.

Oh, I'm careful. I don't do a damn thing without getting the go-ahead. I didn't get this far by lacking self-restraint and discipline. I get what I want because I'm smart and I'm patient, not because I reach out and take what's mine before it's freely offered. But make no mistake about it, that boy belongs to me. From the tips of his lily-white toes to the top of his shiny, shaved head, he's mine. Doesn't matter that he's gay and I'm a dyke. Doesn't matter that he lives in a different country or that he's ten years older than I am. Doesn't matter that he's never sucked any kind of cock that didn't grow on its owner. I'm his Daddy, and he knows it, and the fat head of my dick is going to find a very warm, wet, happy home a few inches down his sweet little throat someday very soon indeed.

We met at one of those stupid contests. You know, with all the weekend warriors wearing exactly the same expensive cow. A fucking herd, I'm telling you. I heard dykes were welcome at the after-party. Ha! Like they were doing us a favor or something. No wonder barely half a dozen of us showed up. I'da left except we saw each other across the room. Locked eyes. You can always tell when they're hungry. Didn't take long before he was buying me a beer and listening all attentive-like. Fine by me. I'm not rich. Plush hotel bars don't sell cheap drinks. He's some sort of big-shot American lawyer. This shit was pocket change to him. Wonder what his lawyer friends would say if they knew he was all tatted up under that Gucci suit, had a PA hanging like an anvil in his pants? Wonder what they'd say if they knew he flew to big cities all over the world on the weekends, trying to find a Daddy who could fill him up and take him down? Wonder what the guys in that bar woulda said if they knew what was really going on between him and me?

But good Daddies don't fuck on the first date.

We kept in touch some. He wrote me the other day to say he was having a rough time. Had just come home from the hospital. I can read between the lines. Stupid, lying little sack of shit. "Accident" my ass. He tried to off himself. Do you know how hard that is for me?

What the fuck was he thinking, the little punk? No, I didn't want to go take care of him, hold his hand, make sure he felt okay. Hell no. It was all I could do not to hop on a damn plane, find my way to his swanky New York apartment, and bang on the door 'til the maggot let me in.

And then, you bet your ass that Daddy wouldn't be offering cuddles and cookies. Nuh-uh. This Daddy woulda given him exactly what he deserves: a right sound ass-whipping. No warm-up. Take his damn fancy jeans down to his knees, bend him over at the waist, and let loose on that pale, muscled little bubble butt 'til it's striped good and fair. After that, a lecture. Standard style, the kind that's best aimed at someone whose ass is already smarting, but not hurting so bad that he can't still feel the crack of my hand on his face too, while I hold him steady with a fist around the collar of his polo shirt. "You will never, and I mean NEVER, try to take what's mine away from me, ever again. Is that clear, boy? IS THAT CLEAR?"

Then, I'd wait. Wait for the apology, for him to drop to his knees and blubber some. Make him push his nose into my crotch the way a good little boy does when he's been taken down a peg or two. And then, do you think I'd let him get his mouth on my dick? Hell fucking no. My hard-on's too good for a little fuckwad who can't even be trusted to take care of his damn self. Not to mention that was a damn long flight. I'd throw some blankets on the floor for him if I was feeling real nice, lie down in the bed and have myself a deep, long sleep. The next morning, the work would begin.

Yeah, I said work. What, did you think this Daddy shit was all fun and games? Did you think it was some sort of erotic role-play thing, that you flag hunter green for a few hours 'til you get your dick sucked and then drop the hanky on the floor next to your boots at the end of the night? Well, you got another thing coming. Oh, I sure do like getting my rocks off, don't you worry, and there's plenty of it that comes with the territory. A boy needs to know his place, and the simplest way to do that is to let him know just whose fun comes first and who has to work hard to get who off before anyone else gets to come. That, and some good old-fashioned discipline. None of those pretty toys. My belt does the job just fine.

Yeah, sure, I get laid. But mostly, I make sure that pansy-ass little shits like this one do the right thing in the world. The right thing, in this case, is some serious therapy. Progress reports. Maybe some happy pills to get him through the rough spots. Visits to the gym five days a week. Jerking off every Wednesday and Sunday. Vegetables. You heard me. Actual green ones, from a market, not a fucking can. Yes, every day. And a plane ticket after six months to come get a treat for good behavior.

What do you mean, what do I get out of it? You serious?

Okay, I'll lay it out. All this stuff I'm talking about?

This is foreplay. The day my boy is a man? Can stand on his own two feet? That's the biggest fucking come of all. Cocksucking is fine and good. But this? This is sex.

You don't have to get it. I do. He does.

But like I said. I'm a patient kind of gal. When my boy needs his Daddy, he'll call. Just like boys have been doing since pay phones cost a dime—since when there were pay phones. Since forever.

I can wait. Won't be long now.

NIGHT NURSE

Giselle Renarde

I don't know about this…"

Joanne clawed at the covers, kicking her feet beneath the sheets. "Oh, come on! Who can resist a sexy night nurse?"

"I guess." The bathroom door opened and Steve emerged, fresh as a daisy. "But I doubt this is what *most* men have in mind."

Joanne sat up in bed, giddy as hell. "Oh, baby, you're making me drool."

He turned to trace both hands down the curve of his ass. "Does this dress make my butt look big?"

"No way, baby." Joanne kicked off the covers. "I'm ready for my physical, but I must admit, I'm a little nervous."

"You're not the only one, sister." Steve pulled on

the tight, white minidress Joanne had coaxed him into wearing. "Why is this thing so short?"

"It shows off your thighs." Her gaze scanned the length of his stellar, white stockings. "And, baby, you've got *sweeeet* thighs."

When she reached for them, Steve hit her hand away. "That is not proper patient behavior!"

"I'm sorry, Nurse...what's your name?"

"Ratched."

Joanne laughed out loud. "No!"

"Okay, it's Nurse Betty."

"No!" She rolled around the bed, in fits. "Pick another one, baby."

"Settle down, now." Steve pinned one shoulder to the bed, and the warmth of his hand on her bare skin sent a pulse straight between her legs. "That's a good girl."

Her breath grew shallow as she looked up at his closely shaved face. He'd put on a touch of lipstick, a little blush, and some subdued eye shadow. The mascara made his blue eyes pop. When he smiled, she nearly passed out.

"I like your hair."

Steve cocked his head, twisting strands of the blonde wig around one finger. "Oh, you! Flattery will get you everywhere."

"Will it get me here?" Joanne asked, sneaking her hand underneath his starched cotton dress.

"Naughty, naughty!" Steve clicked his tongue,

moving Joanne's hand to the mattress. "Were you raised by wolves, young lady? Let a girl do her job."

"Lift your skirt. I'll give you a job that'll blow your mind."

"Hmm? What was that?"

"Nothing, Nurse."

Steve set his hands on his hips and shook his head. "No wonder none of the other clinics will take you."

"You know it." She reached for his crotch. "I'm bad."

With a squeal, Steve shuffled backward. His cute canvas tennis shoes squeaked against the hardwood floors. "Keep those hands to yourself, young lady, or I'll have to bring out the restraints."

Joanne arched forward. "You wouldn't dare."

"Just watch me!" Steve grabbed the Velcro pads from the dresser and strutted haughtily to the bedside. "Hands up against the iron posts."

"Make me!"

"You're fighting a losing battle, young lady." Steve grabbed both wrists as she tussled against him. "Don't even bother. You'll never win."

"Yes I will!" She kicked her feet and whipped her hair while Steve Velcroed her wrists together. Of course he was right—he was too strong to beat, and his muscles surged as he secured her hands to the iron bars of their headboard.

So she bit him.

"What the hell!" Steve jumped away from the bed,

cradling his wounded arm. "You little bitch! I'll have you locked up for assaulting a medical professional."

"Do your worst, and I'll do mine."

Steve's eyes narrowed. "What's that supposed to mean?"

"What do you think it means?" Joanne struggled uselessly against the Velcro. "It means you've got a dirty little secret and I could easily expose it."

"Expose it?" Steve's cock jumped so hard Joanne could see it through his skirt. "Why, whatever do you mean?"

"I think you know." Her feet were still free, and she grabbed the hem of his skirt between her toes, lifting it up. "Well, well. What have we here?"

"Brat!" Steve quickly covered himself, but the image of his thick cock branded itself on Joanne's brain.

"I saw it," she cooed, picturing the bulge of his cock-head beneath those tight white stockings. "You've got a big, hard cock under that skirt."

"How dare you?"

"Don't deny it." Her foot found his erection and stroked it under his skirt. "Oh, you like that. My little foot rubbing your fat cock—you like it, don't you?"

"This is most inappropriate," Steve said, but he didn't push her away.

"You're a naughty night nurse. You just love it when wayward patients dig out your dick. Don't you?"

Steve's eyes flashed. "I'm a medical professional, young lady."

"Oh yeah?" Joanne put on her brattiest airs. "Well then why haven't you examined me yet? If you're such a professional, do your damn job."

Squirming toward the edge of the bed, Joanne opened her legs. The position was a little awkward, with her hands bundled over her head and secured to an iron rod, but she'd give anything to feel his hands on her just now.

"I will do my job," Steve said, picking up a pair of latex gloves. "And I'll do it by the book, thank you very much."

Joanne's pussy pulsed as she watched her husband snap on those sheer gloves. They clung to his fingers the way those white stockings hugged his firm erection. God, she wanted that monster in her mouth. Steve looked so hot in his naughty nurse getup.

"Where do you want to examine me?" Joanne asked.

"Right here is fine."

She giggled like a schoolgirl. "I mean where on my body, silly."

"I see." He set his palms on her splayed thighs and pressed down. His strength surged through the muscles in his arms. "This is as good a place as any."

"Oh." Joanne gazed at him through the valley of her breasts. Her skin jumped when he opened her pussy lips with his sheathed thumbs. She could feel his heat right through the latex. "You've done this before."

He raised an eyebrow. "It's my job."

"In your professional opinion, Nurse, would you say I'm sufficiently juicy, too juicy or not juicy enough?"

"That's easy." Steve pierced her with one thick finger, and her cunt rang out with a wet squelching sound. "Hear that? You're wet enough for two."

"Ooh!" Joanne's muscles seized as Steve rubbed that sensitive spot just inside her pussy. "That feels good."

"It's not supposed to feel *good*," Steve clucked as he jammed another finger inside of her. "I'm measuring your cunt capacity. It's a scientific procedure."

"Like hell it is."

Steve said, "Fine," and pulled out his fingers.

Joanne put on a pout. "I didn't say stop."

With a smirk, he shoved them back in, filling her cunt so full she thrashed against her bindings. It hurt so good, the way he stretched her open with those thick, firm fingers. This felt different with gloves, strangely naughty. Those weren't her husband's fingers, oh no. They belonged to the naughtiest of night nurses—the one who'd secretly shared her bed for nearly twelve years.

She squealed when he dove between her legs.

"Just testing your reflexes," Steve cried, crawling up the bed.

When his tongue met her clit, every muscle tensed. "Oh no."

"Oh yes, young lady." He wrapped his mouth around her pussy, sucking every swollen fold. Joanne hollered and shrieked, but she couldn't fight him anymore—she wanted this too much. His lips traced sticky, pink gloss all over her pussy lips. He kissed them like a mouth.

How was he doing that?

Pressing her heels into the mattress, Joanne hoisted her hips up, feeding Steve her pussy like a warm slice of strawberry pie. He growled as he ate her, cupping her asscheeks with two gloved hands. She missed his fingers, but if all went as planned, she'd surely get a crack at the huge, throbbing cock beneath that prim white skirt.

A ball of fire lit in Joanne's belly, and she bucked against Steve's face. Her body had a mind of its own. Rubbing her fat clit up and down his hot tongue, she cried, "Yes, you naughty bitch! Eat my fucking cunt. I'm gonna come so hard."

Steve grunted his approval, letting her stroke her eager cunt against his tongue. Would she have gotten off so fiercely if he weren't wearing the wig and the makeup? It seemed like she always came hardest when Steve was dressed to impress. There was something about seeing her guy dressed like a girl that really put her over the edge.

"Eat me!" She rammed her wet cunt against his face, finding the rhythm and the speed that took her up and over. "Yes! Right there, you naughty thing. Just like that."

He kept at her as she came, and even when it felt like too much, he refused to let up. Her pussy fluttered, her belly flipped and the muscles in her thighs locked tight. She struggled to get away, but it was no use. Velcro was a powerful tool when it wanted to be, and Steve's gloved hands clung to her ass. No chance of being set free.

She arched higher off the bed when his tongue found some forgotten spot between her thighs. The edge approached faster than before, and suddenly she was over it again, free-falling off the precipice of orgasm. How did he do that? The man in the nurse's uniform made her scream until her throat ached. She couldn't get enough.

Well, that was a bit of an exaggeration.

"Too much," she said, closing her legs to push his head away. "Too much. Oh god, I can't take it anymore."

Steve backed away from her swollen pussy, grinning like a demon. "Your reaction times are beyond reproach."

Joanne couldn't stop panting, but she managed to giggle.

"Make no mistake," he went on. "I'm not done with you yet."

She caught her breath just long enough to say, "I sure hope not."

THE ROPE GAME

Kathleen Tudor

"Are you sure about this?" Kira's husband spoke mildly, as if merely curious.

Kira snorted and turned around, baring her back to her husband, and he chuckled as he patted her ass through the sundress.

"First things first," he said, and bent, reaching up under her dress to draw her panties down her thighs. She sighed as his hands eased down her heated flesh, and stepped helpfully out of the sparkly blue thong. "Open."

She opened her mouth obediently, and he stuffed the panties inside. Kira struggled to get her tongue between the fabric and the back of her throat, gagging at first as the cloth was jammed deep into her mouth. She had barely managed to find a comfortable way to hold them in her teeth when a strip of duct tape came down across her mouth, and she moaned; she had a love/hate relationship with duct tape.

"That's my pretty girl. Now put your hands back, I have something special for today." She reached up behind her back, grabbing her opposite elbows to allow him to bind her wrists in his favorite position. The rope scratched roughly at her skin, and she gasped, nearly choking herself again on the panties as she released them in surprise. This was not the soft slide of the silken cords they usually used....

"Do you like it? I thought that a kidnapping fantasy deserved something special." The rope dug into her flesh, harsh and rough, and Kira bit down on the panties and moaned. She closed her eyes, wanting to focus on the sensations. As her left wrist was bound fast to her right elbow, the rough rope scraped over her skin painfully. She bit off another moan as he brought the rope up between her arms and her back, letting it drag slowly across her exposed arms as he wrapped her up like a neat little package.

By the time he had finished tightening the knots that bound her right wrist into position, Kira's cunt was throbbing with wetness, her arms were throbbing with abrasions, and she was sure that he could smell her arousal in the close air of their bedroom.

Alec leaned close to whisper in her ear. "Do you want to fight me?"

She immediately jerked her head toward his, and he

dodged out of the way, laughing. It was easy for him
to get a foot between her legs, and Kira tumbled sideways and hit the ground with a painful huff. She held
herself still until he bent to grab her, and then kicked
out, catching him on the hip as he turned to evade her.
He growled as he fell, then he pounced on her, angling
himself to pin her facedown on the rug.

Kira snarled, making animal sounds of rage and frus-
tration through the gag, and Alec laughed. He pulled the
skirt of her sundress up, rubbing roughly at her swollen
cunt. "Look how wet you are, you slut," he said, and
Kira bucked again, snarling at him even as she yearned
to have him plunge his hard cock into her, here and
now. But that wasn't the game today, and she counseled
herself to patience, even as she fought him.

Alec ground his erection against her hip and moaned.
"I should take you right now, you filthy little whore. But
you and I, we have bigger things to do today. You're
coming with me." He turned so that he was seated on
her back, facing her feet, and grabbed her legs as she
attempted to kick at him.

He was quick with a rope, and soon the same rough
bindings were wrapped around her ankles, holding her
feet together. Kira bit down on her panties and held back
a moan as she felt the rasp of the rough rope digging
into her legs, abrading and arousing her. He ran another
length of the rope through her leg bindings, and she felt
him attach it to a loop he must have left in her arm
binding, pulling her feet painfully up toward her back.

Kira tried to pull free, but the pain in her back as she pulled told her that she was caught. She turned her head to glare at him, and he laughed as he shoved her over onto her side. "Not so tough now, are you? Wait here, I need to pull the car into the garage." He paused as he stood, looking down at her. "One long blink if you're okay, two quick if you need out."

Kira blinked once, holding her eyes shut for a three count. When she opened them again, he nodded, leered at her and left the room.

He was back quickly enough, lifting her up and carrying her awkwardly through the house and into the garage, where his car was waiting, trunk open. He dumped her in and arranged her carefully so that she wouldn't be hurt by the closing lid, then he placed something cool in her hand. "Airhorn. Honk it if you need out while I'm driving, and I'll pull over. Go ahead and try it." She found the trigger and depressed it, startling herself with the loud horn.

He nodded, and his face changed again, back to the leering sneer of her captor. "You and I are gonna go on a little trip," he hissed, "and then we're gonna have a whole lot of fun." He grinned and reached down to tweak her nipple, giving it one rough twist before he slammed the trunk shut. Kira shuddered with anticipation. He was playing it up, and the rough treatment was even better than she'd hoped.

As the car started, Kira focused on taking slow, deep breaths. She had been worried that she would be too afraid of the enclosed space to enjoy this part of the game, but she soon forgot about the dark and the confinement, instead letting it highlight the senses she could still use. Her nose brought her the smell of her own arousal, hot and sweet in the closed space as she felt it soak the insides of her thighs. The muscles in her arms and back ached, but they were easy to ignore in favor of the rough rope digging into her arms and ankles.

Under the smell of her own arousal, Kira could sense the plastic smell of the harsh acrylic rope that bound her. She shifted, trying to get more comfortable, and moaned as the movement coincided with a turn and her shifting weight pulled against her bonds.

The silky ropes they usually used were wonderful, and the sensation of being unable to move had always left her hot and happy, and she certainly wouldn't like ropes like this all the time, but... But still, it was perfect. They scraped and scratched at her skin, digging in and reminding her that she was a captive—a prisoner—and helpless. The cold of the can in her hand did nothing to offset that delicious feeling of being totally under his power.

She was nearly delirious with excitement by the time the car crunched over gravel and the engine stopped. Alec popped the trunk and reached down, feeling her feet, then her hands. "Any tingles or pain?" She gave another long blink, and he smiled again as he slipped back into his role.

"Look around," he invited, stepping out of her way.

They were in a parking lot, from the looks of it, but in the middle of nowhere, with plenty of trees at the edges and no other cars that she could see. She whimpered in anticipation. "This factory shut down two years ago, and no one comes out this way anymore. Do you know what that means? No one is going to interrupt our little party."

He ran his fingers over her face, and she jerked her head away, her breath coming fast in arousal. "I can be real nice to you if you're nice to me," he said, and pulled a knife out of his back pocket, flipping the blade open. She whimpered again, and he held it close to her face for a moment before sliding it behind her and slicing through the rope that held her wrists to her feet. She moaned in relief as the cramps in her back eased, and hardly noticed as he tossed her over his shoulder.

Alec carried her to an area just inside the tree line and tossed her down into the leaves. She grunted as she landed hard on her arms, and he paused, watching her face for a moment before his leer returned full force. He knelt beside her, and Kira's every exhale was accompanied by a low moan as his hands roamed up between her legs and found her dripping cunt.

"Mmm, looks like I won't have to tell you what's what," he said. He thrust two fingers deep inside her, and although Kira struggled to bring her legs together, she was working against her own horny instincts.

Alec reached up with his other hand and grabbed one of her breasts, mangling it roughly in his large hand and then twisting her nipple. Pain and pleasure washed over Kira, and as she struggled against the pain, the ropes only tightened on her wrists and ankles, driving her even higher into an aroused stupor.

She was close to orgasm—so close—when he pulled his hand free, grabbed her by the waist and flipped her over. She made a startled sound as her face hit the dirt, too surprised even to struggle as his arm around her waist pulled her hips up and back to expose her hot cunt.

He shifted behind her as she struggled to regain her bearings, then she screamed with pleasure as he thrust deep inside her before she remembered that she was supposed to be struggling. Fortunately for her, each futile buck seemed to drive him deeper even as it pulled against her bonds and sent waves of pleasure from the ropes straight to her core. It was only seconds before she had forgotten the struggle entirely, pushing back into him as she moaned in mounting pleasure. She convulsed when her orgasm took her, and she felt his cock pulse inside her spasming cunt. She distantly heard his shout of pleasure behind her.

He let her collapse completely to the leafy ground, and she heard the *snick* of his knife again. Her bonds jerked, sending one last pulse of pleasure to her cunt, then parted under his blade, and he rubbed the circulation back into her fingers and toes. When she felt recovered enough, she took a deep breath through her nose, squeezed her eyes shut and ripped the tape away. She squeaked with the pain of it and spat the damp panties into her hand, then collapsed against him, spent.

"You okay?" he asked, and she moaned an affirmative. "You leaving under your own power?" She moaned again, and he laughed and lifted her, cradling her in his arms this time as he carried her back toward the car.

Kira rested her head against his chest, admiring her bruised and scraped wrists as she snuggled up to him in languid pleasure. "Can we do that again soon?"

He laughed and kissed the top of her head in answer.

THE THIRD
FLOOR

Amanda Earl

"Mandy, I think it's time we meet. Time for you to serve me in person," John said.

I paused. Aimed the cell phone camera away from my cunt. Shut it off. Put the dildo down.

I didn't know what to say. Of course I was tempted. After all, I'd done everything he'd told me to do. Opened my cunt wide on command. Slid my fingers over my lower lips. Diddled my clit to the sound of his heavy breathing. Moaned for him. Come when he ordered me to.

"Is it all just make-believe, Mandy? Are you a mere phone slut? Just a cocktease? Unwilling to kneel in person? To serve my cock?"

I sighed. Maybe he was right; maybe I was just a tease. A timid mouse.

"You've done everything I've told you to do for

months, girl. You've buggered yourself with a dildo for me. You've dug your fingernails into your tits and shown me the marks. You've shoved a carrot up your twat. Didn't you say you'd do anything for me, Mandy?"

I had said that. I'd done everything he'd asked.

On the phone.

I'd sent him photographs upon command. Picked the thickest carrot in my fridge, washed it, warmed it with my hands, then slowly pushed it into my hot and aching cunt, imaging it was his cock forcing its way inside me. And been turned on by it. Because I was serving him. Doing what he told me to do. But this was different. What if he was dangerous? What if he could indeed get me to do anything in person? As he had over the phone.

I was tempted. I needed something more. I felt such a longing to obey him. So I took a deep breath and answered his question.

"Yes, Sir, I want to serve you in person."

"Good girl. Now come for me, Mandy. Stick your fingers inside that wet, hot cunt. Soon it'll be my cock filling you up, mastering you."

The authoritative tone of his voice sent shivers through my body. Turned my nipples hard. Soaked my cunt.

"That's right, Mandy," he whispered. "Open up that needy little hole. I want to hear you moan for me, girl. Moan nice and loud. Come for me. Right…now."

I humped against the fingers inside my cunt. Imagined his fat cock fucking me hard. I humped and humped.

Sighed. Groaned. Sweated. Turned on my stomach. Pressed my aching vagina against my fingers. And came.

"Very good, Mandy. Tell me...whereabouts do you live?"

Still under the influence of the orgasm, I told him.

"Downtown. In a walk-up apartment. On the third floor."

"Thank you, slut. That should suit. I'll email you about meeting soon."

Afterward I turned off the speakerphone. What the hell had I been thinking, agreeing to meet a stranger? And even more stupid, meeting him at my own place? Sure we'd been chatting online and talking on the phone for many months. Actually, we'd been cybering and having phone sex.

That's all I did with dominant men. I didn't meet them. I was too afraid of what they'd try to do to me. Of what I would let them do to me. This guy had gotten a lot farther than most of them ever did. Usually we'd hook up online for a few sessions. Then it would get stupid. They thought submissive meant doormat. They told me to do stupid things: bark like a dog; meet the pizza delivery guy at the door naked; lash my body with a belt. Even though I didn't have the slightest idea about how to whip myself without doing damage. It was all crazy. Senseless.

Not to mention so many of them were poor writers with limited imaginations. John wasn't like that. He knew the difference between what he could get me to do, what was plausible and what was dangerous, or silly. Not to mention he was well-spoken, articulate and erudite.

I knew he was much older than me. That was part of the turn-on. He was an experienced Master. I craved to kneel at his feet. To worship his dick. The very thought made me wet again. I stripped naked. Fondled my tits until my nipples were hard. Squeezed them. Imagined my fingers were his fingers twisting my nipples cruelly. Because he assured me he was ever so cruel.

I kept checking my email. Then going back to my bed and humping when nothing was there. I wanted to serve him. I didn't. I did. Jeezus. I thought I was going to go mad.

Finally his email arrived. I was to give him my address. He would arrive at four p.m. and call me on my apartment intercom. I was to meet him in the lobby wearing a short skirt with no underwear. A subtle yet revealing top with no bra. A pair of fishnet stockings. Not nylons. Stockings. So he could part my legs as we climbed the stairs. So he could feel my naked, shaved cunt. So he could make sure I was wet.

I was to put on the highest heels I had, preferably stilettos. Preferably strappy. I didn't have to buzz him in if I didn't like the way he looked.

I hadn't even seen a picture of his face. He could be some grizzly, old hunchback for all I knew. I was torn. Should I give him my address? Shouldn't I? Why shouldn't I? I wanted it. I wanted him to use me in every way possible. One fantasy he spun for me was that of putting me in a cage on a table. So my tits rubbed up against the bars at the front of the cage. Making me kneel on all fours so my ass was against the other end. Ready for his use.

I'd seen photos of his manhood. Because that was the part of him that he wanted me to serve. The part of all men that he said I should serve. I loved that thought. It got me turned on all the time. I was made to serve cock. To worship it.

I didn't even know if I could take his up my ass. He was hung like a fucking horse. But I knew. If I met him, I would be expected to. Take his cock. Up my ass.

I humped my needy cunt against my chair while I typed in my address.

Very well, slut. I'll be there at four p.m. Be ready. Don't fuck yourself. Wait for me, you horny little bitch.

Yes, sir.

Fuck. That was it. I was going to serve him. I knew I was going to let him in. I knew I was going to let him use me. I knew I was going to let him do whatever the hell he wanted with me. There was no turning back now. Whatever he ordered me to do, I would obey him.

With trembling hands, I closed my email program. I was fucking drenched. My juices flowed down my thighs. I returned to the bedroom. I wanted to lie on the bed. Shove the vibe up my cunt. Give myself some release. But I knew I couldn't. I'd promised him.

I took a hot bath. I knew he liked a clean, shaven cunt. I opened the can of shaving gel. Parted my labia with one hand. Slid the razor along first the left, then the right lower lip. Diddled my clit a bit. Then stopped. It was already so swollen. I had to stop. I didn't know what he'd do if I fucked myself before he got there. But I knew I wouldn't like it. I knew I would like it.

Did I want him to punish me? Did I want him to remove his thick leather belt? The one he'd told me about? Black and wide with a solid silver buckle. Purchased from a fellow dominant who was also a leathersmith. Who knew how to create a belt that would be strong enough to exact punishment on a misbehaving brat like me.

The tub water turned cloudy white with my cum. I knew I was going to be punished. Could I handle it? Could I handle his big, firm, strong hand on my naked buttocks? Could I handle the red, raw licks of pain that would stripe my ass? From his hands or from even worse his belt? Buckle side down?

I watched the tub water spiral down the drain. I was spiraling too. Letting my need to be mastered control me. I knelt by the tub. Caught my breath. I wanted to be on my knees for this man. To worship him. It was all I needed. It was too late for regrets. It was too late to cancel.

I opened my closet. Found the clothing John required. Sat on the bed. Counted heartbeats. Counted breaths. I waited. I thought of one of the stories he'd told me. I was on my knees beneath the dining room table. A bunch of his poker buddies were playing the game. Their flies open. Their cocks hanging out. Every once in a while, one would gesture beneath the table. I would crawl over. Take his cock in my mouth. Suck it till he emptied his load down my throat. Cum or piss. I was the game ho. I was the toilet. An object to be used.

I came hard when he told me that. When he called me his little toilet. Told me that one day he'd have my throat. Have it for his cum. Have it for his piss. One day he'd invite his friends over to fuck the living daylights out of me. To use all of my holes in whatever way they wanted.

That was the day he'd made me take a champagne bottle up my twat. Up to the label. Then send him pictures. He told me he was going to email the photographs to his friends. To let them see what they were in store for. Fuck. He drove me wild.

I misted my naked body with fucking Shalimar. He'd told me it was his favorite perfume. It means *abode of love* in Sanskrit. The sweet vanilla scent mingled with my dark, musky need, to create a seductive blend.

I shimmied into my tight brown corduroy miniskirt. I buttoned up my low-cut, V-neck, knitted sweater. I painted my lips a scarlet, whore red. I thickened my eyelashes a dark black. I ran the matching eyeliner along the rims of my eyes. I stepped into my strappy six-inch stilettos. I waited by the intercom. I stood there. Panting like a fucking dog. I felt like a tart.

3:15 p.m.: My nipples are hard as stones. My hands shake. I imagine kneeling for him as soon as we cross the threshold. For this is indeed a threshold I am crossing.

3:30 p.m.: I move my right hand to beneath my sweater. Raise it to my naked tit. Squeeze. I am so horny. I am so scared. What if he sells me as a white slave? My fucking imagination is working on overdrive. Yet still I wait. From here on in, there's no limit to what I will do. And there's no limit to what he will ask me to do. I know this right down to my bones.

3:45 p.m.: I pace back and forth. Go to the kitchen. Drink water from the tap. Fuck. I've wrecked my eye makeup. I return to the bathroom. Do a quick fix.

3:48 p.m.: My whole body is trembling now. With fear. With desire.

4:00 p.m.: I stare at the clock on the wall. I can't breathe. My chest heaves. I'm all want now. All object. The instrument of his desire.

4:05 p.m.: The intercom. Finally. Chimes.

"Mandy?" he says. His voice sounds strong. Deep. Masterful.

"Yes, Sir. I'll be right down."

I clatter on my stilettos until I find my balance. I carefully walk down the stairs. Take deep breaths.

He is there. At the door. A tall man with silver hair. He smiles. So fucking calm. He's wearing a dark-blue overcoat. It's raining outside. I watch the light from passing cars reflect in the puddles. I look up. I look into his dark brown eyes. I open the door. I let him in.

METHOD ACTING

Thomas Roche

One thing Hank really appreciated about the Hubbards: they were one prompt fucking couple. He guessed it came with being as bourgeois as all fuck—or maybe they weren't from California. Either way, he appreciated it. When he arrived at their condo five minutes early, it didn't matter. Kyle Hubbard was ready.

In fact, Kyle looked *hella* ready, and then some. Kyle opened the door looking fine as wine in a pair of pink panties, black fishnets, fuchsia pumps with high heels and a padlocked collar. The pinks didn't match and it all sort of clashed like a nightmare. Nonetheless, Kyle's lanky body pulled it all together somehow, maybe because Kyle was *hot*. The sexy little fucker even wore lipstick.

Hank tried not to look too surprised; after all, he was the Daddy here, and this crap was to his specifications, right? At least, that's how the story went. Truth be told, Kyle was the one who got into all this cross-dressing shit, but what the hell? He had the body to pull it the hell off. Normally, the last thing Hank looked for in guys was lipstick, with panties and fishnets and heels each a close second, third and fourth, respectively. But there was something he loved about the submissive shame that flashed in Kyle's eyes.

"Hello, Master, welcome, Master." Kyle's voice was soft and sweet. "Thank you for coming." Kyle stood aside, holding the door as Hank stalked his way into the living room like he owned the place. The door shut with a clunk, and Kyle scampered after his Master, tottering wildly on those heels—four or five inches, maybe six, Hank figured.

By the time Kyle caught up with his Master, Hank had planted his ass on the soft leather sofa and his boots on the expensive coffee table. He watched Kyle's eyes, fiery blue with excitement as they lavished shamed affection on Hank's oiled Corcorans. Kyle couldn't have looked more distressed or turned on if Hank had just taken a dump on the sofa. He didn't dare say a word, though; he just looked with longing at those giant boots, as if his Master's putting his boots on the goddamn coffee table had established Hank as the rescue remedy to everything yuppie-suburban.

Kyle kept on stealing looks at Hank's big boots as he

spoke in a soft, girlish voice: "My Mistress is still getting ready, Master. May I get you a drink while you wait?"

"Beer and a shot," said Hank with a glare. "Whatever you got. You like these boots?"

A visible ripple went through Kyle's half-clad body. "Yes, Sir. Very much, Sir," he said. "They're very sexy."

"Know where I got 'em?" growled Hank.

Kyle's halfway-plucked eyebrows rose slightly, his red-painted lips hanging open.

"I took 'em off the last married bitch whose hot wife I fucked senseless," sneered Hank. "You believe that? The little sissy thought he could wear real boots, like a man." Hank's contemptuous chuckle was equal parts Jabba the Hutt and Burt Lancaster in *From Here to Eternity*. He wasn't particularly proud of it, but it sure as hell did the trick for Kyle, who wiggled his hot little butt as if someone was pulling some Wartenberg shit up and down the backs of his pretty little thighs. So help him, Hank liked it when Kyle Hubbard wiggled.

He barked: "I said, *you believe that shit*?" This time Hank thought his bark sounded more like Nurse Ratched or maybe the Wicked Witch of the West. But that shit didn't matter one damn bit to Kyle, who shivered all over and said: "No, Sir, that's totally crazy. A sissy? In *those* boots?" His face had turned red; he could not take his eyes off Hank's boots. "What a...*sissy*," he added.

That last word, "sissy," came out kinda weak and unconvincing. Hank figured maybe Kyle wanted to say something nastier—the F-word?—but knew better, what with Hank being...*you know*. Hank didn't think he would particularly care if Kyle called himself a faggot, but since Kyle *wasn't* a faggot in anything like a meaningful sense, Hank appreciated the little fuck's concern for using PC language. Specifically, he liked the way insecurity played across Kyle's lips as his face reddened. It inspired Hank to go very much in the opposite direction, which he'd always done somewhat naturally. Hank swore like a sailor at the best of times, and this was far from the best of times. Foul language was called for.

"You sick, disgusting pervert!" he snarled. "Are you getting a hard-on?"

This time Hank couldn't help it; he sounded one hundred and fucking ten percent like Neely O'Hara in the midst of a doll-fueled breakdown. Too many goddamn drama classes in college had left him desperately in need of a rehearsal before he could nail any given role, but you didn't get a rehearsal when it came to perversion, did you?

It didn't matter. Cute little Kyle bought it, trying to cover the front of his swelling panties with both of his red-nailed hands. Hank aimed his index finger at the bulging front of Kyle's panties and crowed: "That sad little thing of yours is actually—fuck, you sick weirdo, is that as big as it gets?"

Kyle looked like he was about to faint.

He crossed his hands in front of his crotch and whimpered:

"No, Sir! No Sir, no, Sir, why—why would I get a—
Sir, let me get you that beer!"

"Yeah, you do that," snarled Hank as Kyle scampered away. He called after him: "You better lose that
wood! If I see those pink panties stretching when you get
back, bitch, I'll—!" He left the threat hanging, ambig-
uous, as he watched Kyle's butt wiggle down the hall to
the kitchen.

Kyle had thoughtfully placed a pile of porno magazines on the end of the coffee table, pleasingly fanned
like the *Ladies' Home Journal*s at a dentist's office. *Shit,*
Hank thought. *They still publish these things in print?*

Hank retrieved a *Hustler*, saw it was from 1990, and
almost laughed his ass off. He paged through the picto-
rials with a furrowed brow, thinking, *Huh?* He began to
feel mildly anxious. Was it weird that he was about to
receive Mrs. Lisette-*superfuckable*-Hubbard, and...*do
something* with her? He hadn't had time to think about
it, really, until he looked into the weird, gooey Grand
Guignol of pussy...or something like it. *Vaguely* like it.
Truth be told, Hank didn't remember them looking like
that. He'd seen plenty of sex-party snatch, and not a
damn one looked like that thing in the magazine. Maybe
he'd been out of the game longer than he'd thought.

But hell, it wasn't *that* weird to have sex with a
woman, was it? It's not like Hank hadn't been with
females before. It'd just kinda, you know, been a while.
He'd been to plenty of mixed-gender sex parties, right?
Didn't that count, kinda?

As unfamiliar as women's bodies sometimes seemed to him, there was little question in Hank's mind that he was still bi, whatever that meant nowadays. After all, it had gotten him hotter than hell to see Lisette sitting there holding Kyle's leash as he sucked Hank's dick at the Queen Goddess party three weekends ago, and then she'd got all up close and personal right along with her husband when they'd met at Steam Boys' first mixed-gender night. Hank hadn't even been all that weirded out—certainly not as much as the several times he'd tried to make it with bi girls over the years. In fact, it was kind of a thrill to feel soft, wet lips like Lisette's all over his balls and his taint, while her red-faced husband smeared lipstick all up and down his joint. Hell, he'd always been bi, right? At least on paper. And he'd definitely always liked straight guys anyway; something about forbidden fruit. Hank wasn't exactly a fan of drag, but he had to admit, Kyle wore it well.

He'd taken to dominating Kyle with a natural's grace. There was a different technique required, but it wasn't difficult at all. All he'd really had to do was dig into that deep reservoir of internalized homophobia and misogyny, smear it all over his dick and start whapping the guy with it. Pink this, sissy that, panties, small dick, blah blah blah. The strange truth is that Kyle Hubbard actually had a hell of a *nice* cock, and plenty big. How did someone like that develop a kink for getting told his more-than-adequate junk was so small it required lepre-chauns to rent time on an electron microscope to give him a hand job? Hank didn't know, but he'd said some weird-ass shit to other guys over the years, in bedrooms and dungeons and rest stops and, you know, wherever. He was more than willing to meet any freak on his own terms, and Kyle was hot enough to make it worthwhile, even though—or maybe *because*—he had a wife.

Hank was so lost in the weirdness of the Clinton-era *Hustler* that he didn't hear the *click-click-clicking* of Lisette Hubbard's stilettos until she was almost literally on top of him. She stood by the sofa, towering over him on six-inch heels, wearing nothing at all but those six-inch Steve Maddens and a padlocked black leather collar, just like the one on her husband. The key dangled from a silver chain in her hand.

"Yum," she said. "I mean, yum, *Sir*." She held the key out. "May I give you this?"

"You may," he growled. Hank's eyes went roving up and down Lisette's body gratefully as he tossed the *Hustler* to the far end of the couch. He snatched the key and the chain from Lisette's slender fingers and shoved it into his front jeans pocket.

Without being told, Lisette lowered herself to her knees.

Kyle came scampering in again, holding a tray with a bottle of Pabst, a shot glass of whiskey and a glass of red wine. Hank eyed the Pabst with a wary frown and regretted his order of "beer and a shot." It had seemed like the manliest thing to demand from his slave, even though he would really have preferred a gin and tonic.

Like he was going to order that shit from a guy in pink panties when it was his job to make the guy tremble with erotic humiliation? He didn't even order mixed drinks at the Boxcar, because those wicked, bitchy leather queens never let a guy live that shit down.

Hank thought, "May as well get it over with." He plucked the shot from the tray and slammed it. It wasn't bad whiskey, but it sure as hell wasn't a gin and tonic. He took the beer and watched Lisette's candy-green eyes flicker longingly over the glass of wine.

She asked softly, "May I, Sir?"

Hank retrieved Lisette's wine from the tray and held it out of her reach.

He said, "No. Beat your husband first."

Lisette looked a little surprised, but only a little. It was Kyle whose eyes went all buggy-scared and freaky. Hank felt proud of his choice of words: *beat*, not *spank*, *whip* or *punish*, just flat-out "beat," which might mean anything.

Lisette's eyes sparkled. Hank thought he saw a smile forming at the edge of her lips.

She said, "Yes, Sir. Of course, Sir. May I ask why?"

Hank guffawed. "Look at that boner," he sneered. "Yeah, I know it's hard to miss, but…"

Lisette picked up on Hank's line of reasoning and added: "Yes, Sir. It certainly is, Sir. Very tiny, Sir. I can barely feel it."

"Is that as big as it gets?"

Lisette's bright smile hid behind her hand, as if she

were embarrassed. She was *not* embarrassed; the look in her eyes told Hank this girl was probably *wet*.

"Yes, Sir, I'm afraid it is," she said. "Much to my chagrin." She made eye contact with the red-faced Kyle. Hank could practically feel the heat between them— invisible pleasure, like the radiation from the core of a nuclear reactor. The icier Lisette's voice sounded, the redder Hank's face got. It was positively frigid as she said: "My husband's small dick is why I have to fuck other men. Real men. Lisette's hand snaked its way up to Hank's crotch. "Men with real dicks. Big dicks. Dicks that can satisfy me. Isn't that right, Kyle?"

"Yes, Mistress," said Kyle, his voice soft and rich with submission. His dick was as hard as Hank had ever seen it. Its bulbous tip threatened to breach the top of his skimpy panties.

"Go get the flogger," said Lisette to Kyle. Then, softly, to Hank, she said: "A flogger? Is that okay?"

"Whatever you use," said Hank, "make it something that hurts."

"Oh," said Lisette with pleasure. "The flogger hurts. It hurts *bad*. Doesn't it, baby?"

"Yes, Mistress," said Kyle. He left, his butt wiggling as he hurried down the hall again.

Hank felt slightly weird as Lisette and he were left alone. He really wasn't very used to this; when he'd made out his New Year's resolutions, the last goddamn thing he'd thought to put on there was "have a hot girl kneel and worship you." But that's what she seemed to be doing. Lisette looked up at Hank in a deep, easy kind of submission. She blinked her emerald-green eyes as if waiting for something she needed very badly. Hank just wasn't quite sure what it was. It had been a long damn time.

Hank froze a little. He thought about breaking character or something and making sure this was all Kosher. But what the hell? Lisette seemed perfectly capable of giving him the hairy eyeball if he did a damn thing that she didn't like. So far, she'd piggybacked just like an expert on every mean thing Hank had said to her husband. She seemed to be even more of a natural than Hank was.

Besides: like drinking the whiskey, he may as well get the scary part over with.

Hank reached out and hooked his finger in the D-ring of Lisette's collar. He tugged her face closer to his crotch. Lisette went nice and easy.

"Say hello, slave," he ordered, pointing her face at his crotch.

Lisette got his gist immediately. Her slender hands came up to unbuckle his belt and unfasten his pants. Her hand eased its way into his jockey shorts, tentatively, as if she wasn't quite sure what she'd find in there. She found him half-hard, not quite ready but getting there quickly as she gently caressed him.

Lisette Hubbard wrapped her red lips around Hank's cock and started to suck. She made eye contact as she did: someone had trained her how to give a properly submissive blow job. Hank couldn't take his eyes off her face. It had been a long time since he'd observed a face like Lisette's from this vantage point. Excepting the scene at the Steam Boys' coed party, where she'd mostly just lapped at his balls while her husband did the heavy lifting, Hank hadn't gotten a full-on blow from a girl for like, what…five years? Maybe more?

To his relief, he quickly got all the way hard. He lifted Lisette's wineglass to his lips and drained it in one slurp. It cut the hard burn of the whiskey and the sharp bite of the Pabst.

Lisette really went to town, opening wide and gagging herself on his cock. She appeared to like it messy, which more or less matched with her husband's technique. By the time Kyle Hubbard reentered the living room, Lisette's face glistened with drool and Hank's jockeys were practically soaked.

When he saw his wife sucking Hank's cock, Kyle looked like he was damn close to fainting. His erection had mostly softened while he was gone, leaving a shiny little smear on the front of his panties. Now, it grew inches in seconds. Kyle stood there watching, red-painted lips opened wide in an O of surprise and fascination, out of which came a soft and sad moan of arousal-dismay.

Hank made eye contact pointedly with Kyle. Then Hank dropped his eyes to Kyle's stiffening cock and said: "I guess your wife couldn't wait. I guess it's been a long time since she had some real dick, hasn't it?"

Kyle answered quickly, his voice soft and desperate.

"Yes, Sir, it certainly has, Sir." Kyle's erection had grown to its full size again—maybe even bigger and harder than before. He didn't try to conceal it this time. He just watched in fascination as Lisette worked her lips up and down Hank's shaft. Lisette made eye contact with Hank now and then, but didn't stick to it; she lost herself in the task before her, which was damned fine with Hank. But every now and then, she'd look up and make sure her husband was watching. Then Hank could feel a shiver go through her, a sinuous undulation working its way through her tongue and the soft, wet snugness at the back of her throat. She pushed down onto Hank with increasing force. She kept deep-throating him with mounting eagerness, seemingly going out of her way to drool, slurp and gulp. Hank understood Lisette's adoration for sloppy head when he saw Kyle's reaction. He looked ready to faint all over again. He could not take his eyes off his wife's drooly face, or Hank's cock thrusting up between her messy lips.

"Don't you touch that!" barked Hank when he saw Kyle's hand moving surreptitiously down toward the front of his panties. Kyle put his hands at his sides, the fronds of the flogger trailing on the floor. To Lisette, Hank said—sort of absently, with the blow job and all— "Your sissy wants to touch his little dick. You believe that shit? Does a dick like that *ever* get touched?"

Lisette shook her head. She mewled, "Mm-mmm, Sir, no Master, never, Sir," or something like it—it was damned hard to tell, with her mouth full of dick and all. Hank watched her pretty face for a while, loving the way her eyes got all wet from the repeated violation of her gag reflex. Hank would have liked seeing Lisette's eyes wet about as much as he liked it on guys, except for one thing: guys don't wear mascara. There was something so hot and filthy about the way Lisette's eyes got all black-rimmed and nasty-looking. It called attention to the eager effort she was putting into sucking his dick. What's not to love about that?

In fact, Lisette's effort was so damned eager that Hank knew he couldn't last long if she kept that shit up, and he'd be damned if he was going to blow his load before Kyle even writhed in pain for him. That just wouldn't do.

Hank slid his hands into Lisette's long dark hair and eased the eager cocksucker out of his crotch. She came free with a pop, strings of drool running down over her chin and onto Hank's balls.

"Slave, beat your husband," said Hank.

"Yes, Sir," said Lisette, getting up from her knees.

To Kyle, Hank said: "Give your wife the whip, slave. Then take over."

Kyle played at being shocked. "You mean," he squeaked. "You mean—" His eyes rambled over Hank's spit-shined cock.

Hank said, "I mean, suck my dick. Or else. Come on, slave, your wife got it started for you…"

"Yes, Sir," said Kyle softly, lowering himself to his

knees. He looked shy and scared as he gazed up at Hank. For the first time, Hank noticed that Kyle was wearing mascara. How had he missed that? Damn, Hank decided. This was gonna be good.

Kyle's face hovered over Hank's crotch. He whimpered softly, "Sir, you mean...you want me to...?"

Hank grabbed Kyle's hair, pried his mouth open and shoved his dick in. Kyle gagged and whimpered and choked a little, but it didn't take long before his lips were tight around Hank's shaft, working as wetly and eagerly as his wife's had. Hank didn't let that stop him, though; he slid his hand into Kyle's hair and gripped it. He pulled his dick out of Kyle's mouth and slapped him across the face with it. Kyle gasped a little.

"I told you to *suck*!" he snarled. "Now *suck*!"

"Yes, Sir!" Kyle bleated, just in the split-second before Hank shoved his dick back in Kyle's mouth. The sissy choked and drooled, just like his wife; she'd probably taught him to suck, hence the similarities in their styles. Hank would not let Kyle run the suck just yet, though; he kept his firm grip on Kyle's hair and put his hand on his throat, just to let Kyle know that he could. The harder Hank topped him, the more Kyle's tongue worked against Hank's soft underside. It was right there on the checklist: *FORCED ORAL,* with six checks and three smiley-faces, just in case Hank had any questions about whether Kyle was a real sissy or not. Kyle liked to play hard-to-get; he was good at it, too. Almost as good at it as Hank was at playing hard-to-resist.

"May I whip my husband, Sir?"

Hank had been so absorbed with subjecting Kyle to the "forced" blow job that he'd barely noticed the breathtaking ivory-skinned woman standing there behind him. She was poised, gorgeous and pale. In her hand was a flogger that looked like it must have been made to whip misbehaving Brobdingnagians.

"Yeah," grunted Hank, thoroughly absorbed in the warm wetness of Kyle's hot mouth. "How many times do you whip him for getting a boner?"

Lisette seemed to be scrambling slightly, but she came up with a quick answer:

"When a real man's around? Ten strokes at least, Master."

"Give him twenty."

"Yes, Sir." Lisette's lips, no longer red but a messy, smeared pink, twisted upward in a savage smile, as if it pleased her that Hank, *Master*, was willing to be even crueler than she.

Lisette's hand spiraled two or three times in the air and described a graceful arc. The flogger hit with the force of a freight train. The cracking sound filled the small condo's living room. Kyle surged forward onto Hank's cock, choking on the thickness of Hank's shaft. Hank immediately regretted saying, "twenty"—what was this, the fucking Inquisition? But Lisette seemed to know what she was doing; after the first brutal stroke, she eased up somewhat; the next few strokes were a little bit lighter. That first one had just been intended to get her

husband's attention. Lisette landed each blow with the
grace of an angel, counting: "One, Master, two, Master,
three, Master..." Hank supposed Lisette counted because
Kyle *couldn't* count, with his mouth being full of Hank's
dick and all. Then again, from the rapture in her voice
with every number and every "Master," Hank thought
maybe it just made her pussy wet.

With the incantation of "Twelve, Master," roughly,
Lisette stopped playing nice and went back to hitting
her husband *hard*. Kyle wiggled and writhed, shoving
his pantied ass high up into the air as his wife punished
it. Hank watched eagerly as the tension built in Kyle's
slender body. His cock was still hard, a fact Hank could
tell when he nudged his big boot up to rub it a little.
Should he up the punishment or something? Or was
Kyle being a good little slave, now, popping a boner
while he served his Master? Hank couldn't decide, but
he knew with the slave's eager sucking, he wasn't going
to last...and he no longer wanted to. Every hard stroke
that landed on Kyle's upthrust ass dragged Hank closer
to an explosive orgasm.

Between "Fifteen, Master" and "Sixteen, Master,"
Hank interrupted Lisette's work:

"Slave! Pull your husband's panties down."

With an excited, "Yes, Master," Lisette obeyed, dropping down to one knee. Kyle's hard cock bounced free,
scattering droplets of precome on Hank's boots. Lisette
pulled Kyle's panties down to his knees; Kyle never
stopped sucking. Lisette returned to her whip-wielding

position, but before she could start, Hank slid his hand into the narrow inside pocket of his leather vest and tossed something to her. She caught it neatly, as she did the little pillow of lube Hank followed it with.

"When he's taken his punishment," Hank said. "He should get a little something, don't you think?"

"Yes, Sir," Lisette said happily. "If you do, Sir." Her whip once again drew its savage arc through the close air of the condo and made explosive noises on her husband's shaved butt. Kyle sucked Hank's cock with increasing abandon, maybe fancying that proper obeisance could earn him some mercy.

And it did. With Lisette's rapturous, "Twenty, Master" still fresh in Hank's hungry ears, Lisette dropped to her knees behind her husband. She snapped the rubber glove over her hand and broke open the lube with her teeth.

She wasted no time at all; Hank couldn't see how many fingers she shoved in her husband's hole, but it sure as hell got his attention. Kyle practically squealed. He never stopped sucking, though; his wet mouth and soft, open throat still pumped hungrily onto Hank's cock. Hank had to hand it to Kyle. For a guy who wanted to be "forced" to give head every time, he sure got the hang of things fast.

Lisette's hand was well into her husband when Hank realized he was going to come—and come *hard*. It's not exactly that he wanted to do something nice for Kyle; he just loved the way the sissy's hard cock felt against the toe of his boot as he kind of kick-rubbed it. Hank wanted more, and he knew damn well that Kyle wanted *way* more.

So Hank barked: "Put your hand on your dick, sissy. You wanna jack off so bad? Fine...come on your Master's boots."

Kyle tried to grunt something like, "Yes, Master," but didn't dare take Hank's dick out of his mouth. Kyle's hand went to his dick and wrapped tightly around it; he started pumping furiously.

"Keep fucking him," Hank said to Lisette. "Fuck him harder."

"Yes, Master," she purred with a smile on her messy face. Lisette looked gorgeous back there; she seemed to be trying very hard to shove her whole hand up her husband's ass. Hank could see four fingers buried up deep in Kyle's tight hole, and Lisette's thumb was tucked right where a thumb belonged when it was about to go somewhere very, very special, like maybe all the way up Kyle's butt with the rest of his wife's hand.

Hank flat-out lost it. It was too much to take. He realized there was a very real chance of hot little Kyle kneeling there, ass in the air and face stuffed with dick, while Lisette rammed her whole hand into him. Maybe not now, not *right* now, but—damn, Lisette had her hand pretty far up there...

Hank gave up trying to hold himself back. He arched his back and pressed his shoulders into the soft, supple leather of the couch as he let Kyle finish him. The sissy was down hard on Hank's big cock when Hank came, the head tucked firmly into the back of Kyle's throat. He didn't gag once, this time; he didn't choke, drool, or sputter. He just opened wide and took hot streams of Hank's jizz down his throat.

Kyle's hand never once stopped jacking. His mouth was still clamped tight around Hank's softening shaft when a series of spasms went through Kyle's body. Hank had forgotten all about keeping his boot right there up against the tip of Kyle's dick, but it was okay; Kyle had impeccable aim. He laid maybe half a dozen wet streams of jizz on Hank's boots, shuddering with each glistening string that poured from his cock.

"Clean it up." Hank's voice was hoarse. Lisette backed off to let her husband kiss his way down Hank's legs to plant his red lips on the glistening black leather surface of Hank's Corcorans. Lisette's hand hadn't made it all the way into Kyle's ass, but Hank didn't mind. The night was young.

"That's good, slave," Hank said. He wasn't talking to Kyle, but to Lisette. "You can stop. We'll fist-fuck him later." Hank felt a ripple of fear and excitement go through Kyle's body as his tongue lapped his come from Hank's boots.

Lisette said, "Yes, Sir," and snapped the wet glove off her hand.

"I think you could probably use that wine," said Hank.

"Yes, Master," said Lisette. She eyed her husband's bobbing head as Kyle lapped up his come from Hank's boots. She took obvious pleasure in the sight. "I'll get it myself, Sir...I don't want to stop him. Would you like anything, Master?"

Hank eyed the half-drunk Pabst on the coffee table. He frowned angrily at it.

"Yeah," he said. "I want a gin and fucking tonic."

"Of course, Sir," Lisette said. Neither she nor Kyle seemed bothered in the least by his choice of a mixed drink, Hank noticed with pleasure. Maybe he really was a natural at this, after all.

While Lisette got the drink, Kyle continued to worship Hank's boots. They'd long since been cleaned of his come, but Hank didn't stop Kyle. The guy looked too goddamn good doing it. He could go on forever, far as Hank was concerned.

LITTLE ANGEL

Evan Mora

I hate him.

It's instant. Fiery hot, burning through my veins like a volcanic eruption.

"Isn't he sweet, pet?" Mistress laughs, ruffling the shiny black hair of the grinning boy at her side.

"Yes, Mistress," I reply, jealousy splashing and churning in my belly like acid.

"His name is Gabriel. When I saw him up on the stage tonight in his cute little collar, I just couldn't pass him up!" She pinches his cheeks, making him blush. "He's going to be my little angel, aren't you Gabriel?"

He nods, still grinning, which earns him a swat on the behind and a look that promises more.

"I mean, uh...yes, Mistress." He looks proud of himself, and Mistress has a hungry gleam in her eyes that I know only too well.

"You can head to bed, pet. Breakfast at eight please," she says without taking her eyes off the boy.

"Yes, Mistress," I say again.

She hooks a gloved finger through the D-ring on the front of his collar and leads him down the hall to her room.

For a moment, I remain kneeling on the cool marble of the entryway floor, a riot of thoughts racing through my head. I've never seen Mistress with a boy before. I know she's taken male lovers in the past, but not in the year since I've been with her. Is she not happy with me? She hasn't said anything to that effect, and she's definitely not one to hide her displeasure. She only casually mentioned attending the auction tonight (which wasn't even a real auction, I might add), and certainly said nothing about buying some pretty boy who looks barely old enough to drink! And he *is* pretty; even I can't deny that. I sigh, getting slowly to my feet and padding down the opposite hallway to my small room.

Once inside, I close the door and slide between the soft cotton sheets of my single bed without even turning on a light. I barely notice the pleasing feel of the cool sheets on my naked skin—such is my agitation. I wonder what they're doing. I wonder if he'll kneel between Mistress's thighs, caressing her with his tongue while her fingers delve into his hair, holding him fast. I wonder if she'll stoke her desires first with flogger and paddle, heating his skin until it's as hot as hers; until the demands of her body make her lay down her tools and open herself to him. The familiar pulse of arousal begins to beat low in my belly, and I roll onto my side with a groan, knowing that relief will not be mine tonight.

Sleep eludes me. I feel like I've been staring at the wall for hours when suddenly my door is thrown open and I bolt upright as Mistress shoves the boy, now naked and tearful, into my room. Barely over the threshold, he collapses into a heap on the floor, sobbing pathetically.

"Mistress?" I ask.

"Ugh. He's completely useless. No skill whatsoever with oral sex, and he came all over my Persian rug while I was spanking him. I should've known better—all Dominic sees is a little submissive with a pretty face…" She lets her sentence trail off.

I'm not surprised. While Dominic's charity auction is rightly lauded for its support of many worthy causes, it's also a notoriously bad place to go looking for a well-trained slave. A superior smirk tugs at the corner of my mouth and I quickly school my features.

"How can I be of service, Mistress?"

"You can take his place in my bed. And you," she points to the boy, "you'll sleep on the floor here. I'll see about a room for you tomorrow."

She turns on heel and heads back toward her room, leaving me to close the door behind her. For one brief moment, I allow myself a triumphant smile as my eyes sweep over the sniveling boy. *Good night, little angel.*

* * *

"Mmm...pet, you are divine," Mistress says, chest rising and falling rapidly in the aftermath of her orgasm. Her cunt is still spasming around my fingers, and my face is wet with her juices. She tugs my hair, drawing me up out of the cradle of her thighs and into her embrace, my head resting in the hollow of her shoulder as she runs her fingers through my hair. This is my very favorite place to be.

"You could teach that boy a thing or two," she continues.

I don't want to teach him anything.

"In fact..." her voice takes on a contemplative quality, and little pinpricks of apprehension skitter over my skin, "I think you *should* teach him!" she laughs. "Oh, this is too good..."

I frown, trying to imagine the boy servicing Mistress while I lean over his shoulder and offer pointers; frankly, it doesn't seem like a terribly sexy scenario.

"You've never been with a boy, have you pet?" she asks.

Wait. What?

"No, Mistress." She can't possibly mean—

"I want you to train him." She props herself up on elbow, looking down at me with an excited intensity. "You know exactly what I like, and moreover," her voice turns sultry and she runs a fingertip down my belly to my sex where she lingers, circling my clit, "I happen to know it's what you like as well."

"Mistress, I—"

"Besides, I can't even entertain the thought of fucking him until he learns to control himself."

She rises gracefully, slipping into her peignoir and taking a seat at her vanity where she picks up her hairbrush and runs it through her dark, shoulder-length hair.

"I leave for Brussels tomorrow evening. You can have him for the week." She eyes me speculatively through the vanity mirror. "I'll be curious to see what you've accomplished."

Oh god. Panic makes me swallow convulsively, makes my palms sweat and my mind race. I can't do this. There's no way I can do this.

"Mistress…with respect, I don't think…" The words come out slowly, carefully.

Her eyes narrow and the rhythmic brushing stops. I blunder on quickly, knowing I shouldn't even as I do. "I can't train him. I can't teach him—I don't know anything about boys, and…and I've never disciplined anyone in my life. I'm a *slave*—"

I break off with a jolt as Mistress's hairbrush connects forcefully with her vanity.

"Yes, and you're *my* slave." She rises, coming back to sit next to where I'm huddled on the edge of her bed. "And you can, and *will* do as I say." She grips my chin in her hand, holding me with her powerful gaze.

"Yes, Mistress." I say quietly.

"Because you don't want to disappoint me."

"No, Mistress."

"Good."

She stands, and I do the same, allowing her to guide me out the door.

"And pet," she pauses, and there's something in her eyes that I can't define, "this isn't just for the boy."

"Yes, Mistress."

The door closes and I'm left to wonder at her meaning.

At first, I don't even go near him.

Mistress left the boy in a tiny room adjacent to mine after handing me a bag of toys ("nothing you can hurt him too badly with"), and making sure we both understood what was expected of us in her absence.

Thwap.

Right in the center of the pillow. I pull back my arm, the soft tails of the suede flogger brushing against my skin, concentrate and let it fly again.

Thwap.

Another hit. I tell myself I'm getting a feel for it—and it's true, I am. After all, it would be irresponsible of me not to practice a little before I use it on the boy.

Thwap. Thwap. Thwap.

But the truth is, I just don't want to do it. I sigh, letting the flogger dangle loosely in my grip. I've spent the better part of the morning abusing my pillow, but the fact remains that if I can't teach this boy a few things before Mistress comes home, I'm the one who'll suffer for it. Resolutely, I toss the flogger back into the bag of toys, grab it by the handles and pad the short distance down the hall to his room.

When I open the door, he's sitting on the bed with his back against the wall and his legs drawn up in front of him. Thick leather cuffs adorn his ankles and wrists, but his collar, I notice, is nowhere in sight. His head is bowed slightly and dark hair falls across his forehead. He hasn't heard my arrival, and there's a quiet vulnerability in him that I hadn't noticed before. I clear my throat to alert him to my presence and he startles, his eyes immediately jumping to mine. They're beautiful, like brilliant sapphires fringed by the kind of impossibly long lashes that make women weep with envy. Its no wonder Mistress wants him, I think with a sinking stomach, he's just so...pretty.

"Hi," he says.

"Rule number one: don't speak unless you're spoken to." I move briskly into the room, dropping the bag on the end of his bed.

"Okay."

I glare at him pointedly.

"Sorry." He has the grace to blush a little.

"Now get up," I say, the words awkward in my mouth.

He complies, getting uncertainly to his feet, his hands moving as though to cover his genitals before dropping to his sides.

"You might as well get used to being naked," I say.

"Mistress prefers her slaves unclothed while in the home."

His eyes slide shyly over my body. For the first time in a long time I'm conscious of my own nakedness, and I frown as a flutter of awareness stirs in my stomach. Mistress has always liked my appearance because it differs so greatly from hers: my figure slim and firm where hers is lush and curved; my skin pale where hers is a rich olive; my light hair and green eyes a striking contrast to her dark hair and even darker eyes. I wonder if the boy finds me attractive, and the thought both confuses and appeals to me.

His body is as beautiful as his face, lean and muscular without being overly large, his chest smooth but for a light dusting of hair that begins at his navel and swirls its way down to his cock. I've seen plenty of cocks in my life, Mistress has several that she likes to fuck and be fucked with, but this is the first time I've really been close to a naked man like this, and his cock looks so... soft. It seems so unimposing, resting between his thighs, and yet even as I watch it seems to lengthen and swell. I wonder if it feels warm....

The boy's hand rises into the air, like a schoolboy waiting to be called on.

"What is it?" I'm sharper than I mean to be, unsettled by my thoughts.

"It's just that...I don't even know your name. I mean—what should I call you?"

What indeed? I'm Mistress's pet, but he can't call me that. Ma'am? Definitely not.

"Ashley." I say it out loud and it feels rusty on my tongue. "How about...Miss Ashley?"

"Miss Ashley." He smiles. He looks at me expectantly, but honestly, I don't know what comes next. I remember the first night I spent with Mistress, how she spent hours learning all the nuances of my body, how unhurried she was while she played with me, discovering how my body responded to different sensations.

I step closer to the boy, my eyes on his chest, and lick my lips nervously. I raise a tentative hand and brush a fingertip over the flat disc of his nipple. He sucks in a breath and I watch as the skin tightens into a hard nub. I do the same to his other nipple and it hardens too, and he exhales shakily. I glance down, curious. Yes, the boy likes this. Bolder, I circle one nipple with my finger, then roll it between my thumb and forefinger, gently at first, then with increasing pressure until he gasps. I look up into his eyes and am struck by the familiarity of his expression—hurt, need, desire—it's all there.

"You like that, don't you Gabriel?"

He nods. "Yeah."

I pinch his nipple painfully and he gasps again. "Yes, Miss Ashley!" He says quickly, eyes wider now.

Arousal, hot and sweet, fires in my blood and moves swiftly to my sex. It's a heady feeling, and yet so unexpected that I drop my hand, momentarily unnerved. I look at the boy, wondering if he senses my confusion, but he looks at me with such expectation, such trust, that I know there's no choice but to continue.

This time I place both hands on his chest, palms over the slight swell of his pectoral muscles, his heart a rapid staccato against my skin. I move my hands upward, tracing his collarbones and the breadth of his shoulders before moving down again, grazing his nipples with my fingernails. He makes a small sound of pleasure and I do it again, flexing my nails like a cat, scoring the tender skin there and lower, across his ribs and stomach, a host of red scratches rising in my wake. He moans, eyes closed, his cock thick and hard just below his navel, and I bite my lip against a moan of my own because I know *exactly* how good that feels.

I also know what Mistress would reach for next if she were playing with me, and I leave the boy for a moment, drawing a short leather crop from the bag of toys on the bed.

"Have you ever played with a crop before, Gabriel?"

"Yes, Miss Ashley," he answers promptly and politely. A small smile tugs at the corner of my mouth.

I tap the end of the crop against his belly and watch his muscles instinctively clench while his cock bobs just a little. I feel a tiny bit sadistic and for the first time, I consider that I might actually enjoy teaching this boy a few things after all. What was it that Mistress said? No control, and no skill with oral sex.

I begin tapping out a light, steady rhythm across his torso, just enough to warm his skin a little. I love when Mistress does this—it feels like she's waking me up, like my skin comes alive, every inch of it, and it practically sings with pleasure.

"Do you remember rule number one?" I ask, continuing the same steady rhythm.

"Don't speak unless I'm spoken to?"

Whap. He jumps a little and his breath hisses out.

"Yes," I say, "though if you can't speak respectfully, Mistress isn't likely to let you speak at all." I throw in another hard *whap* for emphasis.

"Yes, Miss Ashley. Sorry, Miss Ashley," he says with a wince. I circle around behind him, warming his back and buttocks with the same light strokes.

"Rule number two," I continue, "is don't come unless you're told to."

"Yes, Miss Ashley."

His skin is beginning to take on a soft, rosy blush, so I make my strokes a little firmer.

"Coming without permission makes Mistress very upset."

I change my rhythm, interspersing hard with soft: *tap tap tap* WHAP *tap tap tap tap* WHAP. He doesn't answer other than to moan, which I figure is okay, given that I didn't really ask a question. I keep my rhythm unpredictable, focusing on his ass, watching the muscles there clench and unclench as he tries to antici-pate where the next hard stroke will fall. It's an impos-sible task, I know, and yet it's almost equally impossible to stop that reflex.

Watching him struggle fuels my arousal, though

whether it's because I'm the one in control, or simply because I know what he's feeling, I can't honestly say. I want to take it farther though—him, me, both of us—that's what I know. That, and I'm missing the sweet spot.

"In fact, I suspect Mistress was so upset the other night that she didn't punish you properly for making a mess on her rug, did she boy?"

"No, Miss Ashley."

"Hands on the bed then, bent at the waist."

He moves into position without objection, exposing the tender skin at the juncture of his ass and thighs. I run the end of the crop across this untouched skin, then between his legs, stroking it gently across his cock and balls. He moans and rocks his hips forward, seeking more contact. I pull back and immediately deliver a sharp smack right on the underside of his ass. He cries out, a mixture of surprise and pain, and the sound goes straight to my pussy. I do it again, this time on the opposite side, and he grunts and then sucks in a breath, but otherwise holds still.

He's ready now; he knows what's coming, so I go to work in earnest, peppering both sides of his ass and thighs with a series of deliberately hard strokes, and though his thighs tremble and his skin turns a deep, rich rose he maintains his position. I watch his body to try and gauge where he is: at first he's stiff and stoic, but then, as the endorphins start to kick in, his moans become less restrained and his back arches ever so slightly.

Now for the lesson.

"Stand up, boy." I say, and he complies, turning to face me. His eyes are hazy with pleasure and his cheeks are flushed, and I know a pang of longing so intense it makes my breath catch in my chest. What I wouldn't give to be in his position right now. And yet, the feel of the leather grip in my hand, the sheer number of things I could do to him...or have him do to me; knowing that I'm the archi-tect of his pleasure and pain right now, all of these things are so much more intoxicating than I'd imagined.

I run the tip of the crop down the center of his chest, over the fine hair below his navel and down to his cock. When he moans again, I'm bolder, tracing the rigid length of his erection, swirling the leather against the moisture that glistens at its tip.

"I want you to stroke your cock for me, Gabriel," I say, my voice husky with desire, "I want you to show me what feels good to you." I move the crop lower, brushing it against his balls as he takes his cock in his hand, pumping it slowly.

"But if you come before I tell you to," I pause, the crop resting snugly against his tight sac, "I'll make you regret it. Do you understand?"

"Yes, Miss Ashley." He licks his lips, eyes on mine while he strokes himself. At first he's almost leisurely, but gradually his tempo increases, his breathing becomes more erratic and I can see his muscles beginning to tense. I tap the crop lightly against the side of his balls and he jumps, breath hitching a little.

"Not yet." I shake my head and he nods that he understands, taking a deep breath and slowing his tempo. This time, I keep the crop moving, stroking it against his balls and the base of his cock. Before long, he's close again, and I give him another tap, though harder this time than before.

"No," I say, and for a moment he stills his hand and closes his eyes, swallowing rapidly. When he resumes, I start tapping his balls gently, rhythmically, just as I warmed him up earlier.

"This time when you get close, I want you to ask me to come, boy."

"Yes, Miss Ashley." He speaks quickly, voice rough with arousal. I can feel my own arousal pooling between my thighs, and I marvel that this slave, this boy, can have such a profound effect on me. Mistress knew though. Sometimes I think she knows me better than I know myself.

"Can I come, Miss Ashley?" he asks, before hastily adding: "Please?"

I smile wickedly.

"You've got to do better than that, boy," I say. I know he's a heartbeat away from coming, and holding there, on that edge, is the hardest thing in the world right now, but he does it, muscles straining visibly as he pumps his cock.

"Please, Miss Ashley," he says. "Please can I come now?"

"Yes, boy."

He throws his head back, eyes shut, and his whole body shudders as he comes, thick white jets spurting from his cock and trickling down over his fist.

I sit down on the bed, my clit pulsing insistently, watching him as the aftershocks of his orgasm pass. His legs look as wobbly as a newborn foal. *Fortunately*, I think, patting the spot next to me as I recall Mistress's other complaint about the boy, *he doesn't need to be standing for what comes next.*

"Come here, little angel," I say.

ABOUT THE AUTHORS

VALERIE ALEXANDER (valeriealexander.org) lives in Arizona. Her work has been previously published in *Best of Best Women's Erotica 2, Best Bondage Erotica 2013, Under Her Thumb* and other anthologies.

ZOE AMOS (Lesbian.com/blogs) enjoys writing stories of lesbian interest. Her work appears in numerous erotica and romance anthologies. For more stories, please search for Zoe Amos on Amazon.

LAURA ANTONIOU (LAntoniou.com) is best known for her Marketplace series of BDSM erotica. She has also lectured, ranted, read and presented on kinky sex at over one hundred events worldwide. Her novel, *The Killer Wore Leather*, a comedy murder mystery set within the leather/BDSM world, won the 2013 Rainbow Award for Best LGBT Mystery; her stories and essays have appeared in dozens of anthologies.

RACHEL KRAMER BUSSEL (rachelkramerbussel. com) is the editor of over fifty anthologies, including *Gotta Have It: 69 Stories of Sudden Sex, The Big Book of Orgasms, Baby Got Back: Anal Erotica, Serving Him, Going Down, Flying High, Lust in Latex, Best Bondage Erotica 2014* and others.

Called a "legendary erotica heavy-hitter" (by the über-legendary Violet Blue), **ANDREA DALE** (AndreaDaleAuthor.com) likes to toy with expectations, both in fiction and in life. Her work has appeared in more than one hundred anthologies from Harlequin Spice, Avon Red and Cleis Press, and is available online at Soul's Road Press.

LILLIAN DOUGLAS lives and writes in the U.S. Midwest. She likes bicycles, language and sex, though not in that order.

AMANDA EARL's (amandaearl.com) BDSM fiction appears in *The Mammoth Book of Best New Erotica, He's on Top: Erotic Stories Of Male Dominance and Female Submission, Surrender: Erotic Tales of Female Pleasure and Submission* and *Coming Together Presents Amanda Earl.*

KATYA HARRIS lives in Kent, in the United Kingdom, with her family and three crazy rat boys. You can find her on Twitter @Katya_Harris and on Facebook. She hopes that you like what she's written and that you'll come back for more.

TILLY HUNTER (tillyhuntererotica.blogspot.co.uk) is a British writer and editor with a wicked imagination and a fondness for quirky stories that usually involve rope. Her work has been published by Xcite Books, House of Erotica, MLR Press and Ryan Field Press.

Like any overly intense Scorpio, there's nothing **ATHENA MARIE** enjoys more than exploring the secret, shadowy depths of the human psyche. And what is more obscured in darkness than our sexual desire? Athena's writing has been published both online and in print.

ANNA MITCHAM is an actress and writer living in Oxford, England. She writes a blog (justresting.org) about being a struggling actress. She is currently working on turning this into a book. As well as taking the occasional acting job, Anna writes erotica.

EVAN MORA's tales of love, lust and submission have appeared in many anthologies, including: *Please, Sir: Erotic Stories of Female Submission*; *Spank!*; *Best Bondage Erotica 11 & '13*; *Bound by Lust: Romantic*

Stories of Submission and Sensuality and *Cheeky Spanking Stories*. She lives in Toronto.

ISEULT REAGE is a French writer of all things erotic and BDSM. She is a kinky Torontonian who has self-identified as a slave since her early twenties. Trained in the arts of tea ceremonies, storytelling and service, she currently travels the world with her owner, assisting him as required.

GISELLE RENARDE is a queer Canadian, avid volunteer, contributor to more than one hundred short-story anthologies and author of numerous electronic and print books, including *Anonymous, Nanny State* and *My Mistress' Thighs*. Ms. Renarde lives across from a park with two bilingual cats who sleep on her head.

THOMAS ROCHE (thomasroche.com) is a widely anthologized author of short stories and an occasional novelist. His 2011 SF/horror novel *The Panama Laugh* was a finalist for the Bram Stoker Award; he's also been a finalist for the John Preston Award for short fiction from the National Leather Association.

ROB ROSEN (therobrosen.net), author of the novels *Sparkle: The Queerest Book You'll Ever Love,* TLA award-winning *Divas Las Vegas, Hot Lava, Southern Fried, Queerwolf* and *Vamp*, and editor of the anthologies *Lust in Time* and *Men of the Manor*, has had short stories featured in more than 180 anthologies.

ANGELA SARGENTI (angiesargenti.blogspot.com) has dozens of erotica and horror stories published all over the web and in various anthologies. Her latest e-book, *So Spankable!,* is available now.

OLIVIA SUMMERSWEET is a California-based freelance editor and former journalist who writes erotica for fun and personal growth. She loves animals and has written about animal protection issues.

KATHLEEN TUDOR (KathleenTudor.com) is currently hiding out in the wilds of California with her spouse and their favorite monkey. Her wicked words have broken down the doors to presses like Cleis, Mischief Harper-Collins, Xcite and more.

Called a "Trollop with a Laptop" by East Bay Express, **ALISON TYLER** is naughty and she knows it. She is the author of more than twenty-five erotic novels, most recently *Dark Secret Love*, and the editor of more than seventy-five explicit anthologies. Visit alisontyler.com 24/7, as she's a total insomniac.

DAVID WELLWOOD lives in Milton Keynes, United Kingdom with his wife and two recalcitrant hounds.

ALISON WINCHESTER is a part-time writer, full-time nerd. When she's not writing erotica, she's probably reading fan fiction, watching a web series, or plotting her next tattoo. By day, she's a wild-mannered freelance writer and editor wielding a mighty red pen, or at least a mean backspace key.

DAVID WRAITH is a Saint Louis native, writer, filmmaker and activist. He's a polyamorous sadomasochist and exhibitionist. He is one of the cofounders of Sex Positive St. Louis (sexstl.com) and he occasionally rants about movies, sex and politics at davidwraith.com.

KRISTINA WRIGHT is a full-time author and the editor of several erotica anthologies for Cleis Press, including the Best Erotic Romance series. She holds degrees in English and humanities and her fiction has appeared in over one hundred anthologies. She lives in Virginia with her husband and their two young sons.

ANDREA ZANIN, aka Sex Geek, runs a book club called the Leather Bindings Society, blogs at sexgeek. wordpress.com and pens erotic fiction when she's not working on her PhD. She lives in Toronto and enjoys cultivating M/s relationships with exceptionally high-quality individuals.

ABOUT
THE EDITOR

Lambda Literary Award–winner and multiple Independent Publisher Book Awards medallist **D. L. KING** continues to work on her home dungeon when she isn't writing or editing smut. *The Big Book of Domination* makes her seventh dip in the editorial pool for Cleis Press. She is also the editor of *Under Her Thumb: Erotic Stories of Female Domination, Seductress: Tales of Immortal Desire, The Harder She Comes: Butch/Femme Erotica, Carnal Machines: Steampunk Erotica, The Sweetest Kiss: Ravishing Vampire Erotica* and *Where the Girls Are: Urban Lesbian Erotica.* Other books edited by D. L. King include *She Who Must Be Obeyed: Femme Dominant Lesbian Erotica, Spankalicious: Adventures in Spanking, Voyeur Eyes Only: Erotic Encounters in Sin City,* and *Spank!.* D. L. King is the publisher and editor of the erotica review site, Erotica Revealed. The author of more than sixty short stories, her work can be found in various editions of Best Lesbian Erotica, Best Women's Erotica, Best Bondage Erotica, The Mammoth Book of Best New Erotica, as well as such titles as *Baby Got Back, Between the Cheeks, Sudden Sex, Ageless Erotica, No Safewords, The Big Book of Bondage, Leather Ever After* and *Luscious*, among others. She is the author of two novels of female domination and male submission, *The Melinoe Project* and *The Art of Melinoe*, as well as a collection of short fem dom erotica, *Her Wish Is Your Command*. Find out more at dlkingerotica.blogspot.com and dlkingerotica.com.

More from D. L. King

Under Her Thumb
Erotic Stories of Female Domination
Edited by D. L. King

Under Her Thumb will whet your appetite for all things femdom. These fierce tops know how to dominate their men—and the occasional woman. Award-winning editor D. L. King serves up a feast to be savored by tops, bottoms and the wonderfully curious.
ISBN 978-1-57344-927-4 $15.95

Seductress
Erotic Tales of Immortal Desire
Edited by D. L. King

A succubus is a sexual vampire, a shape-shifting temptress who steals the life force from her victim—but what a way to go! Award-winning editor D. L. King has crafted a singularly sexy and mysterious compilation that will have you lying in bed all night wondering who might visit.
ISBN 978-1-57344-819-2 $15.95

The Harder She Comes
Butch / Femme Erotica
Edited by D. L. King

Some butches worship at the altar of their femmes, and many adorable girls long for the embrace of their suave, sexy daddies. In *The Harder She Comes*, we meet femmes who salivate at the sight of packed jeans and bois who dream of touching the corseted waist of a beautiful, confident woman.
ISBN 978-1-57344-778-2 $14.95

Carnal Machines
Steampunk Erotica
Edited by D. L. King

D. L. King has curated stories by outstanding contemporary erotica writers who use the enthralling possibilities of the 19th-century steam age to tease and titillate in a decadent fusing of technology and romance.
ISBN 978-1-57344-654-9 $14.95

The Sweetest Kiss
Ravishing Vampire Erotica
Edited by D. L. King

These blood-drenched tales give new meaning to the term "dead sexy" and feature beautiful bloodsuckers whose desires go far beyond blood. Enter these shadowy alleys and dark bedrooms to experience the frisson of terror and delight that only a vampire can inspire.
978-1-57344-371-5 $15.95

Happy Endings Forever and Ever

Dark Secret Love
A Story of Submission
By Alison Tyler

Inspired by her own BDSM exploits and private diaries,
Alison Tyler draws on twenty-five years of penning sultry stories to create a scorchingly hot work of fiction, a
memoir-inspired novel with reality at its core. A modern-day
Story of O, a *9 1/2 Weeks*-style journey fueled by lust, longing
and the search for true love.
ISBN 978-1-57344-956-4 $16.95

High-Octane Heroes
Erotic Romance for Women
Edited by Delilah Devlin

One glance and your heart will melt—these
chiseled, brave men will ignite your fantasies
with their courage and charisma. Award-
winning romance writer Delilah Devlin has
gathered stories of hunky, red-blooded guys
who enter danger zones in the name of
duty, honor, country and even love.
ISBN 978-1-57344-969-4 $15.95

Duty and Desire
Military Erotic Romance
Edited by Kristina Wright

The only thing stronger than the call of
duty is the call of desire. *Duty and Desire*
enlists a team of hot-blooded men and
women from every branch of the military who serve their country and follow
their hearts.
ISBN 978-1-57344-823-9 $15.95

Smokin' Hot Firemen
Erotic Romance Stories for Women
Edited by Delilah Devlin

Delilah delivers tales of these courageous
men breaking down doors to steal readers'
hearts! *Smokin' Hot Firemen* imagines the
romantic possibilities of being held against
a massively muscled chest by a man whose
mission is to save lives and serve *every* need.
ISBN 978-1-57344-934-2 $15.95

Only You
Erotic Romance for Women
Edited by Rachel Kramer Bussel

Only You is full of tenderness, raw passion,
love, longing and the many emotions that
kindle true romance. The couples in *Only
You* test the boundaries of their love to
make their relationships stronger.
ISBN 978-1-57344-909-0 $15.95

Many More Than Fifty Shades of Erotica

Fuel Your Fantasies

Unleash Your Favorite Fantasies

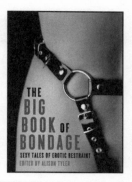

The Big Book of Bondage
Sexy Tales of Erotic Restraint
Edited by Alison Tyler

Nobody likes bondage more than editrix Alison Tyler, who is fascinated with the ecstasies of giving up, giving in, and entrusting one's pleasure (and pain) to the hands of another. Delve into a world of unrestrained passion, where heart-stopping dynamics will thrill and inspire you.
ISBN 978-1-57344-907-6 $15.95

Hurts So Good
Unrestrained Erotica
Edited by Alison Tyler

Intricately secured by ropes, locked in handcuffs or bound simply by a lover's command, the characters of *Hurts So Good* find themselves in the throes of pleasurable restraint in this indispensible collection by prolific, award-winning editor Alison Tyler.
ISBN 978-1-57344-723-2 $14.95

Caught Looking
Erotic Tales of Voyeurs and Exhibitionists
Edited by Alison Tyler
and Rachel Kramer Bussel

These scintillating fantasies take the reader inside a world where people get to show off, watch, and feel the vicarious thrill of sex times two, their erotic power multiplied by the eyes of another.
ISBN 978-1-57344-256-5 $14.95

Hide and Seek
Erotic Tales of Voyeurs and Exhibitionists
Edited by Rachel Kramer Bussel
and Alison Tyler

Whether putting on a deliberate show for an eager audience or peeking into the hidden sex lives of their neighbors, these show-offs and shy types go all out in their quest for the perfect peep show.
ISBN 978-1-57344-419-4 $14.95

One Night Only
Erotic Encounters
Edited by Violet Blue

"Passion and lust play by different rules in *One Night Only*. These are stories about what happens when we have just that one opportunity to ask for what we want—and we take it... Enjoy the adventure."
—Violet Blue
ISBN 978-1-57344-756-0 $14.95

---

* Free book of equal or lesser value. Shipping and applicable sales tax extra.
Cleis Press • (800) 780-2279 • orders@cleispress.com
www.cleispress.com

Red Hot Erotic Romance

Obsessed
Erotic Romance for Women
Edited by Rachel Kramer Bussel

These stories sizzle with the kind of obsession that is fueled by our deepest desires, the ones that hold couples together, the ones that haunt us and don't let go. Whether just-blooming passions, rekindled sparks or reinvented relationships, these lovers put the object of their obsession first.
ISBN 978-1-57344-718-8 $14.95

Passion
Erotic Romance for Women
Edited by Rachel Kramer Bussel

Love and sex have always been intimately intertwined—and *Passion* shows just how delicious the possibilities are when they mingle in this sensual collection edited by award-winning author Rachel Kramer Bussel.
ISBN 978-1-57344-415-6 $14.95

Girls Who Bite
Lesbian Vampire Erotica
Edited by Delilah Devlin

Bestselling romance writer Delilah Devlin and her contributors add fresh girl-on-girl blood to the pantheon of the paranormal. The stories in *Girls Who Bite* are varied, unexpected, and soul-scorching.
ISBN 978-1-57344-715-7 $14.95

Irresistible
Erotic Romance for Couples
Edited by Rachel Kramer Bussel

This prolific editor has gathered the most popular fantasies and created a sizzling, no-holds-barred collection of explicit encounters in which couples turn their deepest desires into reality.
978-1-57344-762-1 $14.95

Heat Wave
Hot, Hot, Hot Erotica
Edited by Alison Tyler

What could be sexier or more seductive than bare, sun-warmed skin? Bestselling erotica author Alison Tyler gathers explicit stories of summer sex bursting with the sweet eroticism of swimsuits, sprinklers, and ripe strawberries.
ISBN 978-1-57344-710-2 $15.95

Best Erotica Series

"Gets racier every year."—*San Francisco Bay Guardian*

Buy 4 books, Get 1 *FREE**

Best Women's Erotica 2014
Edited by Violet Blue
ISBN 978-1-62778-003-2 $15.95

Best Women's Erotica 2013
Edited by Violet Blue
ISBN 978-1-57344-898-7 $15.95

Best Women's Erotica 2012
Edited by Violet Blue
ISBN 978-1-57344-755-3 $15.95

Best Bondage Erotica 2014
Edited by Rachel Kramer Bussel
ISBN 978-1-62778-012-4 $15.95

Best Bondage Erotica 2013
Edited by Rachel Kramer Bussel
ISBN 978-1-57344-897-0 $15.95

Best Bondage Erotica 2012
Edited by Rachel Kramer Bussel
ISBN 978-1-57344-754-6 $15.95

Best Lesbian Erotica 2014
Edited by Kathleen Warnock
ISBN 978-1-62778-002-5 $15.95

Best Lesbian Erotica 2013
Edited by Kathleen Warnock
Selected and introduced by
Jewelle Gomez
ISBN 978-1-57344-896-3 $15.95

Best Lesbian Erotica 2012
Edited by Kathleen Warnock
Selected and introduced by
Sinclair Sexsmith
ISBN 978-1-57344-752-2 $15.95

Best Gay Erotica 2014
Edited by Larry Duplechan
Selected and introduced by Joe Manetti
ISBN 978-1-62778-001-8 $15.95

Best Gay Erotica 2013
Edited by Richard Labonté
Selected and introduced by Paul Russell
ISBN 978-1-57344-895-6 $15.95

Best Gay Erotica 2012
Edited by Richard Labonté
Selected and introduced by
Larry Duplechan
ISBN 978-1-57344-753-9 $15.95

Best Fetish Erotica
Edited by Cara Bruce
ISBN 978-1-57344-355-5 $15.95

Best Bisexual Women's Erotica
Edited by Cara Bruce
ISBN 978-1-57344-320-3 $15.95

Best Lesbian Bondage Erotica
Edited by Tristan Taormino
ISBN 978-1-57344-287-9 $16.95

Read the Very Best in Erotica

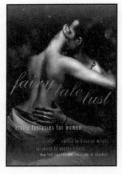

Fairy Tale Lust
Erotic Fantasies for Women
Edited by Kristina Wright
Foreword by Angela Knight

Award-winning novelist and top erotica writer Kristina Wright goes over the river and through the woods to find the sexiest fairy tales ever written.
ISBN 978-1-57344-397-5 $14.95

In Sleeping Beauty's Bed
Erotic Fairy Tales
By Mitzi Szereto

"Classic fairy tale characters like Rapunzel, Little Red Riding Hood, Cinderella, and Sleeping Beauty, just to name a few, are brought back to life in Mitzi Szereto's delightful collection of erotic fairy tales."
—Nancy Madore, author of *Enchanted: Erotic Bedtime Stories for Women*
ISBN 978-1-57344-376-8 $16.95

Frenzy
60 Stories of Sudden Sex
Edited by Alison Tyler

"Toss out the roses and box of candies. This isn't a prolonged seduction. This is slammed against the wall in an alleyway sex, and it's all that much hotter for it."
—Erotica Readers & Writers Association
ISBN 978-1-57344-331-9 $14.95

Fast Girls
Erotica for Women
Edited by Rachel Kramer Bussel

Fast Girls celebrates the girl with a reputation, the girl who goes all the way, and the girl who doesn't know how to say "no."
ISBN 978-1-57344-384-5 $14.95

Can't Help the Way That I Feel
Sultry Stories of African American Love, Lust and Fantasy
Edited by Lori Bryant-Woolridge

Some temptations are just too tantalizing to ignore in this collection of delicious stories edited by Emmy award-winning and *Essence* bestselling author Lori Bryant-Woolridge.
ISBN 978-1-57344-386-9 $14.95

Ordering is easy! Call us toll free or fax us to place your MC/VISA order.
You can also mail the order form below with payment to:
Cleis Press, 2246 Sixth St., Berkeley, CA 94710.

Buy 4 books,
Get 1 *FREE**

ORDER FORM

QTY	TITLE	PRICE
_____	_____	_____
_____	_____	_____
_____	_____	_____
_____	_____	_____
_____	_____	_____
_____	_____	_____
_____	_____	_____
_____	_____	_____

SUBTOTAL _____

SHIPPING _____

SALES TAX _____

TOTAL _____

Add $3.95 postage/handling for the first book ordered and $1.00 for each additional book. Outside North America, please contact us for shipping rates. California residents add 9% sales tax. Payment in U.S. dollars only.

* Free book of equal or lesser value. Shipping and applicable sales tax extra.

Cleis Press • Phone: (800) 780-2279 • Fax: (510) 845-8001
orders@cleispress.com • www.cleispress.com
You'll find more great books on our website

Follow us on Twitter @cleispress • Friend/fan us on Facebook